MR MUO'S
TRAVELLING COUCH

Since the publication of *Balzac and the Little Chinese Seamstress* (published in thirty-eight countries), film-maker and novelist Dai Sijie has become internationally famous. His film of the book was chosen to open the Cannes Film Festival in 2002. *Mr Muo's Travelling Couch* sold over 100,000 copies in its first French edition and has been published throughout the world. Dai Sijie lives in Paris and writes in French.

DAI SIJIE

Mr Muo's
Travelling Couch

TRANSLATED FROM THE FRENCH BY
Ina Rilke

VINTAGE BOOKS
London

Published by Vintage 2006

2 4 6 8 10 9 7 5 3 1

Copyright © Dai Sijie 2003
Translation copyright © Ina Rilke 2005

Dai Sijie has asserted his right under the Copyright, Designs
and Patents Act, 1988 to be identified as the author of this work

First published in French by Éditions Gallimard as
Le Complexe de Di

First published in Great Britain in 2005 by
Chatto & Windus

Vintage
Random House, 20 Vauxhall Bridge Road,
London SW1V 2SA

Random House Australia (Pty) Limited
20 Alfred Street, Milsons Point, Sydney,
New South Wales 2061, Australia

Random House New Zealand Limited
18 Poland Road, Glenfield, Auckland 10, New Zealand

Random House (Pty) Limited
Isle of Houghton, Corner of Boundary Road & Carse O'Gowrie,
Houghton, 2198, South Africa

The Random House Group Limited Reg. No. 954009
www.randomhouse.co.uk/vintage

A CIP catalogue record for this book
is available from the British Library

ISBN 9780099470182 (from Jan 2007)
ISBN 0099470187

Papers used by Random House are natural,
recyclable products made from wood grown in
sustainable forests. The manufacturing processes
conform to the environmental regulations of the
country of origin

Printed and bound in Great Britain by
Bookmarque Ltd, Croydon, Surrey

Contents

I

The Spirit of Chivalry

I

A Disciple of Freud

A metal chain sheathed in pink plastic is reflected, like a gleaming snake, in the window of a railway carriage, behind which the signals dwindle to pinpoints of emerald and ruby before being swallowed up by the mist of a sultry July night. (Only a short while ago, in a squalid station restaurant in southern China, this same chain had bound the leg of a fake-mahogany table to the retractable, chrome-plated handle of a pale-blue 'Delsey' suitcase with wheels belonging to Mr Muo, a Chinese-born apprentice psychoanalyst returned, some weeks before, from France.)

For a man so bereft of charm and good looks, thin and scrawny, a mere one metre sixty-three in height, with an unruly shock of hair, a slight squint and eyes that bulged behind thick lenses in a fashion that could only be called 'Muosian', Mr Muo behaves with surprising assurance: he takes off his French-made shoes (revealing red socks with a hole through which pokes a bony toe, pale as skimmed milk), climbs up onto the wooden seat – a sort of banquette without padding – and places his Delsey in the luggage rack, securing it with the plastic-coated chain and a small padlock. He then rises up on tiptoe to check whether the lock is secure.

Having settled down on the bench, he places his shoes under the seat, puts on a pair of white flip-flops, polishes his glasses, lights a small cigar, uncaps his pen and sets to 'work', that is to say, noting down dreams in a school exercise book purchased in France, this being part of his self-imposed training as a psychoanalyst. Hardly has the train gathered speed when the hard-seat carriage (the only one for which tickets were still available) fills with the bustle of peasant women with large baskets and bamboo backpacks who lurch up and down the corridor offering their wares – hard-boiled eggs and sweet dumplings, fruit, cigarettes, cans of Cola, Chinese mineral water and even bottles of Evian – before getting out at the next station. Uniformed railway staff work their way along the crowded carriage with laden trolleys bearing spicy ducks' feet, peppered spare-ribs, newspapers and gossip magazines. An urchin no more than ten years old sits on the floor vigorously applying polish to the stiletto-heeled shoes of a glamorous woman in her prime, remarkable on this night train for her large dark-blue sunglasses. No one appears to notice Mr Muo, or his maniacal vigilance with regard to his Delsey suitcase (unlike a few days previously when, travelling on a day train – also in a hard-seat carriage – Muo had looked up from his exercise book, having just completed his entries for the day with a resounding quote from Lacan, to see, as if in a slow-motion silent film, passengers so intrigued by the safety measures he had taken to protect his property that they were standing on the bench to stroke the suitcase and tap it with their jagged, black-rimmed fingernails.)

Once engrossed in his writing, Muo is oblivious to the world. His neighbour on the three-seater bench, a dapper fifty-year-old with sagging shoulders and a long swarthy face, keeps glancing at the exercise book, covertly at first, then quite unashamedly.

'Mr Four Eyes, is that English you're writing?' he inquires obsequiously. 'May I trouble you for some advice? My son, a secondary school pupil, is utterly hopeless, hopeless, at English.'

'By all means,' Muo retorts gravely, not revealing any annoyance at being addressed as Four Eyes. 'Let me tell you about Voltaire, an eighteenth-century French philosopher. One day Boswell asked him if he spoke English. Voltaire replied, "Speaking English requires placing the tip of the tongue against the front teeth. I am too old for that, I have no teeth left." Do you follow? He was referring to the way "th" is pronounced. The same goes for me: my teeth aren't long enough to practise the language of globalisation, although there are certain English writers that I revere, and also one or two Americans. However, what I am writing, sir, is French.'

Initially awed by the length and discursiveness of this reply, his neighbour quickly composes himself and fixes Muo with a look of profound loathing. Like all workers of the revolutionary period, he can't abide people whose learning surpasses his own and who, by virtue of their superior knowledge, symbolise enormous power. Thinking to give Muo a lesson in modesty, he draws a game of Chinese chequers from his bag and invites him to play.

'So sorry,' says Muo, in all earnestness, 'I don't play. But I do know exactly how the game originated. I know where it came from and when it was invented . . .'

Completely fazed, the man asks him, before settling down to sleep, 'Is it true that you are writing in French?'

'Indeed it is.'

'Ah, French!' he repeats several times, and the word resonates through this night train like a faint echo, a shadow, a reminiscence of the magical word 'English'.

For the past eleven years Muo has been living in Paris, in a seventh-floor maid's room converted into a bed-sit (no lift and no red carpet beyond the sixth floor), a damp place with cracks all over the ceiling and the walls. He spends every night from eleven till six in the morning noting down dreams. At first, it was just his own; now it is those of others, too. He composes his notes in French, checking each word he is unsure of in a big Larousse dictionary. Oh, how many exercise books he has filled! He keeps them all in shoe boxes secured with rubber bands, stacked on top of a metal shelving unit – boxes covered in dust, like those in which the French invariably keep their utility bills, pay slips, tax forms, bank statements, insurance policies, records of instalment-plan payments for furniture and cars, builders' receipts . . . in other words, the type of boxes that contain the balance sheets of a life. In the decade since his arrival in Paris in 1989 (he has just turned forty – the age of lucidity, according to the old sage Confucius), these notes, written in a French mined word for word from the Larousse dictionary, have left Muo changed, no less changed than his wire-framed spectacles (like those worn by the last emperor in Bertolucci's film), which, as well as being stained with grease and sweat, now have sides so deformed that they no longer fit in any spectacle case. 'I wonder if my head has changed shape, too,' Muo wrote in his exercise book after the Chinese New Year celebrations of the year 2000. That day, he had tied an apron around his waist, rolled up his sleeves and resolved to set his bed-sit to rights. He was in the middle of doing the dishes, which (a bad bachelor's habit) had been stacked up in the sink for days – a sombre mass jutting, iceberg-like, from the surface – when his glasses slipped from his nose (plop!) into the soapy water, on the surface of which floated tea leaves and food scraps, and sank among the reefs of crockery. Unable to see, he was obliged to grope under the suds and fish out chopsticks, rusty saucepans with rice stuck to the bottom, tea cups, a glass ashtray, rinds of sugar melon and water melon, mouldy bowls, chipped plates, spoons and a couple of forks so greasy they slipped from his grasp and clattered to the floor. At last he found his spectacles. Carefully he wiped off the suds, polished the lenses and held them up for inspection: new scratches scarred the glass, and the sides, already bent, had become even more fantastically twisted.

But now, as this Chinese night train pursues its inexorable journey onwards, little bothers our hero: neither the hardness of the seat nor the proximity of the other passengers. He is not even distracted when the attractive passenger in sunglasses (a show-business wannabe travelling incognito perhaps?) sitting by the window (beside a young couple and opposite three elderly women) graciously tilts her head in his direction while resting her elbow on the folding table. No indeed. Rather than riding a train, our Mr Muo is being transported by words and writing, by the language of a distant land and especially by his dreams, which he notes down and analyses with professional rigour and zeal, or rather, with loving tenderness.

Now and then his face lights up with pleasure, especially when he manages to apply to his subject matter an entire paragraph of Freud or Lacan, two masters for whom his esteem knows no bounds. As though recognising a long-lost friend, he smiles and moves his lips with childish glee. His expression, so severe a while ago, softens like parched earth under a shower, his facial muscles slacken, his eyes grow moist and limpid. Freed from the constraints of elaborate calligraphy, his writing becomes a confident scrawl, with strokes growing bolder and bolder and loops undulating and harmonious. This is a sign of his entry into another world, a world ever fascinating, ever new.

When a change in speed interrupts his writing, he lifts his head (his true Chinese head that is always on guard) and casts a suspicious eye overhead to make sure his suitcase is still attached to the luggage rack. In the same reflex, and still in a state of alert, he reaches inside his jacket to feel whether his Chinese passport, his French residence permit and his credit card are still in the zippered pocket. Then, more discreetly, he moves his hand to the back of his trousers and runs his fingertips over the bump made by the hidden stash in his underpants, where he has secreted the not inconsiderable sum of ten thousand dollars in cash.

Towards midnight the strip lights are switched off. Everyone in the packed carriage is asleep, except for three or four card players squatting by the door to the toilet, placing feverish bets – the notes keep changing hands – under the naked bulb of the night-light, whose weak blue glow casts violet shadows on their faces and on the fanned cards held close to the chest, but also on an empty beer can rolling back and forth across the floor. Muo recaps his pen, places his exercise book on the folding table and watches the attractive lady who, in the semi-darkness, has taken off her enormous sunglasses and is smearing a bluish substance on her face, a moisturising or revitalising mask perhaps. 'How vain she is,' he reflects. 'How China has changed!' At regular intervals the woman turns to the window to observe her reflection, after which she removes the bluish paste and starts all over again. It has to be said, the mask suits her rather well. It gives her the mysterious appearance of a femme fatale. Suddenly, a passing train flashes a succession of lights on the window and Muo discovers that she is crying. Her tears stream down on either side of her nose, carving wonderful sinuous striations in the thick, creamy mask.

As time passes the stark, massed mountains and interminable tunnels give way to sombre rice fields and slumbering villages scattered on a vast plain. A windowless brick edifice (a warehouse perhaps, or a watchtower in ruins) appears on a vacant lot lit up by street lamps. In theatrical solitude, it looms majestically towards Muo. Inscribed on its blind, whitewashed wall is an advertisement consisting of a few gigantic black ideograms: 'Guaranteed cure for stammering'. (Who guarantees? Where and how would the stammerers be treated? In the tower?) The oddness of the slogan is emphasised by the vertical stripe of a rusty metal ladder propped up against the wall in the centre of the inscription. As the train draws level with the tower, Mr Muo finds himself only a hair's breadth away from the rusty ladder, while the ideograms swell until one of them fills the whole carriage window as though trying to get inside. Ladders, as every analyst knows, have a special significance, quite apart from the dangers inherent in their height and instability, for they exert a dark, sexual fascination which is purely Freudian.

At this moment, in his hard-seat carriage, Muo is seized by the same vertigo he felt twenty years earlier (on February 15, 1980, to be precise) in a student room measuring six square metres and filled by eight tiered bunks. A damp and chilly room, where the air was thick with the smell of greasy water, instant noodles and various other detritus – a smell which stung the eyes and still pervades the dormitories of Chinese universities today. It was past midnight (lights-out being at 11 p.m.), and the dormitories, consisting of five identical nine-storey buildings, three for the boys and two for the girls, were plunged in obedient darkness and silence. For the first time in his life young Muo, then aged twenty and a student of classical Chinese literature, held in his hand a book by Freud entitled *The Interpretation of Dreams*. (It had been given to him by a white-haired Canadian historian for whom he had spent his winter holidays translating into modern Mandarin the inscriptions on some ancient stelae, without, however, receiving a penny for his labours.) Lying under the quilt on his top bunk, he had read the book by the tremulous yellow beam of his flashlight, poring over the foreign words, carefully tracing one line after another, pausing frequently to focus on some obscure, abstract concept before losing himself all over again in the long, labyrinthine passages that rarely reached a comma let alone a full stop. Coming upon Freud's commentary about a staircase in a dream had been like being hit on the head by a brick. Huddled in his quilt – stained with sweat and other nocturnal emissions – he had tried to make out whether the dream was one that Freud himself had had, or whether Freud had penetrated the meanderings of Muo's own brain to witness one of his recurrent dreams, or even whether it wasn't simply that he, Muo, was dreaming dreams that Freud had dreamed before him, in another place . . . Ah, there is no end to the graces and pleasures books can hold for a young man. That night, Freud ignited a joyful flame in the spirit of his disciple-to-be, who threw down his sorry bed cover, switched on an overhead lamp (despite his room-mates' protests) and, in a state of utter beatitude, read and reread the sentences of this living god out loud, on and on until the burly, one-eyed supervisor stormed in and confiscated the book amid curses and threats. That was when his room-mates nicknamed him 'Freud-Muo', and the name had stuck.

He thinks back to the dormitory and the huge ideogram he had inked on the distempered wall next to his top bunk at the end of that revelatory night: 'dream'. He wonders what happened to his youthful graffiti. He had not employed a simplified modern Chinese script, nor the more complicated classical Chinese, but the primitive writing used on tortoiseshell inscriptions dating back three thousand six hundred years. On those ancient artefacts the ideogram for 'dream' was composed of two parts: on the left side a drawing of a bed; on the right, a flowing line that would not look out of place in a Cocteau drawing, symbolising a sleeping eye crossed by three slanting strokes – the lashes – with a human thumb pointing down at it as if to say, 'Even in sleep the eye goes on seeing, so beware!'

Muo had arrived in Paris after winning a gruelling competition in China and receiving a bursary from the French government to complete his PhD thesis, which was devoted to one of the many alphabetic languages that were spoken along the Silk Road before they were swallowed up by the sands of the Takla-Makan, the Desert of Death. This bursary, which was by no means ungenerous (two thousand francs a month), was accorded to him for four years, during which time he took the opportunity to present himself three times a week (Mondays, Wednesdays and Saturday mornings) at the home of Michel Nivat, a Lacanian psychoanalyst, who invited him to recline on a mahogany couch. Throughout these lengthy confessional sessions Muo kept his eyes glued on an elegant wrought-iron spiral staircase that occupied the centre of the room and led up to his mentor's private quarters.

Mr Nivat was the uncle of a student whom Muo had met in a Sorbonne lecture hall. Neither good-looking nor ugly, neither fat nor thin, he had attained such a high level of asexuality that it was some moments before Muo, on their first meeting, could make out the analyst's gender. He had gazed in confusion at Nivat's shock of hair, the silvery highlights of which stood out against an abstract painting on the facing wall made up of almost monochrome stripes and dots. His clothing was both ageless and sexless, and his voice, although a fraction coarse for a woman, was likewise impossible to define. He paced the room with an agitated, limping step that reminded Muo of another limp in another time and another country: that of his grandmother.

For the four years, Mr Nivat received Muo (gratis, in consideration of the student's modest means) with the calm and patience of a Christian missionary lending a forgiving ear to the fantasies and intimate secrets of a convert newly touched by the grace of God.

The birth of the first Chinese psychoanalyst was a painful process, but not without its comic moments. Having no French at first, Muo spoke Chinese, of which his psychoanalyst understood not a word (even if he had, he would have been hard put to grasp the meaning of the dialect of Sechuan, the province from which Muo hailed). At times, during these early sessions, Muo's super-ego would get the better of him mid-monologue and would cast his memory back to the Cultural Revolution, whereupon Muo would laugh and laugh until the tears streamed down his cheeks and he was obliged to take off his glasses to wipe them under the watchful eye of the Mentor, who, although superficially unperturbed, suspected deep down that the joke was on him.

The rain pours down outside the carriage, as it has done since the train departed. Muo nods off. His sleep is stirred by recollections of his Paris years, the muffled sound of a little cough somewhere in the carriage, the theme tune of a TV soap hummed by a card player in luck, and the presence of his precious suitcase overhead, chained to the rack . . . His drooling neighbour, the father of the hopeless student of English, sags to one side, straightens up, sags again, until his head comes to rest on Muo's shoulder. Just then the train crosses an illuminated bridge over a murky river. For a moment Muo has the sense of bathing in a succession of lights aimed directly at his face, scrutinising him by turns. He opens his eyes.

He can't see very much without his glasses, but he has the impression that there is a stick or rod being waved in front of his nose. Shaking himself fully awake he discovers that the rod is a long broom-handle, and that it is being wielded by a girl, of whom he can make out little more than her blurry outline as she moves about, bending over him to clean the floor under his seat with wide, rhythmical sweeps.

The train suddenly lurches to a halt and, in the jolt, Muo's twisted glasses fall off the folding table on to the floor. The girl with the broom reaches for them, but Muo bends down at the same time and receives a blow to the head from the broom-handle. In this fleeting contact with a girl whom he can barely see, he catches, rising from her hair, the familiar fragrance of Eagle soap, a cheap soap scented with bergamot. His mother and grandmother used to wash their hair with it in the old days, down in the courtyard of their apartment block. He, little Muo, would draw cold water from the communal tap and mix it with hot water from a thermos to wet his mother's silky, jet-black hair (and sometimes the silvery hair of his grandmother), pouring steaming waterfalls from an enamel mug decorated with a picture of Chairman Mao at the centre of a halo of red rays. Crouching on the ground before a basin (enamel, too, but decorated with huge red peonies, symbolising the great revolutionary spring), his mother would rub her scalp with a bar of Eagle soap, the soap that smelled pleasantly of bergamot and genteel poverty and sent iridescent bubbles frothing between her fingers to drift off in the air.

The girl retrieves Muo's glasses and puts them back on the table.

'Tell me, my dear, why are you sweeping the floor at this hour?' Muo inquires. 'Is this your job?'

The girl sniggers and continues cleaning. With the aid of his glasses Muo identifies what she is wearing on top as a man's vest. One thing is clear: she is not a member of the railway staff. With her baggy shorts reaching to her knees, her mud-encrusted, cheap rubber shoes and her grimy, patched cloth bag with the shoulder strap cruelly emphasizing the flatness of her chest, she is the picture of poverty. Muo notes the black tufts in her armpits and the acrid aroma of sweat that mixes with the bergamot from her hair.

'Excuse me,' she says, 'may I move your shoes?'

'Of course.'

She bends down and lifts Muo's shoes delicately, fingers curled respectfully.

'My word, proper Western shoes! Even the soles are lovely. I've never seen such lovely soles!'

'How can you tell they are Western? I thought they were modest enough, my poor shoes, quite ordinary-looking. Nondescript, really.'

'My father used to shine shoes for a living,' she says, smiling.

She puts the shoes down again, sliding them into a corner under the bench, against the side of the carriage.

'He always used to say,' she goes on, 'that Western shoes last much longer and that they never lose their shape.'

'You have just washed your hair, I can tell by the fragrance. It's bergamot, which comes from a South American tree, probably Brazilian. First imported into China in the seventeenth century, roughly at the same time as tobacco.'

'I washed my hair because I'm going home. I've been away a whole year, slaving away in Pingxiang, a dump of a town a couple of stations back.'

'What sort of work do you do?'

'I sell clothes. The shop went bust all of a sudden, so I got the chance to celebrate my father's birthday at home.'

'Have you bought him a gift? Do forgive me for being so inquisitive, but, to be honest, my work consists largely of studying the relations between children and their parents. I am a psychoanalyst.'

'What's that? A job?'

'Indeed it is. I analyse . . . how shall I explain? I do not work in a hospital, but soon I shall have my own private practice.'

'You're a doctor, then?'

'No. I interpret dreams. People with problems tell me their dreams and I try to help them understand what they mean.'

'My goodness! You don't look anything like a fortune-teller to me.'

'I beg your pardon?'

'You, a fortune-teller!' she exclaims, and without giving Muo a chance to redress this common misconception of psychoanalysis, she points to a cardboard box in the luggage rack: 'That's my present, up there. A "Rainbow" TV set, 28 cm screen, made in China. My father would have liked a bigger Japanese one, because of that rotten cataract of his, but it cost too much.'

While Muo raises his eyes to take in the cardboard box overhead, a proof of filial devotion that wobbles on the luggage rack to the bumpy rhythm of the train, the girl drops her broom, takes a bamboo mat out of her bag, spreads it out under the bench he is sitting on, then, yawning discourteously, removes her rubber shoes, places them next to Muo's, crouches down and, in a slow, fluid, feline movement, slides out of view under the seat (where, to judge by the lack of even a toe poking out, and the ensuing silence, she must have drawn up her knees and fallen asleep the minute her head touched the bag serving as her pillow).

The ingenuity of this sleeping arrangement leaves Muo open-mouthed. He suffers with her, empathises, almost as if he were falling in love, blinded by a familiar wave of pity which, welling from his short-sighted eyes, deposits a curious mist on his glasses through which he sees the girl's bare feet as they gradually emerge from under the seat. Such a hypnotic sight, those feet crossing and re-crossing, languidly rubbing together to fend off invisible mosquitoes. The slimness of the ankles, he notes, is not without charm, nor is the hint of coral varnish on the nails of her big toes, a token of her vanity. The next instant, in a rapid flexing of the knees, the girl's feet, none too clean, once more disappear from Muo's view, but the sight of them, crossing and re-crossing, remains fixed in his mind for as long as it takes him to complete his mental picture of the reclining figure in the dark: the scabby knees, the twisted shorts, the man's vest clammy with sweat, the dust clinging to her back, forming a sad little collar at the nape of her neck, and tracing a grimy line beneath her eyelashes, slick with perspiration.

He gets up and, apologising to his sleeping neighbours, picks his way among the passengers sitting in the corridor to the WC. Upon his return his precious seat, that tiny paradise comprising one third of the hard bench, has been claimed by the father of the hopeless English student, whose head rests so heavily on the folding table one would think he had received a couple of bullets to the temple. Leaning against the family man's shoulder is another usurper, likewise with saliva drooling from the corner of his mouth, while the seat near the corridor is occupied by a peasant woman with unbuttoned blouse, squeezing her swollen left breast to suckle her infant. Bitter and angry, Muo accepts his loss and settles down on the floor at the woman's feet.

The night-light shining weakly on the naked torsos of the card players extends its faint glow to the infant's red bonnet. 'Why cover the poor child's head in this hellish heat?' Muo thinks to himself. 'Is there something wrong with it? Is the mother not aware that a celebrated psychoanalyst pointed out, with reference to European folk tales, that a red bonnet symbolises the menstrual flow?'

At that instant a spark is ignited – either by the red bonnet or the idea of menstruation – that immediately sets his brain ablaze.

'Could the girl with the broom be a virgin?'

A thunder-clap resounds in his head. His pen falls off the folding table, bounces on to the floor and skitters away as though taken with a nervous spasm. It rolls to the far side of the corridor, where Muo watches it out of the corner of his eye as it continues on and on with a momentum as impetuous as that of the train. His gaze is still fixed on the baby's red bonnet.

'If she's a virgin,' he thinks, 'that would make all the difference.'

Screwing up its eyes and opening wide its milk-rimmed mouth, the infant begins to cry.

Muo can't abide howling babies. He averts his eyes, preferring to observe the shadows shifting from one face to the next in the carriage, the pulsing lights flitting past outside the window, an empty service station, a street lined with shuttered shops, construction sites with unfinished apartment blocks enclosed by bamboo scaffolding.

The infant in the red bonnet, silent now, leans over and thrusts its puny fist into Muo's face. Its mother is too tired and drowsy to restrain it. Muo receives this battering without flinching, and his eyes fasten on the empty beer can which, just a moment ago, rolled past the card players, and which is now traversing the carriage, crossing a puddle of water (or child's pee), circumventing a gob of phlegm and halting in front of him, so close that he can make out, in the weak light, a dent in the top. He feels warm air tickling his neck and, twisting round, sees that the baby has leaned out from its mother's arms to bury its nose in his neck, as though seeking out some particular odour. It gives Muo a wary, almost hostile look, flares the tiny nostrils and resumes its olfactory exploration. How grotesque! Then it sneezes and begins to cry again.

Its cries this time are ear-splitting. An indefinable shiver runs down Muo's spine as he is seized with anxiety at meeting the stern, accusatory gaze of the child, which seems to say that it knows perfectly well what is lurking at the back of Muo's mind – his strange quest to find a virgin who can help him realise his extraordinary plan.

Abruptly, Muo turns his back on the child, wishing to banish all thoughts that might undermine his gravitas as a healer of souls.

To the accompaniment of the infant's screams, he gets down on all fours and slides into the dense gloom beneath the seat. He has the sensation of being struck blind. The stench is overpowering, and he has to hold his nose to avoid gagging.

For the next few seconds he relives certain smells from an experience long ago, when he was a boy at the start of the Cultural Revolution. He was taken down to an airless basement where his grandfather, a Christian pastor (hardly surprising, then, that Muo should have Saviour-blood in his veins), was being held, along with his grandmother and several other prisoners, in a stink of urine, faeces, acrid sweat, filth, damp, and dead rats who lay rotting on the narrow steps and tripped him up when he descended. With a jolt, Muo realises why the former salesgirl from Pingxiang swept the floor under the bench so vigorously before settling down, and he doesn't dare imagine what the stench would have been like without her preparatory cleaning.

Geographically speaking, the subterranean microcosm is not as small as he imagined. What it lacks in height is compensated for by depth: the space amounts to that of two benches (the one Muo was sitting on before his seat was usurped, and the one that backs on to it). The lighting, entering dimly from left and right, is minimal, infinitely poorer than above and insufficient to see anything by. He can sense, however, the presence of the sleeping beauty curled up on the floor like a heap of rags or dead leaves.

He does not mind having forgotten his matches on the folding table, nor his lighter in his suitcase attached to the luggage rack. He can manage perfectly well without. The darkness enfolding him feels mysterious, welcoming, romantic, even sensual. He enjoys the sense of adventure – the atmosphere of secret passages within pyramids, or blocked Roman sewers leading ultimately to forgotten treasures.

Before crawling all the way under, and by sheer force of habit, he checks routinely whether his wad of money is still in his underpants and his French residence permit in the inside pocket of his jacket. Then he creeps forward in a diagonal direction, thinking he can turn his temporary blindness to his advantage. Suddenly something hard hits him in the face, slamming his glasses into the bridge of his nose. No doubt the girl's bony knee. The pain is so bad it makes him cry out in the gloom, which seems even blacker than before.

The cry of the amorous Saviour does not provoke the least response from the sleeping beauty.

'Listen here young lady,' (the voice reverberating in the dark is low and sincere, as befits the grandson of a pastor), 'there's no need to be afraid. It's only me, the psychoanalyst you were talking to earlier. You interest me. I would like you to tell me one of your dreams, if you can remember any. If not, you could draw me a tree – no matter what kind: big or small, with or without leaves . . . I can interpret your drawing for you and tell you whether or not you have lost your virginity.'

Still on all fours, he waits for the girl to react. Thinking over what he has just said, he is pleased with the authoritative tone in which he broached the subject of her virginity, and believes he has concealed his own inexperience in sexual matters quite well.

There is no response from the girl. In the darkness he feels his fingers coming into contact with one of the girl's bare feet, and his heart leaps into his throat.

'I know you're listening,' he goes on, 'despite your silence. I expect my proposition has upset you. Perfectly under-standable. Let me explain: interpreting drawings is neither a charlatan's trick nor is it something of my own invention. I learnt the technique in France, in Paris to be precise, at a conference for teachers of traumatised children. A conference organised by the French Ministry of Education. I clearly remember the trees drawn by two girls younger than you, victims of sexual abuse. Gloomy trees they were, moist, with huge spreading branches like the threatening, hairy arms of a giant, growing in some no-man's-land.'

As he speaks he feels his subconscious – his own worst enemy – rising up uncontrollably and running riot in his head. He fondles the invisible foot, which feels cold, but silky. His fingertips explore the dainty outline, tracing the bony instep which seems to tremble at his touch. Finally, he curls his hand round the slender, fragile ankle, sensing a delicate vibration of cartilage while his member hardens.

In the near-total darkness, this foot which he cannot see takes on another dimension. The more he fondles it, the more it is transformed, and little by little its essence, its nature, redefines itself as that of another foot encountered by Muo the Saviour twenty years earlier, and so often mentioned by him to his psychoanalyst (although the latter wrongly neglected this train of association in favour of that of childhood).

It was a spring day in the early eighties. The setting: a dimly lit, noisy canteen at a Chinese university, teeming with students armed with enamel bowls and chopsticks. The loudspeaker was blaring poems glorifying the government's latest policy. There were long queues in front of each of the twenty filthy windows; endless rows of good-tempered, dark-haired youngsters jostling in the steamy fug. Glancing round furtively to make sure no one was watching, Muo let go of his soy-sauce-tinged meal-voucher. The voucher whirled away into the general hubbub, landing 'accidentally' at the feet of a female student, whose shoes caught the light of a sunbeam filtering through the cracked glass of a barred window. The black velvet shoes with their paper-thin soles set off beautifully the curve of the white-socked insteps. His heart pounding like a thief's, Muo crouched down as if to reach for the fallen meal-voucher. In so doing he touched the velvet shoes with his fingertips, and thrilled to the warmth given off by the white ankle socks.

Then he lifted his head, and through the spicy vapours of

the canteen noted that the student glanced at him not with curiosity or surprise, but with a tender smile of indulgence.

It was his classmate, H.C., like him a student of classical texts. (H. was her family name, composed of an ideogram whose left section signified 'ancient' or 'old' and right section 'moon'. As for her given name, C., it was likewise composed of two parts, the left signifying 'fire' and the right 'mountain'. Together they made the loneliest-sounding name imaginable – 'Volcano of the Old Moon' – but also the most pleasing to the eye when written, and the most magically melodious when heard. Even today, Muo melts the moment his mouth shapes the two words.)

Once more, he let go of the voucher, which fell to the floor, landing in the same place as before. And again, retrieving it, his fingertips brushed against the long, agile, supple toes under cover of black velvet . . .

Now, in the semi-darkness of the railway carriage, just as the clanking subsides and the grinding wheels begin to slow, he lets out a brief groan: a scalding jet spurts from his groin, staining his underpants and trousers though fortuitously sparing his precious wallet.

The train stops. Bundles of shimmering light enter the carriage from the platform and partially illuminate the space beneath the bench. To his stupefaction, Muo discovers that the foot he has been fondling, the cause of his humiliation, is nothing but the handle of a discarded broom.

Shutting his eyes and putting his hands over his face, he lies back and prays for the train to depart again so that the evidence of his shame will be concealed by the night, but an eerie silence prevails both inside and outside the stationary carriage. Suddenly a voice beside him booms out, 'Where are we?'

Muo turns over on to his stomach as quickly as he can to hide the front of his trousers, dislodging his glasses in the process.

'Who are you?' he asks. 'And where is the girl from Pingxiang?'

'She's gone. Sold me her place for three yuan.'

Muo realises that, in the brief span of his toilet break, the composition of bodies beneath the seat changed significantly, and not in his favour. Was it then that she made off? Anxious to know more, he edges towards the intruder – who has promptly fallen asleep again – and discovers that the girl's rubber shoes have gone. It takes several minutes for it to sink in that his own shoes (Western, sturdy and shape-retaining) have vanished, too.

But he is in for another shock. His clothes covered in dust, his trousers stained, his face grimy, he twists round to look up at the luggage rack. All he can see in the luminous glow of the station lamps is a length of metal chain, dangling in mid-air, severed when and how he does not know.

Aghast, he dashes to the exit and jumps down on to the platform, where the fine drizzle has wrapped the station in a shroud so dense that he believes, for an instant, that he has lost his sight. He runs up and down the platform shouting loudly, but his voice is lost among the gleaming rails, the passengers getting on and off, the railway staff gossiping by the carriage doors, squatting on the platform to slurp their instant noodles, or playing billiards in the station master's office which has recently been converted into a neon-lit karaoke bar. Needless to say, no one knows anything about a pale-blue Delsey suitcase with wheels.

'The train was already pulling out of the station by the time I found a policeman,' Muo writes (in a grey new notebook purchased the following morning, when he also bought himself a boxy black suitcase (without wheels this time), a more formidable chain, and a mobile phone). 'I ran after the train, but couldn't catch up. For a long time I trudged on through the rain, along the tracks stretching away as far as the eye could see, calling out the name of my beloved Volcano of the Old Moon, beauty and wisdom incarnate, and I prayed for her to come to my aid.'

Having written these words in the room of a small hotel, he proceeds to make a list of the contents of the stolen suitcase, item by item, followed by the price in both French francs and Chinese currency, not forgetting to include his shoes, exercise books, thermos flask etc., with the intention of putting in a claim to the Chinese Railways. But before long he is convulsed with laughter: 'Anyone would say I'd forgotten what the great fatherland is like.'

He tears up his list and scatters the pieces out of the window, still laughing.

2

An Embalmer's Prenuptial Drama

'When did you first hear the word "homosexual"?'

'Let me think . . . it must have been when I was about twenty-five.'

'Are you sure? Twenty-five? As old as that?'

'You haven't changed a bit, Muo. Still got that nasty way of opening old wounds. I'm vulnerable, you know, like every woman of forty.'

'Well, I believe that if an old wound hasn't healed properly, then at least I can ease the pain. Forget that I'm thousands of kilometres away in the far south of China and consider this conversation a free therapy session . . .'

'You can stop right there, Muo,' says his old friend. 'You called to wish me a happy birthday, and that's very sweet of you, thank you. But stop fooling around. We're not classmates any more. I'm a widow. What's more, I'm a qualified embalmer.'

'Such a wonderful word – "embalmer"! I don't know the least thing about your job, but I've fallen in love with the word already. A bit like falling in love with the idea of a film before you've even seen it.'

'So?'

'Why so prickly? You know I'll keep anything you tell me strictly to myself. Psychoanalysts are like priests, they never reveal the secrets of the confessional. A matter of professional ethics. Trust me, talking will do you good. Go on, give it a try.'

'The first time I heard about it, you mean?'

'Yes, homosexuality. One would think you were scared of the word.'

'Before the age of twenty-five, I'd never heard it spoken aloud.'

'Do you remember how you first heard it?'

'Yes I do. It was about two years before Jian and I got married, although we were already engaged by then. He was teaching English at a secondary school. It was a Saturday – which was a work day at the time. He cycled over to pick me up at the mortuary, at around 6 p.m. I rode pillion, as usual, while he pedalled . . .'

(Pedalled. Pedal. At the other end of the telephone, Muo mulls over the word, in French: *pédale*, slang for pederast or homosexual. He had often seen the Embalmer's fiancé – a tall, round-shouldered, bookish young man with a thin face and carefully combed, squeaky-clean long hair – pedalling his way towards the grey concrete apartment block where Muo and the young Embalmer lived with their respective families. Jian would slow down and remain motionless on his bike for several seconds, balancing like an acrobat, before slowly, almost nonchalantly, placing his feet on the ground. He always dismounted some distance away, as though afraid his property would go astray in the dark jumble of bicycles parked around the entrance.)

'As usual, we took the road beside the music academy, then past the sweet factory and the tyre factory.'

'By the way,' interrupted Muo, 'I have a little question for you at this point – somewhat personal perhaps, but highly significant for the Freudian analyst that I am. It's about the chimney of the tyre factory. You know, that tall, penis-shaped stack thrusting up to the sky? Does it appear in your dreams at all?'

'No, never. I loathe the way that chimney belches black smoke into the sky, day in day out, sending soot and grime down into the street, on to the roofs and treetops. Worst of all is when the air is heavy just before a downpour and the thick smoke wraps around your head and suffocates you. Awful. What I do like is going past the sweet factory, though. It smells so good. Do you remember that?'

'I certainly do. When we were kids in the sixties there was that special smell of milk mixed with vanilla – I adored those sweets. I've never found anything like them again. Go on, tell me more. You were on the back of Jian's bike, in the black smoke of the tyre factory.'

'All right then. It was already getting dark, and once we were past the Opera House Jian took a short cut.'

'I know the one you mean – the narrow, unpaved alley that goes past that stinking open sewer. It can't have been a very comfortable ride sitting on the back of Jian's bike with all those pot-holes and bumps.'

'No, not really. In fact, hardly anyone used the alley because it was so badly rutted. Halfway down there was a sort of shed – you remember?'

'You mean the men's public convenience?'

'Convenience? You must be joking. A shit-hole, that's all it was.'

'True. A brick building as I recall – gloomy and damp, very run-down and with missing tiles in the roof that let in the light. Thick with flies. No electric lighting. Puddles all over the place. The floor was never dry, even in fine weather. You can imagine what it was like when it rained: you couldn't set foot inside the building. Everyone pissed from the entrance. There would be competitions sometimes, our own Olympics, to see who could piss furthest.

'Well, on that day the public convenience, as you call it, was surrounded by policemen. At first all I could make out were shadowy figures moving around the shed. Then as we drew near, I spotted gun-barrels glinting in the light of the street lamps. The alley was strangely quiet. Then I saw that the place was crawling with policemen in uniform, who had arrested about a dozen men, some young and some not so young. I couldn't see the faces of the stopped figures filing out of the building. Jian and I dismounted and continued on foot. I asked him who these poor men were. "They're homosexuals," he said. It was the first time in my life I had heard that word. I was twenty-five years old.'

'What were they doing in the shed?'

'Jian explained that it was their meeting-place. They passed us as they were led away, cowering, to a police van with barred windows. They resembled broken-backed animals. Even the policemen gave them curious looks. The silence was oppressive. I could hear the telegraph wires humming in the wind, the effluent trickling in the sewer, and my empty stomach rumbling. Jian kept his eyes fixed on the mud-splattered front wheel of his bike. It wasn't until we got on the bike again and I put my cheek against his back that I felt, through his shirt, that he was drenched in cold sweat. I mentioned this to him, but he didn't respond. We never took that short cut again.'

'Did he often pick you up after work?'

'Yes, he used to take me home on his bike almost every day.'

'That was nice of him. Even if I were madly in love I couldn't do that. I'm scared of the dead.'

'Jian wasn't.'

'You're not going to tell me he was fascinated by death, are you? In that case he must have had a mindset akin to that of people in the West. Most intriguing. A pity I didn't get a chance to analyse your husband.'

'D'you know where we met, Jian and me? In the mortuary. In the very room where I still work today.'

'Tell me more.'

'It was in the early eighties. Yes, almost twenty years ago already – I can't even remember what he was wearing that day.'

'Go on, make an effort. It'll come back to you.'

'No, I'm tired. Let's carry on tomorrow, all right?'

'But I really want to know how you two met! Go on, just to please me.'

'Tomorrow.'

'Right, talk to you then.'

'It was getting on for five in the afternoon. My boss and colleagues had left for a friendly basketball game against the fire brigade team. Stepping into the reception room I came upon Jian standing by the body of a woman on a trolley. I remember that his neatly combed hair was so long it brushed his collar. I remember his sad, drawn face, his hollow eyes, and especially his smell – or rather perfume! You know how rare it was back then, in the early eighties, to get a whiff of anything like perfume. Even rich people didn't have any. As soon as I stepped into the room I knew it was the real thing. Geranium with a hint of rose: a subtle, musky, exotic fragrance. In his hand he held a long necklace, which made him look rather girlish and which he kept fingering mechanically like a monk telling his beads. His fingers were stubby and coarse (it wasn't until much later that I discovered that this was the result of his re-education in a remote mountain village during the Cultural Revolution), and his right hand was badly scarred in two places.'

28

'What were you wearing that day?'

'A work-coat and gloves.'

'Was it a white coat?'

'Yes, like a nurse's. I always make sure my coat is clean and smells of washing powder. Not like the others. You should see the state of their coats! They don't bother to launder them until the grime has formed a thick layer of black grease.'

'I see. Jian obviously liked fastidiousness.'

'But he didn't even look at me. He was staring intently at a bluish discoloration near one of his mother's ears. The first sign of decomposition in a corpse. He reached into his pocket for a slip of paper he had obtained goodness knows how from the mortuary director, giving him permission to attend the embalming process as a discreet observer. At that time I wasn't yet a qualified embalmer. The devil only knows what came over me, but I didn't tell him I was just the hairdresser and that we ought to wait for my boss to undertake the real work.'

'Was it usual to have observers at the scene?'

'No, it was very rare.'

'You know, listening to you makes my heart go out to your poor Jian. I bet the perfume he was wearing was his mother's, as well as the necklace.'

'Such powers of deduction, my dear French psychoanalyst! Tell me, why are you not married yourself? Still carrying a torch for that girl at university, Volcano something, the one who couldn't care less about you? What was her name again?'

'Volcano of the Old Moon. But I won't have you taking her name in vain. Joking apart now, tell me more.'

'Where was I?'

'You were going to embalm his mother.'

(In his cheap hotel in Hainan, our psychoanalyst is disturbed by a sudden burst of noise from the room upstairs: water gurgling in the pipes, a man's voice singing in the shower, the waterfall of a toilet being flushed. The sheer force of the din turns the old cracks in the ceilings into gaping wounds discharging plaster dust, which lends a touch of comedy to this session of psychoanalysis-by-phone. Then comes the calmer trickle of the cistern filling up again followed by the throb of a washing machine, a noise that transports Muo back to a spring Sunday long ago, a Sunday whose sounds float into his consciousness like an old song. In his mind's eye he can see a courtyard packed with people, a communal tap, and the Embalmer and her fiancé standing side by side admiring a spanking new washing machine. It was their first joint purchase before they were married. Just watching it fill up with water was bliss for them. They had brought it home by bike. There were no taxis in Chengdu back then. The couple had entered the courtyard on foot, he trundling his bike, she proudly pushing from behind, and on the carrier an 'East Wind' washing machine secured with ropes of plaited straw. It was a momentous occasion, worthy of note in the annals of this courtyard which was home to several hundred families of doctors and medical staff. What an ovation! When they arrived, a mass of children and adults swarmed round the machine amid cries of astonishment and a volley of questions about the price and workings of the wonderful appliance. After unanimous persuasion, the young couple agreed to give a public demonstration. The Embalmer ran inside to fetch her dirty washing, while her fiancé connected the machine to the tap. To Muo, the event seemed rather like the launching of a spacecraft. When Jian pushed the start button, red and green lights started flashing above the round window behind which the clothes slopped and tumbled in the flux and reflux of water, and myriad bubbles burst into multicoloured stars in the spring sunshine. Linking arms with Jian, the Embalmer circled the machine, inspecting it, touching it, giving little cries. The white casing began to shake more and more violently while the noise level mounted until it reached that of an aeroplane just before take-off.

After several minutes of these convulsions, the demonstration reached its apotheosis. The door was ceremoniously opened in full view of the crowd. Kneeling before the machine, the couple reverentially removed the clothes: they were changed beyond recognition, shredded and tattered by the pitiless East Wind.)

'His mother wasn't a pretty sight, I assure you. Seeing her up close was quite a shock. It wasn't the absence of colour that disturbed me, for that was something I was used to, it was her features: they were so twisted it seemed as if she had been consumed by hatred when she died. Her facial muscles were frozen in what looked like a howl of outrage. Eyes wide open, mouth contorted, gums bared like a horse under gunfire. She was a linguist, Jian told me between sobs, in a voice that was barely audible, and she had died suddenly on the Sino-Burmese border, where she had been researching the language of a primitive matriarchal tribe. She had wanted to prove that most of the words of this language derived from the ancient Chinese spoken in the era of the Warring States, before the first emperor. Apparently she had been sounding forth in this unknown language on her deathbed at the local hospital. Not proper words, just the roots of words – strings of strange syllables, isolated vowels and explosive consonants.'

'But aside from these linguistic considerations, what did the autopsy report say?'

'It stated, in specialist jargon, that she had died either from some obscure tropical disease or from food poisoning caused by a toxic plant or mushroom; her liver had crumbled to dust at the post-mortem examiner's touch. Jian was devastated by his loss and also by having to take care of the funeral arrangements. He was all alone, poor thing.'

'What about his father? Wasn't he a linguist too?'

'His father works in Beijing. His parents divorced in the late sixties, and he was raised by his mother. He was desperate for her to look beautiful in death, whatever the cost. He wanted her to wear an expression befitting a great scholar, not that horrible grimace. But the body had been repatriated by plane and, as I told you, it had started decomposing. When I closed her eyes – my immediate professional reaction – I noticed the bluish stains on her temples and neck. I told Jian there was not a minute to lose: we needed to lay her on a bed of ice in the embalming hall. Since the staff that normally ferried the corpses from one place to another had gone off to play basketball with the boss, leaving the lifts reserved for this type of load secured with padlocks, we had to carry his mother up to the first floor ourselves. Her body was quite rigid. We wrapped her in a blanket. I took the shoulders, Jian the feet, and together we struggled to reach the stairs. Jian did not speak. His face was utterly blank. He walked stiffly and jerkily, as if he had wooden legs. He was in a very bad way. To free his hands he had slipped the string of beads round his neck, and he was crying. The staircase wasn't far, but with each step the body seemed to get heavier and slip lower and lower until it almost touched the floor. We had to stop several times for me to get my breath back. I inhaled his perfume. When we paused I sank down onto my haunches with my back against the wall and gasped for breath, resting his mother's head on my knees. I shut my eyes and didn't move. Jian was there, very close to me, but I didn't see him. I didn't even hear him breathing, I just smelled his geranium perfume – sun-scorched geranium, the hint of rose and musk less pronounced than at first. What's that you said? Subjective? Possibly. The fragrance I was so avidly inhaling passed into my body, took possession of me. It was like a dream. There I sat, with my eyes shut and his mother's head resting on my knees, gorging myself on the smell of geranium until I had the sensation that I myself was turning into a long, exquisite seed pod. Ever seen a geranium seed? How can I describe it? It looks something like the beak of a white stork. The same elegance.'

'So how did you get up the stairs? Did you go up together?'

'No. It was a concrete staircase, steep and very narrow. When we reached the foot of the stairs he said the best thing would be for him to carry her up on his own. First he tried gathering her up in his arms the way they do in films – you know, on the wedding night, when the man takes his young bride in his arms and bounds up the stairs two at a time. But Jian couldn't do it. Clearly there was something amiss with this position. He was unable to take a step. Then he asked me to help heave his mother on to his back. That's when I saw that the dead woman's cheeks were even more hollow and her skin even greyer than I had realised, which meant that the muscles were beginning to slacken and her jaw would soon drop. I feared I would have enormous trouble, later on, in shaping the death mask. I tried to secure her jaw by tying a cloth round her head. In the glow of the naked bulb lighting the stairwell, I saw that her eyes had opened again. They still stared, but the look in them had changed. There was less rage, less hatred, but so much sadness, such despair, that I felt ill and turned away from the sight. What a climb! It seemed to me that there was nothing heavier than the body of Jian's dead mother. Jian struggled upwards manfully, step by step. His calves quivered, and the sharp bones of his ankles seemed about to pierce his skin. But he persevered. Then the necklace hanging from his neck suddenly snapped and the beads pattered down on to the narrow steps, bouncing off the concrete, falling, bouncing again and again with a tinkling, crystalline sound. I held out my hands to try and catch them in mid-air, whereupon a burst of laughter rang out above me that made me jump out of my skin. Raising my head I saw Jian almost hysterical with mirth. He looked down at me and apologised, then resumed his ascent of the concrete stairs. With each staggering step he dislodged more beads that had got caught in his hair and his clothes, and the way they pattered and danced before my eyes was very pretty.

(The gurgle of water, a sound less crystalline than that of beads striking concrete, reverberates in Muo's head. It is the sloshing of water in a washing machine, watched with delight by the Embalmer, her fiancé and a courtyard filled once more to capacity, on the Sunday following the drama of the first trial. The couple had taken the defective East Wind machine, that bane of dirty laundry, back to the East Wind factory. Seven days later they returned, trundling a new washing machine on the back of the bicycle, he holding the handlebars and she pushing from behind. Dusk had already fallen, but their arrival in the courtyard provoked an even greater commotion than the week before. A doctor who lived on the ground floor, known for his meanness and his nervous twitch (he was reputed to contort his face five or six thousand times a day), passed a cable out of his window to power a five-hundred-watt light-bulb suspended over the communal tap, beside which the new East Wind stood in readiness. The demonstration was watched, not only by the ardent crowd milling around the machine, but also by curious neighbours hanging out of the open windows of their homes as if they had dress circle seats for a play. Boys threw fire crackers, and girls, glad of the chance to get out of the house, came running, still holding their supper bowls and picking at each other's left-overs with their chopsticks. The mood was festive, abounding with laughter, chatter, flirtation and banter. As the Embalmer had used up all her dirty washing in the first trial, she was obliged to load the machine with clean clothes, which she did, smiling graciously, in full view of everyone. The young couple stood hand in hand as they stared fondly at the window behind which blue jackets frothed and swirled alongside flowered shirts, printed poplin skirts, tops, jeans, a pair of flared trousers that no one had ever seen her wear, and several white T-shirts with slogans – freebies from the mortuary.

Little by little, like the swelling tones in the closing movement of a symphony, the time allotted for the washing cycle
rumbled towards its finale. A sense of nervous anticipation
rippled through the crowd: everyone remembered the nightmarish aeroplane-like roar that had preceded the fatal
outcome of the last demonstration. The five-hundred-watt
light-bulb swung rhythmically in the breeze, and as it swung
to and fro it cast a shadow-play across the faces of the
spectators. All eyes were on the two anxious owners of the
East Wind, who in turn fastened their gaze on the machine's
porthole, now opaque with condensation. So far so good. To
the general relief of the crowd, the machine continued
throbbing in a regular, mechanical, well-oiled baritone.

But once again, just as unexpectedly, the East Wind
struck. The appointed duration of the cycle having been
exceeded, the stubborn contraption refused to stop. Ten
minutes went by, then twenty. Some people wandered off,
others voiced their displeasure. Then someone joked that the
factory had not sold them a washing machine but a zombie
robot, at which everyone guffawed. Muo watched the
Embalmer, flushed scarlet with mortification, try hard to
laugh along with everyone else. The jokes followed thick and
fast until they formed a great flood of mockery that over-
whelmed the couple as they stood there with bowed heads
and sagging shoulders while the fine drizzle danced in the
yellow glare.

Moments later, the courtyard was empty. True to his
miserly nature, the ground-floor doctor with the twitch-
ridden face retrieved his light-bulb, grumbling that he should
never have lent it in the first place and insisting that the
Embalmer refund him the expense of the electricity.

Lashed by the rain, the machine careened on in the semi-
dark as though intent on prolonging its mayhem ad infinitum.
Standing in the porch of the building opposite, Muo peered
through the rainy mist at the ghostly twinkle of ruby and

emerald lights. There stood a cold robot, a hard, inexorable monster doing exactly as it pleased as it sang in the rain. By this time the baritone had risen to a megalomaniac tenor, virile and strident.

Soon the scraps of conversation drifting down from the neighbours' windows turned into protestation and jibes at the two figures standing by the communal tap under Jian's black umbrella, their dull gaze fixed on the rain, the stubborn machine and the flooded courtyard.

Worse was to come. When the front was finally opened with a metallic click and the clothes removed in the flickering light of a torch, they were all, once more and without exception, reduced to a heap of rags.)

'You remember, I told you that I wasn't a qualified embalmer then, not really. I was just doing the hairdressing. Well, until that day I had never prepared a body, properly speaking, nor had I done any cosmetic work. The fact that I had not revealed my true professional status put me in a terrible fix, as you can imagine. Once his mother was laid out on the refrigerated slab, I started combing her hair very slowly, in the hope that my colleagues would not be long getting back from their match. Despite her age, his mother had wonderful hair: streaked with grey and not very thick, but incredibly silky. I washed it, dried it and brushed it strand by strand, then I tied it back in a knot. Jian had told me she used to put her hair up for special occasions: birthdays, new year celebrations and so on. Apparently she used to enjoy the sight of her long elegant neck and her youthful, smooth skin in the mirror. Her hair looked very nice when I had finished. The hairdo made her look intellectual, aristocratic even. Of course it couldn't alter the expression on her face. It was dreadful seeing her like that, all contorted. She looked as if she was in endless torment. My colleagues were taking a very long time, and so I had no option but to act out my role to the bitter end.

'Had you fallen in love with him?'

'I can't deny that I had. But don't you think we've done enough talking for today?'

'No. Tell me what you did with his mother. Let me in on some of your professional secrets. You can be as brief as you like.'

'I had never done it before, but I had watched other people inject the formaldehyde into the veins of the deceased. It's not at all like a blood transfusion. You make an incision in the leg into which you insert a catheter; the fluid is then pumped through the body and out again. It was always the boss who made the incision, no one else was permitted to do it. I had helped reposition the body or passed him instruments a number of times, but for some reason I had always looked away at the crucial moment. A gut reaction. I couldn't help it, something repelled me. It wasn't the actual corpses; I was used to them. It was the boss who turned me off. He had such white hands – so pale, almost ghoulish! His fingernails were straight out of a horror movie. But it wasn't his nails that most repelled me. It was his smell. His breath always smelt of alcohol. I like the odd drink myself, to accompany a good meal or a celebration. But embalming a person's mortal remains . . . you know, it's the last good deed you can do for the deceased, the last token of respect a human being receives on this earth. And the smell of the boss's breath, even a faint whiff of it, sickened me.

'I can't tell you how much I regretted my squeamishness when I found myself having to make the incision myself. I dreaded making a mistake. In fact I was quite terrified, and my hands shook as I laid out the instruments, the fluid and the pump, which was a little rusty but still operational. I rolled up the left trouser leg to expose the calf, which was slender and icy, but misshapen, no doubt because she had been left lying in an awkward position for too long. Then I took the scalpel and made a cross in two unsteady, clumsy strokes. A thick

liquid seeped out, like apple purée mixed with blood. Jian
was as white as a sheet, his eyes were shut and he looked
about to faint. Suddenly I thought I heard the boss on the
ground floor. He was coming to my rescue! Relieved, I ran
out to greet him. I was so scared of making a mistake that I
preferred to confess my intrusion into his professional domain
at once, come what may. I flew down the stairs and along the
half-dark corridor to the entrance, which was firmly shut.
There was no one there. Daylight was fading, and soon the
place would be even gloomier. An evening breeze was
blowing, as icy as Jian's mother's leg. The sound of my own
footsteps in the fake marble hallway, the mute shadows
looming in the corners and even my own shadow made me
shake with terror all over again. I was tempted to run off and
look for my alcoholic boss at the basketball ground, but I
turned round and climbed the stairs again, not knowing what
to do next. Back in the embalming hall I told Jian I'd been
mistaken about the noise and that we'd carry on. He asked if
it was all right for him to recite a poem in English for his
mother. She had taught him English as a boy, and he now
spent every waking hour at the university improving his
knowledge of that language, which was his sole passion. He
told me these things so humbly that I couldn't possibly say no,
and he began to recite the poem in a loud voice. There was
nothing out of the ordinary about the way he spoke (even if
his voice was a touch effeminate), and I didn't understand a
word, but it sounded very beautiful. Beautiful and sad. My
hand stopped shaking, it obeyed my commands and made a
neat cut. The intervention passed without difficulty, amid a
flood of strange and magical-sounding words and phrases. It
was an old Irish song that Jian had come across in a novel by
James Joyce. I asked him what it meant, so he translated it for
me, and I liked it so much that I copied it out so as to
memorise it. I'll recite it for you if you like:

Ding dong, the Castle bell!
Farewell my mother!
Bury me in the old churchyard
Beside my eldest brother.
My coffin shall be black
Six angels at my back,
Two to sing and two to pray
And two to carry my soul away . . .

'Miraculously, his mother's face gradually regained its pinkish colouring, thanks to the fluid filling her veins with the aid of the rusty pump operated by Jian. I set about brushing her teeth. I remember noticing she had a little gap between her front ones, just like her son. In less than an hour the muscles relaxed, first in her chin, then in her hands. The grimace softened until her face was as calm as the sky after a shower. The serene features of a linguist were restored; no longer was she tormented by the dialect of that Sino–Burmese tribe. Jian was so encouraged by this transformation that he said it would be a shame not to make her look even better with some make-up. He went off to fetch his mother's make-up case, leaving me alone with the corpse. I sat looking at it for some time before dozing off. When I woke, it was raining. I don't know what had happened while I was asleep, but something inside me had changed. Everything seemed sweet and gentle; even the patter of the rain sounded like music. I had an urge to sing a mourning song, an ancient dirge that had floated into my mind. You get to hear plenty of laments for the dead in my line of work and I know quite a few. I sang until Jian returned. He liked my song very much, especially the rhythm of it, which he called "luminous and radiant". He asked me to sing some more, which I did. He opened the patent leather case, from which I took the eye-liner and traced a light accent, fluid like a caress, upon his mother's eyelids, after which I smeared her lips with glossy coral and brushed her lashes with French mascara. Finally he placed a gold necklace set with a sapphire around her neck. She was smiling, and beautiful in her own way.'

'I expect that was when he fell head over heels in love with you.'

'Well, that's what I thought, too. But when it comes down to it, you know as well as I do, Mr Psychoanalyst, that a homosexual has trouble making love to a woman. Had this not been the case, Jian wouldn't have thrown himself from the window on our wedding night, and I wouldn't still be a virgin.'

'Perhaps.'

'That's the end.'

3

Games of Mah-jong

The session of psychoanalysis-by-phone terminates at midnight. What a relief! The months Muo has spent crisscrossing China have not been in vain! Successively robbed of his suitcase on a train, his cigarette case in a market, his watch in a small hotel and his jacket at a karaoke club, he had felt himself in a tunnel, without end, constantly prey to crooks and prostitutes disguised as innocent maidens. But now, the confession of his old neighbour the Embalmer that she is still a virgin has struck a light in the dark.

Having put the receiver down, Muo takes a joyful little skip backwards. Buoyed up by a cloud of happiness, his body rises skyward until he lands on his back on his bed, wincing with pain at hitting a hard object lying on the mattress: a porcelain teapot, purchased earlier in the day, shatters on impact. This incident does not, however, diminish his good humour. Despite the late hour, he decides to emulate Michel Nivat, his asexual French psychoanalyst who looked like any ordinary Frenchman in an ordinary film and would go down to the corner bistro to stand a round of drinks whenever he had something to celebrate. He gets dressed and goes out whistling merrily. For the first time ever, the windowless stairwell of the hotel resounds to a Serge Gainsbourg tune.

'*Vive l'amour*,' he murmurs, depositing his key with its carved wooden tag on the front desk. He blows the receptionist a kiss and leaves.

(Nights and weekends, the reception desk is manned by a student who goes round to all the rooms at eleven p.m. offering to procure prostitutes. His Nikes can be heard squeaking to a halt by each room down the corridor, followed by fingers tapping the door as if on a computer keyboard, and his youthful voice calling, 'Anyone for love?' He is the most educated but least helpful of all the local guides engaged by Muo in the course of his laborious quest for a virgin.)

The lamps in the high street are not switched on (for reasons of economy) but the road is bathed in a neon glow by the hairdressing salons where girls (hairdressers?) lounge in doorways or sit in armchairs watching TV, wearing only bras, tight briefs and heavy make-up. They watch Muo as he passes, calling out to him in their quaint provincial accents, provoking him with their lascivious poses. Also open for business are two pharmacies specialising in aphrodisiacs, where cunningly lit windows display live, writhing snakes, counterfeit antlers and rhinoceros horns, dried crabs and a variety of odd-looking plants including a number of hairy ginseng roots. At the end of the street loom the furnaces of a privately-owned brick kiln, which has prospered in the recent construction boom. In the moonlight Muo can see the silhouettes of stooping ant-like workers, loading and unloading bricks. They emerge from the deep maw of the furnaces trundling barrows, and pause to catch their breath before retracing their steps along the thin dark lane to be engulfed once more in the smoke belching from the fires.

Muo steps into a teahouse opposite the factory. It is familiar to him from his visit there a week ago, in the company of another of the local guides he has employed in the course of his, until recently, fruitless quest. He had immediately liked the pitched tiled roof, the little open courtyards, the low wooden tables, the creaking but comfortable bamboo chairs, the damp floor of beaten earth littered with peanut shells, sunflower seeds, cigarette butts, and the sweet familiar smell that reminded him of his boyhood. Best of all was when the waiter brought the tea in a brass kettle with a metre-long spout, down which he poured a jet of boiling water straight into the porcelain bowl on its iron saucer, filling it to the brim without spilling the smallest drop and then delicately placing a white porcelain lid over the hot liquid. But on his second visit Muo receives a shock. The teahouse has been transformed into a vast, smoke-filled billiard hall with hordes of players, some ranged along its twilit walls, some bending over the green baize tables to strike ivory balls against other balls. Under the glare of heavily shaded lamps suspended above the tables, it resembles the Far West in an American B-movie from the sixties – bad set, bad acting, bad lighting. Even the balls knocking together sound hollow and cheap, as if there is something wrong with the recording equipment. Muo swaggers to the bar feeling like Clint Eastwood. For once in his life he wants to act the big spender, paint the town red, invite everyone to raise a glass, not to his own success but to 'American imperialism', and he asks the bartender what the drinks cost. The price of liquor, though not unreasonable, is higher than he expected, so he asks how much the local beer is while simultaneously attempting a head-count of the billiard players. The arithmetic makes him so dizzy that, before the bartender has time to reply, he beats his retreat without having drunk a drop.

'My dear Volcano of the Old Moon, for your sake I shall be sensible and thrifty, I promise,' he vows aloud.

Thirsty and with an empty stomach, he heads out of the

city to the beach, picking his way carefully between mounds of wet rubbish. Crossing a bridge he follows the bank of a murky, sluggish river. Above him the silver disc of the moon rides in an anthracite sky. Crab Bay is not yet in sight, but he can already smell the sea. It is a cold smell, at once strange and familiar, like the breath of a woman borne on gusts of nippy air. To one side are the shacks on stilts used by the crab fishers, who come in from poor villages. He hears babies crying and the doleful barking of stray dogs. The breeze softens. A moth flutters helplessly in a tangle of fishing nets hanging out to dry on the shingle. Muo approaches the nets, drops to his knees and crawls underneath to rescue the delicate creature desperately batting its marbled purple wings while spasms of fear convulse its spindle-shaped body.

'My poor friend, have no fear,' he says to the insect. 'A few hours ago I was in just the same predicament. I too had to extricate myself from an exceedingly tangled web, no less expertly knotted, namely: the Chinese Justice System.'

He frees the moth and takes pleasure in watching it whirr away, like a miniature helicopter.

'Several thousand kilometres across China,' he reflects, 'another delicate creature is asleep in a Chengdu prison cell. How do you manage, my beloved Volcano of the Old Moon? You who always had such trouble sleeping? Do you have a straw mattress? Do you sleep in your striped prison uniform?'

The blood rises to his cheeks and throbs in his head as he stoops to take off his shoes. His feet feel hot, too. He digs them into the grainy sand, then paddles in the greyish water at the mouth of the river. He splashes his face with the warm water. On his return to the shore, he proceeds to undress, not forgetting to take off his watch (which he wraps in a sock and tucks into one of his shoes). Then, scooping up his clothes in his skinny arms, he heads across the sand towards the rocks. Emerald seaweed crackles underfoot; sharp pebbles hurt his feet. The buffeting sea wind almost whips his glasses off, but soothes the fire in his veins. He walks gingerly. He knows they are there, the famous crabs, prized for the whiteness of their meat and their aphrodisiac properties. Monstrous and invisible, armed with mandibles and huge pincers, they lurk at the bottom of the tidal pools, submerged in the sticky sand, hiding under the pebbles, lying in wait for his toes. He can almost hear their conspiratorial whispers planning an imminent attack.

'I'll come back one day, with Volcano of the Old Moon, once she gets out of prison,' he vows as he clambers up on to the rocks. 'I'll push her through the water on an inflated inner-tube so that her feet won't be assailed by the crabs. I can see them now, her bare feet, noble and shapely, encrusted with grains of sand and delicate shards of shell. I can hear her cries of delight resounding in the surf. How wonderful it will be to see her savour her newfound freedom as she rides the black rubber ring, dipping and rising in the surge of the foamy tide! She will have brought her camera, and will take pictures of the toiling fishermen, the poorest in China, if not the whole world. As for me, I will record their dreams and their children's dreams. I will tell them about Freud and his theories, especially about the most important one of all – the Oedipus complex – and Volcano and I will enjoy watching them shake their swarthy heads and gasp in amazement.'

Fishing craft are dotted about the surface of the sea like glow-worms drifting languidly on the current: small wooden dinghies with room just for two, darker than the night, each with an acetylene lamp hanging over the oarsman, whose partner casts nets into the water.

Behind Muo's back, on terra firma, the roar of an engine draws near and a tourist coach pulls up. The passengers, both men and women, spill out on to the beach, no doubt for the express purpose of feasting on freshly caught crab. One man (the guide?) shouts that they want crabs, the smallest ones available, the ones with the whitest meat and the highest aphrodisiac content. An open-air restaurant lights up. Plastic tables and chairs are hastily set up to face the sea beneath a string of brightly-coloured light-bulbs. A few waiters, probably assistant cooks, go to the water's edge and call out to the fishing boats for their catch. At first, in the hubbub of voices and exclamations, Muo is unable to make out where these midnight visitors hail from. Are they from Japan, Taiwan, Hong Kong? When they sit down and start playing mah-jong, he decides they must be Chinese. The empire of mah-jong holds complete sway over a billion Chinese aficionados. How like the Chinese to play mah-jong while waiting for a meal of fresh steamed crab, rather than risk a moment of boredom! His theory is substantiated when one of the men, presumably the driver since he is sitting near the empty coach, takes out his mouth-organ and plays a revolutionary song from the sixties.

'Over in your prison, my dear Volcano,' thinks Muo, 'there are no mouth-organs. Banned. Nor is there crab-meat – just a few slivers of pork twice weekly, buried under slimy cabbage leaves on Wednesdays and floating forlornly on the surface of cabbage soup on Saturdays. Cabbage, day in day out. Boiled cabbage, stir-fried cabbage, rotten, worm-eaten cabbage; cabbage with sand in it, and hairs from goodness knows who or what. Cabbage with rusty nails. Cabbage without end. No mah-jong in prison either. When I arrived back in China and was staying with my parents, I visited you several times. You told me during one such visit that there was only one game played in your cell. You called it Mrs Tang's weewee', Mrs Tang being a doctor's wife condemned for involuntary manslaughter. She had difficulty urinating due to a venereal infection. Each time she squatted over the communal soil-bucket her cellmates would jump with excitement at the opportunity to play their favourite game: as they waited for the amber-tinged, odorous liquid to discharge

46

itself from her poisoned bladder, they placed feverish bets on the degree of compliance that would be shown by her urethra, using as the stakes a few morsels saved from their precious pork rations. A tense silence ensued. If the attempt failed and Mrs Tang was unable to express any urine, those who had wagered that she would indeed fail cheered and danced with voluptuous greed, drooling as if they could already taste the meat in their mouths. As for the others who had wagered the opposite, they rose up and formed a tight circle around Mrs Tang shouting, 'Go on! Push! Relax the sphincter!' as if she were in labour. As a result of their encouragement Mrs Tang might, to the accompaniment of a piercing cry, let a few droplets fall into the bucket. The sound, although barely audible, announced that God had changed sides, granting temporary glee to some and plunging others into renewed frustration.

'I remember well my first visit to you. As I was ushered to the inner recesses of your prison, I looked up and was aghast to see immense black characters daubed on a very long white wall surmounted by barbed wire: "WHO ARE YOU? WHERE ARE YOU? WHY ARE YOU HERE?" (You are my Volcano of the Old Moon, thirty-six years old, unmarried, a photographer who took secret pictures of people being tortured by the Chinese police and took them to the European press. You are in Chengdu women's jail where you await the outcome of your trial.)'

The sea, tranquil now, beckons to Muo, who climbs down from his rocky perch and steps gingerly into the water. He is bothered by his glasses, so he rescales the rocks to put them away in the pocket of his trousers. For a moment he thinks of diving from the rock, but daren't, so he climbs back down and splashes in from the shore. It takes him some time to reach the middle of the bay. He swims at a slow, studied and distinctly unathletic pace, moving his arms and legs in typical Muosian fashion. The rhythm of his strokes is gentle, ceremonious, like that of tai chi, or the cadence of an ancient poem of the Tang Dynasty. Under the violet night sky with its timeless stars and the murmuring, mysterious tide, Muo is reminded of a Schubert sonata that he couldn't abide on account of all those repetitive chords, until, that is, he heard it played by a Russian pianist by the name of Richter. What poetry! Such is the magic that delights our young disciple of Freud.

Suddenly there is a cry in the night, slightly muffled, possibly female, but he is not sure . . .

'Oh Volcano, how you laughed at the way I swam during swimming instruction down at the university pool. With just two or three long, calculated strokes you shot right past me like a giant frog, then turned round to say, "How do you manage to swim so slowly? You're like an old woman with bound feet!" You got out of the pool and imitated my movements in front of everybody. The water dripped from your slender body, with its delightful scattering of faint little chicken-pox scars. Then you sat down on the side and kicked your dazzling legs in the greenish-brown water. I swam over to you and stammered that the only impression I could do was of a monkey, a talent acquired during my years of re-education in the mountains, where monkeys abounded. But you didn't believe a word of it, did you, my sceptical, keen-eyed, proud Volcano of the Old Moon? You simply dived into the pool and sped away.'

The sombre, murky tide complicates Muo's efforts to swim eastwards across the bay. He has heard faint cries in the distance, seemingly drifting in the air somewhere out to sea, and his curiosity is aroused. What can it be? A woman? A siren? After several minutes of vigorous breast stroke he discerns, despite the absence of his glasses, a glimmer of light. A lamp belonging to some crab-catchers, he supposes. The cries fall silent. He can sense that there is something different about this fishing craft, but can't put his finger on it. For one

48

thing, the irregular way the lamp sways above the waves is strange. Either it judders wildly as if the boat were about to capsize in a raging storm (even though the sea is as tranquil as a sleeping infant), or it leans towards the water within a hair's breadth of being extinguished before righting itself again. Although he is so close to the boat that he can see the net rippling on the water, he can't see anyone on the madly tossing craft. Is it an hallucination? A mirage? A vessel in distress? Has the woman succumbed after her final cry for help? Was she a crab-catcher? The survivor of a shipwreck? A clandestine emigrant? The victim of a shark? Of pirates? Of assassination? Fired by notions of good citizenship and chivalry, our Chinese Sherlock Holmes approaches the craft and makes to climb over the side, but is halted by the muffled noises rising from the interior. They don't sound like cries so much as heavy breathing, panting, grunts and groans. His cheeks burning with shame, he withdraws as discreetly as he can for fear of being taken for a nautical peeping tom.

The invisible, muscular fingers of pianist Richter fly nimbly over the keys as Schubert's sonata accompanies the creaking of the craft with its cargo of lust and ecstasy. A sonata in honour of the copulating crab-catcher – a naked prince of the sea – and his unseen partner, perhaps in rags and smelling of fish, but for now queen of the sombre tide.

'One summer evening in Paris, Volcano, my room was wreathed in spicy vapours rising from the pans of steaming broth on my two hot-plates, into which my Chinese guests – all exiles of various kinds, political, economic and even cultural – ritually dipped their chopsticks holding shrimps, shreds of beef, vegetables, tofu, bamboo shoots, cabbage, fragrant mushrooms etc. We were hotly debating something, as was usual in our company of political refugees, students, street artists and a blind poet. I can't remember what. All I remember is that, at one point during the increasingly passionate conversation, the steamy air sizzled with a spray of blue sparks from an electric socket. No one took any notice. The sparks kept coming. Then, in a fit of rage, the blind poet rose, took two hundred-franc notes from his wallet and waved them under my nose, exclaiming, "How can you discuss psychoanalysis if you've never made love!"

'At this, everyone lapsed into silence. The blind man continued: "Here, take these two-hundred francs, jump into a cab, go straight to the rue Saint-Denis and find yourself a whore. *Then* you can tell me all about Freud and Lacan – once you've had a proper fuck."

'He tried to slap the money down on the table, but the bills fluttered away and landed, one in each saucepan, where they floated briefly on the oily broth before sinking to the bottom. Retrieving the money gave rise to an indescribable commotion, which was further exacerbated when the fuses blew and the room was plunged into utter darkness.'

Peering short-sightedly, Muo gropes his way up to the rocky outcrop where he left his clothes and lies down flat on his back. The breeze has softened, and in the lapping of the tide he can make out the rattle of mah-jong tiles and the strains of the mouth-organ. The banquet of white-meat crab is still being prepared in the restaurant. The tune, this time from a Chinese opera, is totally unsuited to the mouth-organ but nevertheless not too badly performed by the driver, who gives it a vivacious and cheerful twist. Muo joins in, first whistling a few bars, then singing along until the driver launches into a sentimental Hong Kong love song. Muo hums it good humouredly and then starts singing old ditties that he remembers, culminating in the rendition of a song entitled *The Mah-jong Player*, during which he displays such fervour that the entire clientele of the open-air restaurant takes up the chorus:

> *Were it not for mah-jong*
> *Our nights would be too long*

Ah mah-jong!
Ah mah-jong
Although I haven't a penny
Joy comes from being many
It's wonderful
It's marvellous

The song is no more incongruous than the sight of the mah-jong players in an impromptu beach restaurant, or the glow of multicoloured light-bulbs on the murmuring tide. A cloud slides slowly across the moon and a shiver runs down Muo's spine as he remembers a remark made by Judge Di, who shares his name with the fictitious Chinese detective Judge Dee, a character from the Tang dynasty invented by the Dutch novelist Robert van Gulik, an author also distinguished for his erudition regarding the sexual habits of ancient China: 'Ah, the pretty little mah-jong tiles, what exquisite freshness – as exquisite as the ivory hand of a young virgin.'

The aroma of steamed crabs wafts towards him on the breeze: a smell of cloves, finely chopped ginger, basil, mountain herbs and white cinnamon, whose fragrance is heightened by the gusty, salty sea air. The mah-jong tiles are brusquely swept into little heaps and make way for steaming dishes, bowls of rice, glasses brimming with Chinese liquor, imitation French wine and fake Mexican beer.

Reclining on his rock, Muo mulls over Judge Di's remark . . .

It was back in May, two months before his suitcase was stolen on the night train and four-and-a-half months before this wakeful night beneath the baroque stars on Crab Bay, that he presented Judge Di with his credentials, in other words with a ten-thousand-dollar backhander.

The Judge's full name is Di Jiangui, Di being his family name – he is from a working-class background – and Jiangui his given name, which is very common among Chinese males whose date of birth coincides with that of the Communist People's Republic in 1949. It signifies 'Construction of the Fatherland', a phrase used in the solemn vows made in Tiananmen Square by Chairman Mao in his somewhat reedy counter-tenor voice. In the early seventies, Di Jiangui joined the police force. He spent fifteen years propping up that pillar of the dictatorship of the proletariat, becoming in the process a member of one of the elite firing squads charged with executions, as well as a good Communist. In 1985 he was rewarded with appointment to the tribunal of Chengdu, a city of some eight million inhabitants. It was the heyday of economic reform and the position was among the most privileged and sought-after. Like most government affairs, especially those involving the judiciary, business was conducted with bribes. Di had been quick to establish one thousand dollars as the fee that would influence his judgement of a criminal offence, an astronomic sum at the time. Subsequently, and in step with the rising cost of living, his fee had increased to ten thousand dollars, which is where it was when Volcano of the Old Moon was arrested and fell into his clutches in what was considered a political affair.

Although our psychoanalyst had been born and bred in this land so dear to his heart, there gaining personal experience of the Cultural Revolution and ensuing innovations, and although he had often told his friends, 'The best saying in Mao's Little Red Book, the only saying with any truth in it is that the Chinese Communist Party makes miracles happen', this particular miracle – the bribing of judges – had shocked him. He did his best not to show his distaste when the lawyer assigned to Volcano of the Old Moon explained the procedure to him. The lawyer, aged thirty-five, was appointed by the tribunal but supposedly independent, although he secretly worked for the tribunal and was, besides, a member of the same Communist cell as Judge Di, i.e. that of the tribunal. (Another miracle, less spectacular than the first but no less revelatory, that shocked Muo.) This lawyer had a reputation for dressing exclusively in black Pierre Cardin suits and bright red neckties (the latter detail having elicited a famous outburst from an illiterate salesgirl in the middle of her trial who, accused of stealing by this same lawyer acting for her employer, thrust her chin in his direction and sneered, 'Why don't you take a look in the mirror, scumbag! Fancy wearing your wife's sanitary towel round your neck!'). He was in great demand because of his bulging address book, his warm relations with judges, and his skill at organising pre-trial banquets in private salons or behind fake antique screens in five-star restaurants (at the Holiday Inn, for example). There he would play host to judges and alleged murderers so that the two parties might negotiate the prison term the former would administer to the latter while savouring together, in the most perfect complicity, an array of exotic delicacies: abalone, a gastropod mollusc from South Africa, or bears' paws imported from Siberia, or the dish called 'Three Cries', which entails the consumption of live baby mice whose squeals resemble those of a newborn infant. (The first cry sounds when they are pinched between the jade chopsticks, the second when they are dipped into a sauce made with vinegar and ginger, the third when they land in the diner's mouth, among the yellow teeth of a judge perhaps, or the dazzling dentures of a lawyer, his red, Pierre Cardin tie stained with grease.)

The dossier on Volcano of the Old Moon proved both complicated and convoluted. In so far as it concerned politics and the nation's reputation, the crooked lawyer was unequivocal: there was no conceivable banquet, however expensive, that could possibly smooth things over; indeed it was necessary to proceed with 'the utmost caution, method and patience, as the slightest false step could prove fatal'.

The lawyer had sat amid the clutter of saucepans in the kitchen of Muo's family home and unfolded his plan with the air of a consummate strategist. Ostensibly ingenious, it revolved around the regularity of Judge Di's weekly jog. From the outset of Di's career as a magistrate, he had been in the habit of 'recharging his batteries' every Sunday morning by going for a solitary run on a stretch of wasteland used for executions by firing squad, whether of individuals or groups. The site, so familiar and dear to this former elite marksman, lay to the north of the city at the foot of Mill Hill. The lawyer's idea was that Muo should meet Di there and introduce himself, not as a psychoanalyst, but as a law professor from a major Chinese university who had been charged with surveying execution grounds in connection with the government's plan to draft new legislation. The encounter was to appear fortuitous. The Judge would launch into an impassioned account of his experiences, to which Muo would respond with such effusive cries of admiration and surprise that the Judge – this was the crux – would accept Muo's invitation to take tea with him. Their ensuing tête-à-tête in the private room of a teahouse would give Muo an opportunity to mention the plight of Volcano of the Old Moon and try to secure her release in exchange for a ten-thousand-dollar bribe.

The following Sunday morning Muo had put on one of his father's old suits, gulped down the bowl of instant noodles with an egg that his mother had prepared for him (his parents, both low-ranking assistants at the faculty of Western medicine and thus reluctant to have anything to do with Volcano of the Old Moon's case, kept a discreet and prudent distance) and had taken a taxi across the city, arriving at Mill Hill soon after daybreak. The fading chorus of toads, frogs and crickets put him in mind of the geographical configuration of the hillside where, as a twelve-year-old, he had spent the summer helping the revolutionary peasants with their work. Setting off up the hill along a footpath that he took to be a short cut, he almost lost his balance several times, not because of any irregularity underfoot but because, each time he encountered one of the rare human shapes on the path, he was convinced, regardless of their gender, that they were Judge Di, and his cheeks would burn, as if his blood had turned viscous and black. At one point he thought he was lost among the multitude of forking paths covering the now deserted hillside. Then he came upon a vast burial ground littered with graves. Some were marked with tombstones, while others, belonging to those firing-squad victims whose families were too poor to claim the bodies, were no more than mounds of bare soil – no stone, no name and no date.

A water-buffalo wearing a bell round its neck appeared at the end of the misty path winding among the graves. The bell clanged, making Muo, who thought he saw Judge Di everywhere, jump out of his skin. Mastering himself, he saw that there were two figures following the buffalo: a young peasant in a Western-style jacket and jeans rolled up to his knees carrying a heavy wooden plough on his shoulder, and a girl in a skirt and high, square-heeled shoes trundling a bicycle. This modern-looking pair did not seem in the least surprised to see him; they pointed him in the right direction and, without interrupting their warm, laughing chatter for a moment, moved away as in a pastoral poem, accompanied by the dulcet tones of the buffalo's bell. 'Such harmony in the morning hours!' thought Muo. 'How wonderful my socialist homeland is, and how deserving of tributes from this errant son!'

Contrary to what he remembered, the place of torture, scene of many a death by firing squad, was utterly unremarkable. No tall yellow grasses swaying and whispering in the breeze, no soil drenched with victims' tears, no drifts of pale mushrooms, fleshy and brooding in the damp undergrowth, no vultures winging darkly overhead. Just featureless waste-land, deceptive to the extreme. Devoid of colour, sound, and meaning. Stonily indifferent to suffering. Once Muo's eyes adapted to the surroundings, he spotted two figures in the distance, soundlessly digging a hole with their spades.

'Could it be,' he asked himself, 'that Judge Di has taken up a new way of recharging his batteries? Or are they ghosts? The souls of two executed prisoners seeking revenge?'

The face of a long-forgotten boyhood friend floated into his mind, causing him to shiver. It was Chen, nicknamed White Hair, the only one of his friends to have struck it rich in the early eighties, when he had married the daughter of the city's mayor (and director of a company quoted on the Stock Exchange), only to end up being condemned to death for trafficking in foreign vehicles. Had he been shot at the foot of this hill? Had he been made to kneel, his back exposed to the barrel of an anonymous gun? Muo had heard it said that much importance was attached to the position of the condemned man's fingers, and that his arms were tied in such a way that the bullets fired would enter the body in the small gap between forefinger and thumb, behind which lay the heart.

The men with spades were dressed in plain military uniforms without officer's epaulets. Neither of them could be Judge Di. The heat drained from Muo's face. One of them wore an oversized metal helmet decorated with a red star, which slipped off when he drove the spade into the ground with his muddy boot and tumbled into the hole at his feet. Bending down to retrieve it the soldier was much amused to discover a green-and-brown striped earthworm wriggling on the smooth dome of the helmet. He shook the creature off and, taking his spade, hacked it into several pieces, each splattering blow eliciting peals of rowdy laughter from the twosome.

It was not the first time Muo had surprised himself, but his ability as an actor was a particularly pleasing discovery. The lies poured poetically from his lips – 'Oh, naked flower of my lips,' as the poet Mallarmé said. Muo even succeeded in imitating the earnest, vaguely academic tones of a law professor from Beijing, and duly impressed the two soldiers with the importance of his governmental mission. He inquired after the purpose of the holes they were digging.

'Without them,' explained the worm-killer, 'the bodies just roll about and spill blood all over the place.'

'Criminals are executed on their knees,' added the other man, who seemed slightly more intelligent, 'and keel over into the hole. If they thrash about in their death throes, the loose earth collapses on to them and pins them down. Next the doctors come to remove the organs. You could get a special permit, if you're interested – for tomorrow. Then you can see for yourself what the procedure is.'

Muo cast a furtive glance at the gaping holes, and felt his blood run cold.

'Your information has been most helpful,' he said, pretending to take notes in his exercise book.

'He's the philosopher of our gang,' retorted the worm-killer, indicating his companion.

Almost cowering with respect, the soldiers took their leave. As they turned to go, Muo caught sight of a man of about fifty running towards them. He was wearing a white shirt with blue stripes rather like a pyjama jacket with two buttons missing.

'That must be Judge Di on his daily run,' observed Muo in a voice tremulous with excitement.

'Judge Di?' the worm-killer asked the philosopher. 'Who's he? Take a look at that shirt – it's just like what they make the half-wits wear at the lunatic asylum.'

'Haven't you read any of that Dutchman van Gulik's detective novels?' replied the philosopher. 'Judge Dee – such a splendid character, such a gifted sleuth! Surely what he is wearing is in fact the robe of a famous Tang Dynasty judge.'

He grinned, a gleam in his eye, and shook Muo's hand, after which he and his fellow digger walked away. Muo hurried after them.

'Please stop fooling with me. The man I am waiting for is the top judge in Chengdu, a man with the power to sentence anyone to death. Is that him?'

'Of course it is,' affirmed the philosopher, winking discreetly at his companion.

'Yes, that couldn't be anyone other than the famous Judge Di, King of Criminal Hell,' concluded the worm-killer.

Sitting on the ground in the middle of the wasteland, Muo watched the man run round in circles. He did not dare approach him yet, so he waited, reflecting that his mechanical, inexorable pace was akin to that of the army of ants bearing away the segments of the mutilated earthworm and embarking on the difficult ascent of a nearby tree trunk. Suddenly, a vehicle hooting in the distance made the presumed Judge Di freeze in a theatrical, listening pose. Muo hesitated. He let another minute pass, during which time there was no further hooting. The runner took a deep breath and carried on running, just as the ants carried on struggling with their load. At last Muo rose and, biting his dry, cracked lip with apprehension, strode towards him.

'Judge Di, I presume?'

The man eyed him in silence. Muo thought he saw a muscle twitch in his face. With mixed emotions – part fear, part respect, part contempt – he studied the man's pale, gaunt features. He was extremely thin, just skin and bone, and the white shirt with the blue stripes flapped around his frame like a shapeless sack. His hair was dishevelled and there were dark, spreading pouches under his eyes. Suddenly Muo was seized by the idea that the man standing before him was just a poor fellow suffering mental anguish, haunted by the ghosts of his victims. A lost soul. Muo extended his hand, forgetting all about the subterfuge he had prepared.

'My name is Muo. I am a psychoanalyst, recently returned from a spell in Paris. It is my belief, your Honour, that I can be of assistance to you.'

'Of assistance to me?'

'Yes. It is clear that you would benefit from psychoanalysis, as propounded in the theories of Freud and Lacan and . . .'

Freud. A name that was anathema to the ears of this individual. Too late.

Before Muo could finish, the presumed Judge Di swung his fist in a punch of such ferocity that it left Muo's glasses embedded in his face. Howling with pain, Muo heard a loud buzzing in his head and saw stars, after which everything went dark. He couldn't understand why he was lying sprawled on the ground, but instinctively tore off his glasses (that vital accessory in the life of a short-sighted intellectual), before passing out from the violent kicks aimed at his skull, abdomen, kidneys and liver.

The presumed Judge Di made off. However, after a few seconds he halted and retraced his steps. He bent over the unconscious body, divested Muo of his jacket and coolly replaced it with his own striped shirt. With a grim smile, he buttoned it all the way up. Once again, he was startled by the sound of a vehicle's horn. Wearing Muo's jacket, he fled, while an ambulance from the psychiatric hospital hove into view, sirens wailing. It rolled onto the wasteland and described a circle around Muo before stopping to let out two hulking paramedics, one of whom held a photograph. The men advanced cautiously towards the prostrate figure.

Muo woke, opened his eyes and looked up to see two stooping giants staring him in the face. At the same time he noticed that he was wearing his assailant's striped shirt, which stank horribly.

'Smells foul, this crazy shirt,' he mumbled, then passed out again.

The paramedics conducted a lengthy comparison with the photograph. Even without his glasses, Muo's face was impossible to recognise on account of the large purple bruises and the blood streaming from his nostrils, but after due deliberation they decided that he was indeed the man in the photograph: the madman who had escaped from the hospital through the main sewer leading from the latrines. (After searching without luck for two days, they had been alerted to his whereabouts by a telephone call from a couple of young peasants.) They tried rousing him by slapping his face. To no avail. Lights flashing, the ambulance spurted away across the execution ground with Muo handcuffed in the back.

As for Judge Di, the real one, he had been unable to recharge his batteries on that particular Sunday: he was felled by a cold, caught whilst up all night playing mah-jong, that irresistible game.

WHAT IF YOU SUDDENLY TURNED INTO SOMEONE ELSE?

From our special correspondent in Chengdu

A week ago Mr Ma Jin, recently escaped from Chengdu Psychiatric Institute, was found in a coma, his face battered and bruised, on the execution ground at the foot of Mill Hill. He was suffering from mild concussion, and was transported back to the Institute where, upon regaining consciousness, he categorically denied his identity, claiming instead to be one Muo, a psychoanalyst returned from France, a follower of Freud (though he found Lacan 'intellectually interesting, blessed with a strong personality, capable of persuading his Parisian clientèle to pay high fees for private sessions that never lasted more than five minutes'.) Dr Wang Yu-sheng, one of China's most eminent psychiatrists and deputy director of the Centre for the Treatment of Mental Illness at Beijing, and Mr Qui, titular Professor of French at the University of Shanghai, were called upon to shed light on the case. They subjected the escapee, the aforesaid Ma Jin, to a series of tests, in the course of which he recited, in a loud voice and in French, entire passages of Freud, phrases from Lacan, Foucault, Derrida, and the opening lines of a poem by Paul Valéry. He also reeled off the names of the street where he lived in Paris, his Métro station, the corner tobacconist (called 'Le chien qui fume'), the café at the foot of his building and the bistro across the street. He invited his examiners to savour the beauty of the French word 'amour' as well as the richness and untranslatable complexity of the word 'hélas'. This brilliant Francophone (Ma Jin or Muo?) claimed to have been attacked and robbed by a jogger, but was unable to recall the reason for his presence at the execution ground. No doubt this memory loss was caused by the blows he sustained.

The two eminent experts issued a formal account of their findings, notably that the case was among the most perplexing in the history of psychiatry, a conclusion that caused an immediate stir among the intellectuals of Chengdu. Professors, researchers, journalists, students of literature, and especially students of philosophy with long-cherished ambitions to become psychoanalysts, flocked to the Institute during opening hours, and the room of the French-speaking escapee was overrun with visitors. It was a single room, high security, with reinforced bars over the window and a nurse who kept guard with his eye glued to the peephole in the door. The patient became the subject of heated intellectual debate and speculation in this city. When I paid him a visit myself, he was being interviewed by a researcher into Chinese mythology, who took copious notes and simultaneously recorded the interview on tape. The researcher's aim was to establish a link between the persona of Ma Jin-Muo and that of the famous immortal cripple, a very popular folk hero. (According to legend, the soul of a monk returned from a spiritual journey to discover that one of his disciples had mistakenly burned his body, which had lain inanimate for the past seven days. The God of Mercy took pity and wrought a miracle, enabling the errant soul to slip unnoticed into the body of a crippled beggar who had been dead only a short while. Picture the scene: the resuscitated body rising up, giving a triumphant laugh and making its way, limping, towards the temple with a view to saving the traumatised, suicidal disciple.) Among the gifts piled high around the patient's hospital bed, I came across a little magazine put together and printed by local students containing an article defending a different hypothesis, according to which the escapee was in fact the reincarnation of a translator from the French who was shot long ago. Sources within the clinic confirmed that agreement had been reached on one point: that the patient was different from all the others. He never complained about the food or the strict discipline. He gave the impression of being content with his situation. He kept saying, without a hint of mockery, that an asylum is the world's best university. A gentle, kind, considerate man who made notes on everything, from the hysterical cries in the night to the after-effects of electroshock therapy and the dreams of his fellow patients, he was described as 'a romantic type' by the nurse who kept watch over him. Despite the sedatives he took morning and night, he regaled me with many salacious and not-so-salacious stories, both Chinese and foreign, and in return asked me to bring him writing paper. He proceeded to compose a succession of very long love letters, in full realisation that they would never arrive at their destination. All the letters were addressed to a female prisoner, his sweetheart, who, he said, had a strange and unforgettable name. But he never told me what it was. It was his secret.

Yesterday Ma Jin's wife, a former opera singer, was summoned by the Institute's governors to confirm the escapee's identity. When she first saw him she seemed shocked. She had not seen her husband, a convert to Buddhism, since he left her to take up residence in a temple three years ago, and since then his appearance has apparently changed almost beyond recognition. She expressed a wish to speak to him in private, which she was permitted to do. They spoke for an hour, at the end of which she confirmed that he was indeed her husband, Ma Jin. She filled in the forms for his release and took him home. But that was not the end of it. That very evening, the supposed Ma Jin, whilst pretending to take a shower, escaped out of the window with the aid of a long rope made of towels and nightshirts knotted together. He has not been seen since.

This morning, the former opera singer told reporters: 'I sincerely hope he will be found.'

4

A Model Aeroplane

The third drawer of Judge Di's desk was open a crack, just as Volcano of the Old Moon's lawyer had predicted. This barely perceptible aperture was the secret sign that an offering would be accepted. The convention was that the corruptor would slip a red envelope containing the bribe into the drawer, while the beneficiary pretended not to notice.

From behind his miraculously intact spectacles, Muo's bleary eyes alighted on the minute opening of the drawer, much as, in a spy film, a secret agent recognises a stranger as one of his number thanks to a prearranged signal. His heart in his throat, he felt a magical wine rise to his head. The Judge's assistant had shown him into the office and then departed, leaving him alone, seated on a leather sofa from which emanated a lingering, musty smell. Muo slipped his hand into his briefcase and ran his fingertips over the envelope, which bulged voluptuously with one hundred brand-new hundred-dollar bills secured by a thin elastic band stretched to its limit.

Muo got up from the couch and sidled towards the desk.

The heat from his face had steamed up his glasses, and he felt light-headed. Never had he come so close to happiness. Before him stood the radiant article of furniture encircled by a brilliant halo, as though Volcano of the Old Moon herself might spring from the third drawer any moment. He feasted his eyes on the resplendent crack he had finally discovered in the armour of the Dictatorship of the Proletariat.

In a flash it dawned on him: of course, this famous third drawer was ever positioned thus. A permanent green light! A message addressed to all and sundry, not just to him. How many times already must the corrupt owner of the desk have opened the drawer and retrieved the red envelopes, without the least regard for the identity of the donor or the reason for his donation?

Sobered by this insight, Muo saw the desk for what it was: a polished wooden cabinet with a dusty marble top, upon which stood a framed photograph of two smiling girls (the Judge's daughters?) and a television that served as a pedestal for a strange-looking object. Glinting in the light filtering through the Venetian blinds, this was the only item in the office that could be said to have any artistic merit – a scale model of a fighter plane made entirely of spent cartridges. Hundreds upon hundreds of them, their copper glittering – each one engraved with a name and a date.

Muo heard footsteps on the marble threshold and then on the wooden floor, and his gaze left the fighter plane to meet that of an elderly man. He wore a navy-blue uniform with, embroidered on the sleeve, the red emblem of the Republic of China and the word 'Magistrate'.

'Good day,' murmured Muo. 'Are you Mr Di?'

'Judge Di,' corrected the old man with the thin moustache as he posted himself beside the desk.

He had a desiccated air. He was no taller than Muo, despite his black thick-heeled shoes. His hair was thinning, too. How old would he be? Fifty-five? Sixty? One thing was certain: he bore not the slightest resemblance to the psychotic escapee Muo had encountered on the execution ground. The old man standing before him could never have dealt all those blows. His violence was of a different, more dangerous order.

Judge Di's eyes were small, but the left one was minute, and almost permanently closed. He opened the first drawer and took out several small bottles, from which he poured a number of tablets and pills on to the marble slab. He lined them up, counting as he went, then took a large bowl of tea and swallowed all ten of them. When Muo introduced himself as the editor of a scientific publishing house in Beijing, the Judge fixed his right eye on him and narrowed the eyelid to a slit, just like an elite marksman coolly appraising his target.

Hardly had Muo embarked on the explanation for his visit – stammering, rolling his eyes and trying desperately to recall the exact words the lawyer had instructed him to use – when he was cut short by the Judge's mobile phone.

The call was about the Olympic Games that were taking place in Sydney at the time. Exulting in the news that China had just won a twentieth gold medal in the women's judo (which put China one place behind the United States but ahead of Russia), the judge switched the television on. Two young women of impressive size were rolling across the screen in slow motion, panting and grunting. The judge's left eye opened, moist with tears provoked by the heart-warming success of the fatherland. Still talking on the phone, he advanced towards his visitor, much to Muo's distress. He had no idea how to interpret this extraordinary breach of protocol.

'Is he going to embrace me?' he wondered.

The judge was jubilant. He raised his arm and kept it up in the air, as if awaiting the same gesture and enthusiasm from his visitor so that they might share a triumphant slap of hands, the way two football players celebrate a winning goal.

In his bewilderment Muo thought it might be another secret sign, some code that the lawyer had forgotten to tell him about. But what did the sign mean? Was he to do the same? Through the mist of his glasses the hand looked ghastly, with some of the fingers barely discernible and others in sharp focus, especially the crooked index finger with its dirty nail, the finger of an elite marksman pulling the trigger. Was he supposed to mimic that gesture? No, that would be a fatal error. But how else should he respond to this secret signal?

Somewhat bemused by his visitor's lack of response, Judge Di lowered his arm and resumed pacing the room. The television screen was filled by the red flag with its five yellow stars (the largest symbolising the almighty Communist Party, the four small ones representing the workers, peasants, soldiers and revolutionary traders) flying over the grandstand in readiness for the ceremony. China's national anthem, rousingly played on trumpets, blared so loudly that it set the miniature fighter plane atremble on the television.

Heaving a deep sigh, Muo took off his spectacles and wiped them on his jacket. This gesture did not escape the notice of the former elite marksman.

'Are you weeping with emotion?' he wanted to know. 'I had taken you for the cold, reserved type.'

Once more Judge Di raised his arm towards Muo, seeking the triumphant slap of hands.

Deciding to risk a response, Muo raised one leg and stood balancing on the other like a pitiful war invalid.

'With the hand, the hand,' the judge said, winking with his right eye in an expression of exceptional indulgence.

Misunderstanding, Muo grabbed his ankle and, with excruciating effort, raised his foot all the way to his shoulder, like a dancer doing warm-up exercises. The judge's left eye closed; the right eye stared coldly. Abruptly, he switched off his mobile.

'What sort of a circus act is this? Do you realise where you are? You are in the office of Judge Di.'

'It's all the lawyer's fault,' Muo murmured, lowering his foot to the ground. 'But . . . it is because . . . forgive me . . . the lawyer acting for my friend, Volcano of the Old Moon . . .'

He was interrupted by guffaws from the Judge. The dark, hoarse laughter chilled him to the marrow. He took it to be the prelude to some cruel announcement. On the television the Chinese judo champion sang with lifted face the national anthem, then faded out for the hockey finals between Russia and Canada.

'Volcano of the Old Moon?' asked the Judge, sprawled on his Grand-Inquisitor throne.

'Yes, she is my friend.'

'How unfortunate! The girl who sold photographs to the foreign press . . .'

'She didn't sell them. They didn't earn her a single yuan.'

The judge's fingers tapped the keys of his mobile.

'Just a moment, I must get in touch with the Party Secretary.'

It is hard to describe the depths of Muo's despair on hearing this. He was terrified. Why would the Judge want to make a call to the Party headquarters? It was sure to be about Volcano of the Old Moon. Was her crime so serious as to warrant sanctions from the Party leader? His shirt, at first drenched with sweat during his clumsy acrobatics, now clung icily to his skin.

A long telephone conversation ensued. Judge Di began by proposing a temporary lifting of the ban on firecrackers so that the people might celebrate the Olympic gold medal. He then turned briefly to matters of general security, enthused about sport, grumbled over budget cuts in the law courts, touched upon the construction of the new Palace of Justice, and ended by suggesting his interlocutor might like to meet for a game of mah-jong. It was at that moment that Muo heard the unforgettable phrase: 'as exquisite as the ivory hand of a young virgin'.

Muo had almost exhausted his strength. The least shift in the judge's tone, the slightest clearing of the throat or harsh word made his heart pound like a frightened rabbit, opening vistas of horror. A misplaced respect for protocol held him back from doing what he was supposed to do: take out his lavish gift, approach the third drawer and slip the envelope inside.

The Chinese sports commentator shrieked when the Russian centre forward shot a winning goal in the final minute of the match. The supporters went wild. The Russian flag was raised over the grandstand.

With faltering step, Muo approached the desk. He had the impression that Judge Di was following his every move. Suddenly he realised what all the posturing had been about: it was an elaborate, well-enacted charade, whose sole purpose had been to steer him towards transferring the envelope from his briefcase to the drawer.

Disgusted by the feeling of being no more than a puppet on an invisible string, he drew back from the drawer and stared at the miniature fighter plane, on which the copper no longer glittered.

By chance he spied a detail: several cartridges bore the same date. The truth flashed across his mind: the name engraved on each cartridge was that of a prisoner shot by the former elite marksman, and the date that of the execution. Each cartridge was the relic of a killer bullet fired into the small wedge of flesh between the index finger and the thumb, behind which resided the heart of the condemned man.

Although he knew about Judge Di's past activities, Muo was deeply shocked by this artefact, fashioned with such care and love. Suddenly the man before him struck him as a devil thirsting after blood, an incarnation of gratuitous cruelty and evil. Surely he should have been surrounded by vengeful spirits. But they were nowhere in sight. Muo, though sceptical about the existence of God, had believed in ghosts since childhood. Now his faith collapsed. He was being forced to pay tribute to a tyrant, whom even the dead dared not disturb. There was nothing to raise a goose pimple; not a single ghost haunted the judge. Muo felt his desire to take action on behalf of Volcano of the Old Moon dissipate, ebb away, recede from him despite his initial resolve. He replaced the envelope in his briefcase and turned to leave the office.

A perplexed Judge Di listened to his increasingly hurried steps clattering down the corridor. Putting his head round the door, the judge saw Muo slip something into the assistant's hand. A twenty-yuan note, no doubt. Here, for you. Mute thanks. Goodbye.

5

Backscratching

For a minute or two at least, Muo thought he was seeing a
revenant ghost. He did not recognise him at once on account
of his bruised eyes. It was merely a sensation of having seen
before the figure poised at the top of the glassed-in escalator
on the exterior of an ultra-modern shopping centre copied
from the Centre Pompidou in Paris. A pair of melancholy
eyes that seemed somehow familiar. But where had he seen
them before? Or was he hallucinating? The crumpled suit,
the pepper-and-salt crew cut, the bony face, the deep lines on
either side of the nose running down to the corners of the
mouth then on past the chin to vanish in the wrinkled neck
– did he know them? Subdued sunlight filtered through the
milky glass of the tunnel. The escalators swished in parallel,
one going up, the other down. The ghost came striding down
towards Muo, who was going up. Again Muo had the
sensation of déjà vu. Who could it be? Muo heard himself
being addressed by his childhood nickname of 'Little Four
Eyes'. It was the voice that revealed his identity: the ghost
was none other than his friend who married the mayor's

daughter, the one condemned to death by firing squad who should have been shot several years ago.

The escalator continued upwards. Muo's arm was gripped by the firm hand of his friend from times past, whose wrist bore the fated number 3519, and, in a daze, he found himself pushing his way down the escalator among the shopping carts and trolleys of the customers going up. A hallucinatory descent.

'What are you doing here?' he asked, so baffled that his own voice seemed distant to him, as in a dream. He was troubled by the words coming out of his mouth, which felt inappropriate to the situation. 'I have just escaped from the madhouse,' he added. 'What about you?'

'I'm on a tour of inspection.'

'Inspection of what?'

'Of restaurants.'

'Are you a restaurateur?'

'Not really. But my prison has opened two restaurants, and I am the manager. My father-in-law wangled it so my death sentence would be commuted to life imprisonment. I was able to persuade the prison governor to open a restaurant and make me the manager, assuring him it would bring in a lot of money. Which it did. As he was pleased with me, he decided to open a second one, here in the shopping mall.'

'You don't look as if you've struck it rich.'

'No. All the profits go to the prison. A reasonable price to pay for my daytime freedom.'

'Why daytime?'

'At dusk I go back to spend the night in a cell for lifers. It's right beside death row. Each time there's to be an execution, a guard goes past the door with a plate of meat and turns the corner into death row, after which you can hear him stop to deliver the plate to the man who's to be shot the next day. That's when I say to myself, "Shit, I've done pretty well to avoid that last supper." '

They went to the prison-owned restaurant in the shopping mall to celebrate their reunion. The Mongolian Saucepan, a self-service establishment operated on the 'as-much-as-you-can-eat' principle. Plate in hand, each diner took his pick (everybody pushing and shoving) from scores of platters set out on long counters: eels, pigs' brains, goats' blood, shrimps, squid, shellfish, snails, frogs' legs, ducks' feet, and so on, all for the single price of twenty-eight yuan (local beer included). Muo took in the hundred tables, the flushed faces leaning over gas rings on which saucepans bubbled, the chunks of meat or vegetable being dipped into a thick, hotly spiced broth. The steam, the aromas, the laughter and the voices of the diners bustling about between the tables and the dish-laden counters all conspired to cloud his mind. He found himself rambling on about the execution ground, the psychiatric clinic, Volcano of the Old Moon's lawyer, Judge Di . . . The floor of the restaurant was slippery with grease and filth, and the diners crossed it cautiously, as if walking on ice. For the elderly or for those who were short-sighted and clumsy like Muo, it was quite a challenge. A drunk in the washroom lost his balance. When he tried to get up, he kept slipping on the slimy floor and ended up falling asleep with his head against the urinal. Of course, The Mongolian Saucepan owed its festive atmosphere and popularity to the 'as much as you can eat for twenty-eight yuan' formula launched by the ex-condemned man. 'It's like a duel between the restaurant and the customer,' he explained to Muo. 'The first to give up is the loser.'

It was raining. The prisoner's car, a splendid, bright-red Fiat convertible with a chauffeur built like a boxer at the wheel, chugged valiantly up the hill to Judge Di's residence. Back in The Mongolian Saucepan, Muo's friend had said he would 'see what he could do', which offer had almost moved Muo, fast losing faith in his humanitarian and amorous mission, to tears.

At the top of the hill the prisoner told the driver to stop. He lit a small Dutch cigar and reflected. The furrows running from either side of his nose seemed deeper than ever. Muo did not dare look at him, let alone talk to him. Was he fine-tuning his master plan? Did he intend to phone ahead to say he was coming? Was he on the point of giving up? Or, conversely, was he mustering his courage? Muo did not know. The chauffeur cut the engine and all three sat motionless. Muo peered through the rain at a stand of poplar trees and a peasant in a straw cape toiling in a distant paddy field. Then his friend motioned the driver to continue. The Fiat spluttered to life then set off slowly, turning into a back street before pulling up at a metal gate in a boundary wall two metres high. The square-shouldered chauffeur got out first and opened the door for the mayor's son-in-law, who headed through the rain towards the entryphone.

The rain did not lift for another hour, during which time Muo stayed in the car. Stars were appearing in the sky; soon it would be time for his friend, manager by day, prisoner by night, to return to his cell. Just as Muo was beginning to feel defeated, the gate opened and out stepped his friend, who came over to the car grinning from ear to ear, thereby transforming the two gloomy furrows into a crinkly smile.

'Done,' he said, sliding into the passenger seat. 'But he doesn't want cash. He's got more than enough of that already. The only thing he asks of you in payment is a virgin for him to sleep with. A girl whose virginity is still intact, whose red melon has not yet been slashed . . .'

This strange expression, the 'slashed red melon', always reminded Muo of a sultry, clammy night, of baskets of freshly caught crabs, of luke-warm hard-boiled eggs, and a cave in the side of a mountain in Fujian, his father's birthplace. It was there that he had first heard it. He was ten years old at the time, and spending the holidays with his grandparents. One of his uncles, a one-time maths teacher now demoted to butcher for political reasons (and, though only thirty, so bent you would have sworn he was an old man), took him for a swim in a mountain river. They were caught in a summer storm and sought shelter in a cave which was already crowded with people of all ages: peasants, passers-by and men carrying baskets laden with dark, stirring crabs fished from a mountain lake and destined for export to Japan. One of the older crab-fishers, whose face was pocked like a skimmer, settled down against a rock. In a low voice interspersed with much spitting and coughing, he embarked on an interminable joke, while Muo shelled a still-warm hard-boiled egg given to him by a peasant woman. Under the Tang dynasty, the crab-fisher began, the Japanese, who had just rallied around their first king, were at pains to create a national flag, so they decided to follow the example of the Chinese. A spy was promptly sent to China, which, being more developed and civilised, was in the golden age of Empire. After many adventures at sea, the spy set foot on the Chinese coast. Night had fallen, and the weather was mild. In the first village he visited he came upon a boisterous crowd singing, drinking and dancing around a white sheet with a large red circle in the middle. The mood was decidedly festive. 'It must be their national feast day,' he thought, 'and that must be the Chinese flag.' He waited in the bushes until everyone had gone home before grabbing the prize for which he had braved months of gruelling travel beset by mortal perils and hunger, and vanishing into the night, not knowing that all he had was a sheet stained with the juice of 'a virgin's red melon slashed on her wedding night'.

The expression provoked waves of laughter throughout the cave. Meanwhile little Muo sat with his cold hands cupped around the shelled egg to warm them. Then, without knowing why, he stood up and marched over to the story-teller sitting by the fire, whose flames lit up the man's bare torso and made his shadow flicker on the wall. With all his might, Muo rammed the egg into the man's open mouth. The man swallowed, almost choked, then leaned back motionless against the rock, his face glistening in the firelight and his small glinting eyes rolling in their sockets. Muo still recalls touching the skin of that gaunt face, skin that resembled waxed paper, and how he counted the smallpox scars and reached out to feel them. That was how the expression 'slashed red melon' came to be etched in his memory: a panoply of colour awash with a shadowy, rustling tide that coursed through his veins and took possession of his body, the smell of the sea in the cave, the jagged rocks . . .

On the way home his uncle proved to be in exceptionally good humour, all things considered. (In the cave he had not dared say a word nor laugh along with the others.) The heavy downpour had lacquered the foliage on the trees. The air was deliciously fresh. The light was lyrical. Muo remembers the pair of them sitting on a slope, wreathed in the fragrance of wet bracken and gazing at an iridescent, snow-capped mountain in the distance. In a low voice, his uncle had taught him a poem from the Yuan dynasty, eight centuries old and forbidden by the Communists. He made him recite after him, word for word:

> A magnificent wedding took place tonight;
> But when I set out to explore the perfumed flower
> I found that Spring had already passed her by.
> Much red, little red, why ask for so much?
> No matter, it is of no matter!
> I am returning to you the length of white silk.

Muo had never imagined, even in his wildest dreams, that he would one day be tormented by the desire of a corrupt old judge to slash, with his bare, marksman's hands, a red melon in the first flush of ripeness. He even had a feeling that such cases as that of Judge Di, or indeed the whole Chinese people, had escaped the notice of his great master Freud, notwithstanding his supposed knowledge of every human perversion. In 'The Taboo of Virginity', Freud argues that the man, suffering from a castration complex, regards the woman at the moment of defloration as a source of danger: 'The first sexual act with her represents a particularly intense danger.' In the man's view, the bleeding caused by the ruptured hymen evokes injury and death. 'The man fears being drained by the woman, being contaminated by her femininity and thus becoming impotent,' Freud goes on, and he entrusts the thankless task of deflowering his partner to a third party.

Freud and Judge Di did not share the same world. In fact, ever since Muo had set foot in China, he had been assailed by doubts concerning psychoanalysis. Take Volcano of the Old Moon: was she suffering from the famous Oedipus complex like everyone else? Were the men she loved, lovers past, present or future, including himself, nothing but substitutes for her father? Why would Judge Di desire to savour a slashed red melon, if it meant losing his penis? How could he not suffer from a castration complex? Muo had a sense of being manipulated by Destiny, of being mocked from on high by a capricious tyrant. These questions kept him awake at night, tossing and turning in bed. He sought answers to them in his books on psychoanalysis, finding it difficult at times to accept wholeheartedly some of the more outlandish explanations. Most of all he was tormented by his inability to put these questions out of his mind, in full knowledge that no straight answers were ever to be had.

From time to time he wondered sadly whether he was cut out for psychoanalysis. He was lacking in self-confidence and experience in sexual matters. People disconcerted him profoundly.

By way of thanks, Muo presented his friend – the mayor's son-in-law and prison restaurateur – with a very pretty fan dating from the twenties and decorated by an artist-monk with a pattern of waxwing sparrows on rocky perches, preening their feathers with ruby beaks. The mayor's son-in-law, for his part, invited him once more to dine with him – not at one of his restaurants but somewhere else at the other end of the city, just for a change of scene. After dinner he took Muo to a tea pavilion on a riverbank, decorated in the Shanghai style of the thirties with lacquered screens, low carved tables and embroidered satin cushions. Soft music, barely audible, wafted towards them from the far end of the pavilion.

'How do you like the girl sitting on the bamboo chair in the hall?' his friend asked.

Muo turned to look at her. She was young, eighteen perhaps. Her shoulder-length hair was dyed red, dull and lifeless. She wore a white shirt that reached down to her thighs. He got up and headed to the men's room so that he might walk past her. In the low, diffuse lighting he noted her plucked eyebrows, her sharp features and, through her unbuttoned shirt, a black semi-transparent lace bra, flat breasts and a bony body.

'A young virgin for the judge?' he asked his friend, returning to their table.

'No, a whore I have reserved for you.'

Muo remained speechless for several seconds. In spite of himself, his eyes were drawn to the girl again.

'Reserved? For me? What do you mean?' he stammered, feeling the blood rush to his cheeks.

'Have fun. It's all paid for. You go ahead and relax.'

'No, no . . . No thank you, I'd rather not.'

'Go on, old friend. Don't disappoint me. Last time we met you earned my respect. Your passion for your photographer friend in jail, and for psychoanalysis, is pretty impressive. But I also feel sorry for you. You're tired. You don't look in the best of health. You're tense. You should follow Judge Di's example: take a girl's essence of Yin to boost your vitality.'

The veils of mystery began to lift. Muo felt he was on to an important discovery. His breathing became fast and shallow, the heat of his eyes misted up the lenses of his spectacles.

'Do you mean to say that when some jerk of a judge wants to take a girl's virginity, it's to boost his vitality?'

'Certainly. To boost his vitality, his power, his health . . . Forgive me for saying so, but an old jailbird like myself can teach you one or two things about sex. When the Chinese make love, it is for two basic reasons, which have nothing to do with each other. The first is to have children. It's mechanical, like work. Ridiculous, but that's the way it is. The second reason is to nourish the self with the woman's energy, with her female essence. And imagine the female essence of a virgin. Her saliva is more fragrant than a married woman's, her vaginal secretions bestow an exquisite grace on the sexual act. It is there, my friend, that you find the most precious source of vitality on earth.'

6

A Travelling Couch

Two vertical strokes crossed by two faint horizontal ones symbolise a bed. Beside it, three child-like strokes represent the lowered lashes of a closed eye. Above, a thumb points down as if to say: even asleep the eye is seeing. Behold the character for 'dream' as it was written three thousand six hundred years ago in ancient Chinese hieroglyphic script. There is a primitive enchantment about the characters, a mysterious grace that hints at the divine. It was this that deeply impressed Muo when, as a twenty-year-old student, he first set eyes on it at the Imperial Museum: an inscription on dark tortoise shell so cracked and transparent in places and so ancient, he half expected it to turn to dust if the air so much as stirred.

The ancient scribe had no way of imagining that, several dozen centuries later, his character would become the logo of a travelling psychoanalyst. Muo set about tracing the outline on to a piece of black silk, taking great pains to adjust the proportions according to the rules of enlargement. He then cut it out and instructed a tailor to sew it to a length of white cotton smelling faintly of washing powder and camphor, purloined from his mother's mahogany chest of drawers when her back was turned. Above the appliquéd logo were printed his title and function in red ink: 'Interpreter of Dreams' (large script), followed by 'Psychoanalyst returned from France' and 'Schooled in Freud and Lacan' (smaller script).

The final stage in the manufacture of his banner consisted in finding a suitable mast. Muo searched the furniture market and compared bamboo canes at length, but none of them had the necessary resilience to support a flag in a brisk wind. Back in his parents' flat he hesitated between the pole upon which his mother dried her washing and his father's collapsible fishing rod, which was made up of several lengths of lacquered bamboo. After due reflection he opted for the latter, less sturdy no doubt but aesthetically far the more pleasing.

Towards the end of a mild summer's night he woke after a brief and restless sleep. Since reading Kafka's *Metamorphosis*, he woke with trepidation every morning. That day, however, he felt curiously refreshed and energetic. He got out of bed, crossed to the window and looked outside. A solitary star, perhaps the Pole Star, was still shining in the Northern heavens. It was the first time since his return that he had seen a star over this polluted city. He gazed at it for a time and interpreted it as a good omen for the psychoanalytic expedition he was about to undertake. Before the star faded, he got on his father's old bicycle and rattled down the pallid streets, drained of colour at this hour. At the outskirts of the city he dismounted in front of a skyscraper whose windows, like a vast mirror, reflected the sun rising over the Yangtze River in all its glory. He took out his banner, hoisted it on the fishing rod firmly secured to the back of his bike, then jumped on to his saddle and sped away with his banner streaming in the wind. Destination: the southern suburbs.

At this point I shall reveal a secret. This psychoanalytic expedition was merely a pretext, a cover for his real purpose: the quest for a girl whose virginity he might purchase as a gift to Judge Di. A great leap forward to secure the freedom of his imprisoned sweetheart, which was his ultimate and clearly defined goal.

'And like an old flag volleying in the gale/Your whole flesh shudders in the blasts of sin . . .' These lines from Baudelaire went round and round Muo's head as he pedalled along.

Little by little he left the city behind. After an hour's cycling he arrived at the Red Gate commune. The first village, known as Jade Bamboo, presented a ghostly spectacle. It had been selected for modernisation: parcels of land had been sold off, the old houses razed and replaced by high-rise office blocks rearing their unfinished carcasses, left abandoned (no doubt for reasons of economy) without roofs, floors or partitions. They were edifices that had simply ceased to exist. The empty frames of doors and windows were fringed with yellow wildflowers springing from cracks in the cement and brickwork. Muo ventured into one of the buildings to relieve himself, and found the ground floor invaded by a lush, strong-smelling weed, wet with morning dew, and a flock of happily grazing sheep who took no notice of him whatso-ever. Now and then, long-drawn-out bleats of contentment stirred this pastoral scene, blending with the faint rush of urine hitting a wall.

It was in this fragrant ruin, open to the sky, that he gave his first dream interpretation. Muo may have made errors of judgement at times — especially in his day-to-day life where he could be singularly inept — but as soon as psychoanalysis came into play, particularly when applied to the domain of dreams, his knowledge was vast.

His first client was the owner of the sheep, a crippled man aged fifty-four, who hobbled towards him on two wooden crutches. Although Muo tried not to stare, he noted that one of the man's legs was shorter than the other, and surely thinner too, for his trouser-leg flapped and his foot was hidden. The man bargained Muo's price down from twenty yuan to ten, which Muo accepted without further ado.

Smoking a cigarette, the owner of the sheep related a dream in which he was walking, or rather wading, in a shallow stretch of water, probably the Yangtze River, in the company of a fifty-year-old woman with whom he had slept several years previously. Their picture had been taken by a neighbour who worked at a tourist site. In the dream his former mistress roused him from sleep some days later to show him the photograph: the Yangtze was so clear you could see the water plants and pebbles on the bottom; midstream was a barge with a line of washing hanging out to dry; the woman was holding the smiling man by his elbow; his trousers, although rolled up, were wet, and from his gaping fly protruded a very long, very straight rod reaching down to the surface of the water. The rod shimmered with colour like crystal.

For Muo, this dream was easy to decipher, and he offered his interpretation with the ease of a chess grandmaster playing against a mere beginner. Without hesitation or the need for further questioning, our psychoanalyst warned his client that another handicap – sex – had him in her sights, and that Sin, known by the religious as Satan and as 'devil's delights' by those of a more literary bent, was about to elude him. He advised him to have recourse to medication.

Hardly had he uttered these words when he regretted having spoken. He remembered his goal, his mission: to find a virgin. He tried to steer the conversation towards the object of his field study, but it was too late: his client was shaking with rage. Narrowing his mean, beady eyes, he showered abuse on Muo, berating him for being interested only in making fun of a man's disability. He flung his cigarette-butt in his face and, leaning on his left crutch, he swung the right one at Muo's jaw. Muo turned and fled, his banner fluttering. The hopping cripple pursued him, leaning on one crutch and swinging the other overhead as in a Kung-fu film, railing all the while. The sheep panicked and scattered in all directions as, in a blind dash, Muo escaped into the morning mist, without receiving payment for his services.

So began Muo's suburban tour as an interpreter of dreams, his private Long March. It was a test of patience. Every day for three whole weeks he set out in the early morning on his father's old bike. By midday the heat was so intense that the tarred surface of the road melted and he felt as if he were advancing through a bog. It was a sweaty, dusty undertaking. On one occasion his front tyre got a puncture, and he pushed his bicycle for a whole hour, panting all the way in the oppressive heat. By the time the flat tyre had been mended in the next village, the saddle was too hot to sit on.

As soon as Muo arrived in a new settlement, his banner streaming from the fishing rod, he would tout for clients. He kept up the pretence of charging a twenty-yuan fee, but often lowered it to one yuan and sometimes even waived it altogether. At night, when he returned to his parents' flat, he was wrung out, his legs buckling.

There were days when the old bike seemed to carry him of its own accord, without him pushing the pedals. Then the fragrance of the countryside, the buffalo in the paddy fields, even the cars, everything struck him as beautiful. He sped along the roads shaded with plane trees, and sometimes spied pretty girls riding bicycles (he always thought women cyclists looked particularly sexy, and dreamed of organising fashion shows with models bicycling down the cat-walk).

But his search for a virgin made little headway, largely because the majority of the younger generation had abandoned the countryside to earn a living in the city and, of the remaining few, it was hard to tell how many were virgins. On a professional level, he encountered several interesting cases. Back home he took out his exercise books and his hefty French dictionary, and proceeded to write up his notes in the language of Molière. Among his exploits as interpreter of dreams, one or two deserve to be cited.

One morning in June, having turned off Highway 351 into a calm and verdant valley, his bike swerving to avoid the puddles on a dirt track, he came upon a lone house with a tiled roof and wooden walls. It had a raised threshold half a metre off the ground and heavily carved double doors several centuries old. In the large courtyard sat two old women next to two spanking new wooden coffins placed one on top of the other under the eaves (the coffins were presumably for their own use, the local custom being to prepare the coffin of an elderly parent well ahead of time and to put it on view until the final day, as a sort of guaranteed residence in the next life). Muo parked his bike, crossed the high threshold and headed towards the gossiping old women. Over the scent of freshly cut timber from the coffins, he caught a whiff of something strange and indefinable. Like an itinerant hairdresser, knife grinder or cock castrator advertising his services, he proposed dream-interpretation, best quality at the best price.

The two old women – he could tell they were sisters because they resembled each other like two peas in a pod – cleared their throats and expressed not the slightest interest in his exposé of the magical method invented by his master Freud.

He was unperturbed. This was nothing new. He did not seriously think the old sisters would tell him their dreams, and anyway he was not sure they were still of dreaming age, what with their two coffins placed under the overhanging eaves. After circling round the subject for some time, he was on the point of asking if they happened to know of any virgins in the area when one of the sisters declared in a sardonic, rather irritating tone, 'We are sorceresses, and we are famous in the region. Our father was a medium who specialised in dreams. He certainly knew a lot more than your foreign master.'

At this news Muo was overtaken by a coughing fit. Suddenly he realised what was causing the strange smell lingering in the courtyard. He laughed. Excused himself. Laughed again, and started back towards the gates. But he could not resist the temptation to provoke the two old sisters, and turning back to them, asked, 'You weren't in love with your father, by any chance?'

The question, posed in such an innocent tone of voice, had the effect of a bomb exploding in the courtyard. Even the coffins seemed to shudder. Muo continued:

'According to the theory I am applying, every girl, at some stage in her childhood, feels the desire to sleep with her father.'

He was expecting a reaction of outrage, and it was not long in coming, albeit from one of the sisters only. She threatened to cast a spell on him, whereupon her sibling frowned and put her in her place.

'Not all of what he's saying is nonsense, especially with regard to you. As soon as Mother got up you used to skip into bed with Father. He had to keep chasing you away. Don't you remember?'

'That's absurd! It was you, you sneaky cat, he kicked out of the bed. You even hid in the dark to spy on him when he peed. You were fascinated.'

'You're lying! Only a few weeks ago you told me how you had dreamed of him peeing in the courtyard, and that you'd imitated him and made him laugh. True or false?'

Muo moved away at a deliberately slow pace so as not to miss a word of their mutual recriminations. Back on his bike, rolling down the dirt track towards the other villages in the valley, he regretted not having seen them break down and cry. In a sense he felt a deep sympathy for the two sisters, more in fact than for his other 'clients'. He loved it when the settling of old scores was like a river overflowing its banks and breaching the dykes during epic full-moon floods. Revelations, confessions – the magic of psychoanalysis! Long live the uninhibited tongue!

Further exploration of the valley proved disheartening. There were two or three villages, but all the young people had moved to the city years ago, leaving only the old villagers with their coffins in their courtyards, and women with babies strapped to their backs working in the fields and feeding the pigs. For a moment he thought Fortune had smiled on him when he spotted a plump girl of barely eighteen behind the counter of the only shop for miles. He eyed her intently as she made entries in a ledger and then stuck a postage stamp on an envelope addressed to the Tax Office. She looked brave, determined to keep her business afloat. However, Muo's hope soon evaporated: the almost child-like face of the girl was marred by the imprint of fashion – plucked eyebrows. The ensuing session of dream-interpretation, which was held free of charge, turned into a tearful confession. She wept over her brief sojourn in the city, where she had worked in a restaurant and lost her virginity in a vain effort to keep her job. What a shame! When Muo asked for the washroom she escorted him to the first floor, held the door of a grimy cubicle open and quietly slipped in behind him. They were met by a swarm of buzzing, whirring bluebottles.

'Shall I help you open your flies?' she asked with the breezy air of a practised prostitute.

'No thank you,' he said, taken aback.

'My price is a mere snip for someone as rich as you, Mr Teacher.'

'Get out!' he cried. 'You must be out of your mind. Besides, who said I was a teacher?'

At this she left meekly and returned to her seat behind the

counter. Had she insisted, had she pleaded for the sake of her business or her family, had she acted the damsel in distress, it might have ended quite differently.

Muo the incorruptible! Muo the true! Muo the knight in shining armour! Like Don Quixote, he invoked the name of his lady love, Volcano of the Old Moon, and pictured her in his mind as he pedalled along the bumpy road with his dream-logo banner streaming behind.

The highway was not yet in sight, but he could already hear the agitated honking of lorries. In the distance he spied two black dots in the middle of the track, close to the old wooden house. The bicycle clattered, the carrier creaked, the handlebars shook, and the chain seemed about to snap with each thrust of the pedals. He was thirsty. He longed for a lick of ice cream. The two black dots swapped position. He was labouring uphill, the slope was long. His front wheel ceased turning, time stopped, and then, in a spurt, everything started up again. Oh, for an iced lolly!

Muo was sweating so much that his glasses were foggy. One moment the two black shapes vanished from view, the next they reappeared, becoming ever larger as he approached, until they revealed themselves to be the two sorceresses, barring his way. Their presence alone was enough to make him dismount. Sweat coursed down his body in cold rivulets. At no time since the start of his psychoanalytic expedition had he sweated so profusely. But he was welcomed most cordially by the two sisters. They apologised, saying they had every confidence in him after all. They even professed an interest in psychoanalysis. He could barely believe this volte-face, and made to continue on his way. They would not hear of it, pressed him to park his bicycle and to step into their house for a bite to eat.

The walls of their low-ceilinged dining room were papered with old newsprint; the floor was of earth. Hanging between the two closed windows was a framed photograph of an old man, no doubt their dead father. A smell of Tibetan incense filled the air. Above a hearth – hollowed out of the earth in the middle of the floor – were suspended two impressive bows, red in colour, which looked as if they were used for shooting arrows at demons. A fire was burning. Water was on the boil. Tea would soon be served.

Muo had to concede: their noodles, their spicy carp broth and their pork kidneys with chives were well worth experiencing. While he savoured this true feast of the culinary arts of boiling, frying and stewing, the two sorceresses told him a dream they had never succeeded in clarifying, as their late father had never initiated them in the meaning of dreams. (Not a single female initiate is mentioned in the Chinese annals of this art, although they are as vast as the ocean.)

The dream had been dreamt by the elder sister's son, who had died two months previously aged thirty-five. The causes of his death were natural; there was no trace of violence. He was most likely killed by a collapsed lung. He had been working for some years in Chongqing, five hundred kilometres away, in a marble quarry. An X-ray had shown up a shadow on his right lung, a frequent occurrence among quarry workers. When he was given five days off to celebrate the 1st of May, he had taken the opportunity to return home to see his wife and family in the house he built the previous year. It was one of the prettiest houses in the village: two storeys, balconies, and an exterior decorated with thousands of white tiles personally affixed by his mother and his aunt while standing on bamboo scaffolding. The poor man had not had time to admire his dwelling, each square centimetre of which he had paid for with his marble-cutter's blood and sweat. When he arrived it was already dark, and he was so tired from the journey that he had no desire to eat or take a bath. His wife filled a wooden basin with hot water and washed his feet for him. Then she helped him off with his clothes and into a clean T-shirt and underpants, after which he went outside to urinate. He came back in telling his wife he wanted to say a prayer before going to sleep: he was a disciple of the forbidden sect of Falun Gong. By the time his wife joined him after finishing her work about the house, he was asleep. The next morning she woke at seven and found him dead beside her. As he had been a member of the Falun Gong, she did not have a post mortem done for fear of involving the police.

On his way home from the marble quarry, the elder sister's son had dropped in on his mother and his aunt. He had stayed for about a quarter of an hour, during which time he checked the state of their coffins and told them what he had dreamed the night before he left Chongqing: he was riding a powerful motorcycle along the Yangtze River; looking down, he noted that his wheels left the gravelly sand of the riverbank divided down the middle – dry and white on the right, damp and dark on the left.

The dream was a veritable enigma. While he listened to the two sisters' story, Muo had kept his eyes fixed on the dusty portrait of the father, the medium of dreams. The man inspired certain thoughts of a particularly Chinese complexion, but not the solution to the dream. Muo asked the old sisters for a few days' respite and returned to his parents' home. The following nights he was unable to sleep more than two or three hours, and smoked more cigarettes than his lungs permitted. He often thought of that famous English detective who could tell when footprints had been made by walking backwards. He continued his daily expeditions, but his mind was elsewhere. One day he came across a decrepit old man trying to hitch a ride by the side of a road that never saw a bus service. Touched by the old man's frailty, Muo obliged. The man settled himself on the luggage carrier and promptly fell asleep. Engrossed in his attempt to analyse the enigmatic dream, Muo rode for about an hour without hearing a word from his hitchhiker. Indeed he had forgotten all about him until he slowed to a halt in the shade of a tall gingko tree and looked over his shoulder: the old man was missing, fallen off somewhere along the way.

In the end Muo decided to try to sleep for a few days and nights, with a view to unravelling the mystery of this dream by having some of his own. He woke one morning as the pale blue light of day was sliding across his window, having dreamed of Volcano of the Old Moon in striped prisoners' garb, accusing him of having forsaken her. At that very moment everything seemed to fall into place. He returned to the sorceresses with the answer to the enigma. The dead son's dream was premonitory: he had an unconscious suspicion that his wife was having an affair with another man, possibly a neighbour by the name of Fong, forename Chang, who would later murder him. (The Fong character is composed of two parts, the one on the left representing water, and the one on the right a horse, i.e. the motorcycle. Two suns symbolise two men – who share the same girl – and two superimposed suns make up the name Chang.)

The elder sister – the mother – broke down in sobs. The younger sister laughed, for they did indeed have a neighbour by this name in the village. A few days later the two sorceresses managed to persuade the police to arrest him. He admitted his crime after ten minutes of interrogation.

Muo paid a heavy price for having dreamed another man's dream. At any time, night or day, the motorcycle would make its entrance, ridden by himself, roaring on the bank of the Yangtze. The machine was black, the river bottle-green. The sand on the left was dry, on the right it was moist, while Muo the rider was mobbed by seagulls whipping his face with their white wings. The image was further enhanced by a sailing boat in the background and a child peeing from a jetty.

Another dream, told by the night watchman of a building site, likewise deserves mention. Muo had met him in a tea-house late one afternoon and had been invited to his home.

'We'll have fun tonight, with some girls from work,' boasted the watchman, a man of about thirty, as short as Muo, but more energetic and very drunk. They arrived at a shack with a corrugated iron roof, illuminated from time to time by the headlights of passing lorries, only to find the door securely padlocked. When the watchman realised he had lost the key, he staggered around in search of a rusty crowbar, with which he eventually forced open the door with a deafening noise. As Muo stepped in, the corrugated iron roof was still reverberating from the shock.

Inside, the place was a shambles, although the refrigerator was not empty. The man gave him a beer and asked if he would pay for two whores: 'We'll have a foursome.'

'Two whores? No! All these whores, I'm sick of them,' said Muo, after a moment's pause.

He decided to abandon his pose and, despite his preference for obliquity, force himself to be direct.

'You don't by any chance know any virgins do you?' he asked nonchalantly.

'Any what?'

The night watchman stepped up to him and slapped him on the shoulder.

'Virgins. Girls who are innocent and pure, who haven't ever . . . you know . . . Virgins!' he repeated, lingering over the word as if it were obsolete, savouring its unfamiliar ring.

The watchman screamed with laughter. Suddenly, Muo felt almost sordid. When the drunkard's unseemly mirth had subsided, he grabbed Muo by one arm and propelled him to the destroyed door, sending him packing as if he were a raving lunatic.

Muo did not lose his composure, he merely adjusted his banner and walked off slowly, trundling his bicycle along the gravelly track. Passing a construction site with an almost finished building, he paused to take a long look at the bamboo scaffolding towering into the sky like a vast chequerboard. 'Life is a game of chess,' he reflected, 'and my quest for a virgin is no exception to this rule. At which point did I make a mistake? Is the game already lost?'

The night watchman's laughter came back to him, making him see the glaring absurdity of his cause.

He noticed there was a metal ladder spiralling up through the scaffolding. He was seized with longing for a cigarette. Why not have a quiet smoke at the very top of these unfinished premises? The idea appealed to him, and he began his solitary, nocturnal ascent. Being unaccustomed to climbing such a narrow ladder, he slipped and almost fell. He laughed. He felt slightly less depressed. He thought of his bicycle: it would be disastrous if he were to go down to find the bicycle gone. It would take him several hours to get home on foot. He peered over the side and, mercifully, it was still there. He climbed down, lifted the bike on to his shoulder and started to make his way up again.

The roof was a vast expanse of tar, a more or less finished terrace. Muo jumped on to his bike and, standing on the pedals, raced along a section that was fenced off with steel cables. Winded, he dropped back on his saddle and free-wheeled for a time before returning to the middle of the roof, where he halted, resting one foot on the metal drum of a roller. Still on the saddle, he lit a cigarette and took a long puff, abandoning himself to the combined narcotic of tobacco and depression and then, pushing off sharply, sped away again.

His friend, the night watchman, had by this point joined him on the roof. Fearing an accident – or worse, a suicide – he ordered Muo, in an unprecedented show of concern for his safety, to dismount at once. But Muo just carried on, extending his act to include shouting at the top of his voice the following phrase by the most illustrious of English poets, 'I have stolen the moon, the sea, the stars,' to which he added, 'and the virgins.'

Behind him, the banner inscribed with the dream logo fluttered and streamed in the wind. Muo could not make up his mind whether it was bearing him aloft or impelling him to plunge over the edge of the building. He was drenched in sweat. The wind suddenly rose, howling and gusting so hard he was afraid the fishing-rod mast would snap, but then it died down just as quickly with a soft moan. The air became as limpid as water and the sky seemed lower than usual. Muo felt like a giant, as though he could touch the sky just by reaching out his hand. Some of the stars shone so brightly that they dazzled him.

The watchman's voice reached his ears, but instead of telling him to get down, the voice spoke to him of a dream:

'It was neither myself nor my wife who had this dream, but someone who lived in our building in the southern district of Chengdu. He was a retired doctor of traditional medicine, who still supplied herbs or plants to the neighbours on occasion. He was also an outstanding acupuncturist. He told me about a dream he had had early one morning. It was about my wife. In front of a shop in a deserted street, she went down on her knees to gather up her own severed head from the pavement. She replaced it on her neck, rose to her feet and hurried down the empty street holding her head in place with both hands. She ran past him without seeing him.'

Muo, who felt inspired and in excellent form, interrupted the night watchman.

'Do you want to know what this dream signified?'

'Yes, please.'

'Your wife was going to die quite soon, probably of some disease of the throat. Cancer, maybe.'

No sooner had he spoken these audacious words than the night watchman fell to his knees before him, apologising for his rudeness and admitting that his wife had indeed died one month after the retired doctor's dream.

Despite this surge of esteem for our psychoanalyst, the

watchman was unable to find Muo a virgin, for the simple reason that virginity had ceased to exist among 'the girls from work' or his female acquaintances. The best he could do was to take Muo to the domestic workers market, where he thought he might have more luck.

7

Mrs Thatcher and the Domestic Workers Market

Muo had never believed such a dreamscape existed: a realm of girls. Upon entering the domestic workers market he was deeply moved. Despite pangs of conscience at the social injustice of it all, his entire body was set alight by the sheer number of young women and the feminine fragrance they exuded. Even the sound of their voices struck him as carnal. 'My God,' he thought, 'what I wouldn't give to stay right here and be of service to these girls – loving them, kissing their young breasts, caressing through their jeans their firm buttocks, and offering them something infinitely more valuable than work or money, namely love and affection.' His knees were shaking: never had he come so close to his goal.

Situated at the foot of a rocky mountain, the domestic workers market occupied the full length of a gently sloping, paved alley, still known by the name it had been given in the Revolution: Great Leap Forward Street. It bordered the Yangtze River, often swathed in mist, and was frequented by well-off women, mostly city-dwellers, seeking domestic servants. Leaving their cars parked on the far bank, they crossed the river in small motor boats, slipped into the alley and, much as at a vegetable market, compared the merchandise and haggled over the price. Half an hour later they left with a girl in tow to take the same throbbing, clanking boat back across the famous Yangtze, whose churning brown waters bubbled with sewage and industrial waste.

The market was run along very strict lines by Mrs Wang, a fifty-year-old policewoman of great determination and efficiency. From a distance, she did not lack charm, and her trim waist, short hair and fine wire-framed glasses suggested a certain stylishness. It was possible to imagine that she might have been an attractive young girl, but, alas, her beauty had been ravaged by smallpox in her teens, leaving her with a face like a colander. Her frugality bordering on avarice, her love of money, and her strict discipline (which ensured that no one had ever stolen so much as a yuan from her) had earned her the nickname 'Mrs Thatcher'. She was clearly not unaware of this appellation, for when Muo went to her office to apply for a permit to analyse dreams in the market, the first thing he noticed was a biography of Margaret Thatcher. It stood on a shelf beneath the portrait of the current Chinese president, tucked in among the usual government-issue publications and volumes of the collected writings of diverse Communist leaders.

Mrs Thatcher listened to three minutes of Muo's laborious explanations before interrupting him with a wave of her hand.

'We Communists are atheists, as well you know.'

'What's that got to do with psychoanalysis?' he stammered, baffled.

'What you call psychoanalysis is nothing but fortune-telling.'

Muo looked her straight in the eye (he had been told that

97

she couldn't stand anyone flinching from her gaze). 'If Freud had heard what you just said . . .'

But he lost heart before he could finish his sentence. He was repelled by the sight of her face and longed to turn away. Instead he summoned all his courage and opened his eyes as wide as he could.

'Who is this Freud?' she asked.

'The founder of psychoanalysis. A Jew, like Marx.'

'Stop looking at me like that,' she said in a timid, girlish tone, which gave her words an artificial ring. 'I'm old and ugly.'

'You're too modest.'

'It is you who are too kind,' she said, touching the sleeve of Muo's jacket. 'I will tell you a dream, and if your interpretation is correct, I will give you permission to ply your trade in Great Leap Forward Street.'

Sunday 25 June. That bitch Mrs Thatcher is driving me insane. This is the first time I have used coarse language in my psychoanalytic notebook (my aim being to employ only neutral, objective words), but only the immediacy of a blunt and brutish vocabulary can do justice to my nightmarish encounter with this representative of authority. She has literally driven me mad. From the start she fazed me with her pockmarks. During my brief career as an interpreter of dreams, I have always shut my eyes to listen to my patient's dreams so that I can sense the presence of the invisible forces that drive them. The narrators fade, their words become distant, but I can feel which words are charged with extra meaning; when I hear them it is like a flash of lightning or a thunder-clap. That is my method. Today, however, I was unable to apply it. Mrs Thatcher cannot abide it when her interlocutor shuts his eyes in front of her. I forced myself to

look at her while she was relating her dream, and I had a vision of her brain riddled with smallpox. Although I had a vague perception that she was talking about a stuffed dog that appeared in her dream, I was filled with a strange sense of powerlessness the moment she opened her mouth. I shuddered at how slowly my brain was working. It was filled with thoughts of psychoanalytic dictionaries, the theories of Freud and Jung all mixed up with Chinese words and the teachings of Confucius. In my confusion I felt I had to confront the situation, conform to her expectations: tell her fortune. What kind of event would be inescapable in the life of a woman of power?

'The stuffed dog is a premonition that you will be invited to a sumptuous banquet in the near future,' I told her. (Will you ever forgive me this sacrilege, Master Freud? It was the smallpox driving me insane.)

'When?' she asked.

'Tonight or tomorrow,' I replied, shutting my eyes, and as I did so strange black blobs appeared on my eyeballs.

She gave a delighted laugh, and again pawed my sleeve. Her laughter was theatrical, like an exclamatory affirmation of her power, contorting her features so that her pockmarks seemed to crinkle and bubble, hundreds of tiny pits opening on her face, growing and growing like dried peas in water, bursting and popping – exploding in my face. The woman scares me. I don't think she'll ever give me my blasted permit. That would be too bad, now that I have fallen in love with the domestic workers market. After all my fears, it promises to be a veritable goldmine in my quest for a virgin.

Monday 26 June. It's done. I can take up my notebook again. Mrs Thatcher has given me my permit. I am proud to say that everything is going in accordance with my wishes and predictions: yesterday evening she received a last-minute invitation to attend an official dinner hosted by the regional authority.

This afternoon I hoisted my banner in the middle of the market. (Psychoanalysis has always brought me good fortune.) My official installation in Great Leap Forward Street proves, beyond a doubt, that the mission I must accomplish on behalf of Judge Di is entering a crucial phase.

At this juncture I would like to mention that I am beginning to enjoy my life as an interpreter of dreams, especially the fortune-telling aspect.

Tuesday 27 June. Sometimes the reality of life conforms but little to the dream. Today's field study was disappointing. The women who came to consult me belonged, for the most part, to the minority I would classify as 'semi-old'.

The wooden crate, which I acquired from the only food shop in the alley, makes an uncomfortable seat. I perch on it during my sessions with clients, for whose convenience I have rented a chair from a pensioner down the road. It is a low reclining chair made of bamboo, vaguely resembling the psychiatrist's couch of my colleagues in the West. I have positioned it beneath my banner.

My first clients were wealthier than the later ones. The consultation fee, which I had fixed at three yuan, was derisory, but treating oneself to a dream-interpretation nevertheless represented a small bourgeois luxury that set the 'semi-old women' apart from the girls. Most of them had previously served company directors, doctors, lawyers and professors, or people working in film or the theatre. The bamboo chair creaked as they reclined. No one wished to remain thus for very long. 'My God! What torture,' they said, laughing – they preferred an upright position. They tried hard to conduct a conversation with me, but with little success. Although they were eager to tell me their dreams, the content eluded them and they kept getting side-tracked. The more they talked, the more muddled their stories became. Some of them wanted to tell me all about themselves, to pour their hearts out, but they lacked the means. The details were often incongruous: a vase shattering spontaneously, half a green apple, the Grand Master of Falun Gong, a dried fish, hair turning white overnight or falling out by the handful, a flickering candle, a rat squeaking in the dark, their own skin shrinking or wrinkling like that of a snake.

Despite my modest fee, I took my psychoanalytic endeavours very seriously. Whenever my memory permitted, I paid tribute to my masters by quoting a passage from Freud, Lacan or Jung. It must be conceded that the language of psychoanalysis, with its specific terminology and phrasing, does not lend itself to translation. When I recited such passages, not in Mandarin but in the melodious dialect of Sechuan, the cabbalistic vocabulary took on a comic edge which provoked such uproarious laughter among the women crowding round to listen that you would have sworn I was engaging in stand-up comedy – a genre I normally despise.

My first client, a woman of fifty, had permed her hair and wore a fancy ring on her finger. She had dreamt of catching a fish. I asked her if the fish was large or small, but she could not recall. To convince her of the significance of this detail, I attempted to translate what Freud has to say on the subject: small fish stand for human sperm and big fish for children. As for the fishing rod in her dream, it obviously stood for the phallus. An indescribable pandemonium ensued, with all the women shouting and cheering at the tops of their voices. My client blushed and hid her face in her hands, while the crowd broke out in deafening applause. From one moment to the next the fear of unemployment vanished from their faces. I have the feeling they have adopted me and that Great Leap Forward Street has accepted me as a public entertainer.

A recurrent feature in their dreams is the domestic iron, symbol of conflict and servitude. ('It means you wish to be in a different situation,' is the diagnosis I give women who see irons in their dreams.) One woman had dreamed of yawning while she did the ironing (as in the painting by Degas, which bears witness to his compassion for the poor). She had yawned and stretched unrestrainedly, and had noticed that she was wearing clothes belonging to her boss's daughter, aged ten.

That night, before shutting up shop, I received a visit from Mrs Thatcher. Unlike the others, she had no problem lying back in the bamboo reclining chair. Her face was drawn, her eyes firmly lowered. Her body gave off a strange smell, which was neither perfume nor the local eau-de-Cologne. She spoke haltingly, in a low voice. She made me think of Freud's description of hysteria in women.

'I dreamt of the same stuffed dog again last night.'

I tried to wrest some more details from her. Was the dog in the same position? Was it the same size? The same breed? Had it looked at her? Had it barked? She was unable to reply. She had seen the dog in a dream, that was all.

'Astonishing, isn't it?' she said.

'No. The return of the already-known is a typical manifestation of the psychical unconscious. Freud, in the early years of his practice, made it an object of special study. He said: "The repetition of an action in time is habitually represented in dreams by the multiplication of an object, which appears any number of times."'

She seemed dismayed. I could not be sure that she had heard the end of my translation, for the crowd roared with laughter as soon as I uttered the Master's name. A few young bystanders even took to chanting it.

'So who is this Freud person?'

'I told you last time: he revolutionised the interpretation of dreams.'

'Well, it doesn't make any sense to me.'

'He is teaching us, quite simply, to trawl our childhood

experiences for the origins of what we dream. Do you remember the first time you saw a stuffed dog?'

'No, I don't.'

'Please try and remember. One of Freud's great discoveries is the nefarious role of such repetition. The point is not to decode a dream or solve an enigma, but to find some way of putting an end to the repetition to which one is subjected, and by so doing clearing a path to further possibilities . . .'

Once again guffaws from the audience obliged me to suspend my precis of Freud. The policewoman's brow was furrowed.

'What does the stuffed dog mean, that's what I'd like to know. I'm sick of your Freud.'

Abruptly she sat up. Her voice became sharp, almost hysterical, and she clicked her tongue nervously.

'Now I remember. It was a dog with a strong smell, it stank of mildewed books!'

She thrust her face close to mine.

'Rather like you.'

'The stuffed dog is an omen that you will soon develop a limp.'

This was not a serious thought on my part; I just had a sudden urge to vent my anger by insulting her. I can't think how I allowed this lapse to occur. No doubt my subconscious was to blame: the Chinese refer to people with a disability as 'pocked, lame and lousy'.

There was a hush, in which the only sounds were the creaking of the bamboo chair, the clicking of her tongue and the whispers of the bystanders. Then she laughed.

As I wheeled my bicycle on to the boat, the ferryman told me that the market women were already placing bets on the future of Mrs Thatcher's feet.

At two a.m. I woke with a start. I got out of bed to jot down notes on the dream I had just had, but it was too late – the essence had slipped through my fingers. What I did remember was a sequence of horrible images. An open-air political meeting in Great Leap Forward Street, awash with black-haired girls. Myself on my knees in front of a grandstand. It was very hot, the loudspeakers were blaring. A heavy slab of cement hung round my neck from a wire so deeply embedded in the skin as to be invisible. Written on the slab were my name and my crime: stealer of virgins. Mrs Thatcher was talking into the microphone, clearly denouncing me, but I could not make out what she was saying. It was too hot, the sweat was dripping from my forehead, creating a puddle on the ground. Then, with the absurd suddenness of dreams, I found myself lashed with ropes to my father's bicycle (the front wheel mud-flecked and spinning), with my dream-interpreter's banner streaming behind me. In a pandemonium of shouting and screaming, the girls threw me into the Yangtze River. The dark, deep water was choppy; below me plants (or grass or some kind of algae) were swaying over the riverbed. The water, black at first, became emerald green, then darkened again to take on an olive sheen. The banner detached itself from the bicycle, eddied around me for a while, then drifted quietly downstream.

Wednesday 28 June. I was obsessed by my dream during the arduous journey to the domestic workers market. I pondered: if the first image, that of the political meeting, belonged to the category of dreams about trials (remember, Muo, the famous opening of Kafka's *Trial*, the most spine-chilling first lines in the history of literature: 'Someone must have been telling lies about Joseph K., he knew he had done nothing wrong but, one morning, he was arrested'), the second image, that of being cast in the river to drown, was the logical and chronological signifier of the verdict of this trial. You did not need to be a psychoanalyst to recognise the shadow of danger hovering about my head, of catastrophe about to strike. I could already see the policewoman's gun levelled at my poor dream-interpreting head. The hand of Destiny. I tried to banish my anxiety by shrugging my shoulders, which is a gesture of mental resignation, but my shirt was drenched with ice-cold sweat.

However, I was not entirely convinced. My sense of logic, my fear and certain tenets of my venerated masters fought for space in my head. Standing on the bank of the Yangtze River, waiting for the boat to ferry me across, something Jung once said with reference to water flashed into my mind. Eureka! This was surely the explanation for my strange dream: the trial signified that I was hiding something (my project? my plan? my love?); as for my being cast in the river, it was the water that played the leading role, for, according to Jung, it was the primitive symbol of unpredictable yet fecund forces. The title of Jung's work escapes me for the moment, but I would be able to locate it in the library of any university in France. I remember feeling so elated by this new perspective that I pulled out my thermos and took a few sips of green tea, relishing it as one would an exceptional whisky. Removing my shoes, I tied them together by the laces and hung them over the handlebars, after which I rolled up my trousers and stepped into the water, carrying my bicycle on my shoulders. As I waded with faltering steps towards the waiting boat, my shoes dangled and bobbed on the ends of their laces. Once on board I looked around with delight and a sense of relief. The clouds were vanishing quietly, melting into the blue. The prow of the boat danced on the river. The current sang, as if to infuse me with renewed strength.

'Thanks to Judge Di,' I said to myself, 'I am experiencing life in the raw.'

In no way was I expecting the ecstatic welcome awaiting me in Great Leap Forward Street. My arrival was met with an outbreak of shrill cries like the sound of chirruping crickets and a whirlwind of excited, admiring women, who bore down on me, whispering in my ear: 'Mrs Thatcher has developed a limp. Stepping off the boat yesterday evening, she sprained her left ankle.'

Thursday 29 June. Poxy Mrs Thatcher did not show up yesterday, nor today in fact, which is unlike her. The cause of her twisted ankle remains to be clarified. In all likelihood it has to do with the law of psychology that I call 'counter-suggestion', namely that the more one fears an imagined danger, the more cautious one is and thus the more one invites mishaps. It has nothing to do with any prowess in the art of fortune-telling on my part.

Be that as it may, for two whole days I have reaped the benefits of what is rapidly becoming a legendary reputation, and my clientele has expanded accordingly. Suddenly everybody had a dream to tell me; they even dream during their brief post-prandial snoozes, sitting on the ground in the street. I am particularly pleased to find that my contact with the younger women at the market is intensifying. (The eye of the virgin-snatcher is ever on the alert, without pity or complacency.)

I can well imagine the purely physical joy experienced by a botanist exploring a new continent. Forgetting his plant-finding mission, he immerses himself in the new bittersweet odours – the tangy, musky perfumes – savouring strange and exquisite forms, and hitherto unseen hues. During these two days I have feared that my memory might fail me altogether in the face of all the different items these girls dreamed about: a mirror, an iron gate, a heavy wooden door, a rusty ring, a card stained with soy sauce, a mother-of-pearl scent bottle, a cloudy water glass, a long thin cake of soap in a black box, a revolving lipstick display in a department store, a collapsed bridge, a flight of steps hewn out of a rock with treads widening and narrowing by turns, a handful of crushed charcoal, a first fall from a bicycle with a tasselled saddle, an antique belt, red patent sandals on a muddy footpath . . . Never do the dreams of these poor young girls, most of whom come from the mountains, feature such things as dolls, teddy bears or cuddly elephants, let alone white or pale-pink wedding gowns.

'My dream . . . [giggle] I often have the same dream. It's like the movies . . . [giggle] I'm acting in a film. Which one? Can't remember. A scene? Wait. For example, I dreamed I was playing a girl who was about to be kissed, or who was watching other people kissing . . . very embarrassing really. Yet I know, even before waking up, that I'm in a dream. Do you see what I mean? I tell myself I'm dreaming, but I carry on doing so . . .'

The girl was one of the youngest at the market: barely sixteen, undeveloped breasts, a pretty comb in her hair, bare feet. (Stretched out on the bamboo chair, she rubbed the arch of her left foot up and down the mud-encrusted calf of her right leg.) I remembered seeing her two days before on the riverbank, having an argument with some other girls. As I listened to her, I glimpsed on her finely turned thighs the 'diaphanous, featherlight down, evoking the bloom on a peach' so highly praised by the poets of the Tang dynasty. I took this to be a sure sign of her virginity, and had to fight back tears of emotion.

'How old are you?'

'Seventeen.'

'I don't believe you, but no matter. I just want to return to one point you made. You said you dreamt you saw people kissing. Have you had any personal experience of such physical contact?'

'You sound like some kind of professor.'

'Indeed, my mother very nearly became one. But please answer me, it is important for the interpretation of your dream. Have you ever kissed a boy?'

'Oh no, sir. Not in real life, anyway. But I did once dream that I was at home watching a film on television, and it was me acting in the film. There was a boy, played by a famous actor, who wanted to kiss me. It was dark, and we were standing on a bridge. He came up close to me, but then, just as he was about to kiss me, I woke up.'

'Congratulations, my dear girl, there is about to be a change in your situation. That is what your dream foretells.'

'Really? Will I get a job?'

'More than that, I assure you.'

My pronouncement elicited astonishment and envy among the crowd of bystanders. I decided to draw our session to a close for the moment, and to talk to her in private later on. She was succeeded in the bamboo chair by other girls, some of whom tried to extract a similarly heartening interpretation from me. When I had finished with them my little film-dreamer had gone.

Friday 30 June. This morning, I woke up fully dressed including my shoes, feeling like a chess champion who has been awake all night planning a tactical offensive. Unfortunately my trousers as well as my shirt were so badly wrinkled I needed to change. A frantic search in my wardrobe ensued. Not only did I fail to find anything decent to wear, my right index finger got stuck between the stealthily swinging doors. At my howls of pain (my finger was bleeding), my mother put her head round the door. She chose this moment to tell me that my three other pairs of trousers were tumbling round in the washing machine – another bright idea of my mother's. Having no option but to wait for the end of the cycle, I paced the shabby living-room in my underpants, fuming. It was unbearably stuffy, and I kept glimpsing my ugly body and incipient paunch in the pitiless mirror. At one point I brushed lightly against a porcelain dish, causing it to fall off the table and shatter on the floor.

In the end I put on a pair of trousers that were still damp, and rushed away in such haste that I forgot to bin the plastic rubbish sack my mother had charged me to take down. I didn't realise this until I was several streets away, when I was flagged down at a crossroads by an old man wearing a Road Safety armband. He sniffed the air suspiciously until his eyes came to rest on the rubbish bag swinging from my handlebars, whereupon he approached for a closer inspection. A trickle of dark liquid began leaking from the sack. Luckily, just then the light switched to green, so I stood on my pedals and shot away like an arrow.

Reaching the suburbs, I dismounted to dump the rubbish. There was too much wind for flying my banner, but as I pedalled along I felt a sense of tranquillity and fulfilment, and gradually my confidence returned. I was tempted to slow down and feast my eyes, perhaps for the last time, on the pretty countryside of southern China, the misty slopes, the paddy fields on either side of the road, and the villages screened by thickets of bamboo all along the Yangtze River. I was optimistic about finding the film-dreamer again, the girl whose virginity was assured, and told myself that, if she accepted my proposition, it would mean that I had brought my latest psychoanalytical endeavour to a successful close. I would treasure my dream-logo banner for ever as a memento of my profound and eternal love for Volcano of the Old Moon.

The boat was waiting for me, and as I got on with my bicycle, the ferryman quietly slipped an envelope into my hand.

'A letter for me?' I asked in surprise. 'Who gave it to you?'

'The policewoman.'

He cast off and the craft chugged slowly towards the opposite bank. I opened the envelope and glanced at the letter. My heart sank and a shiver of distaste ran down my spine. Yet another vile twist of fate. Without reading to the end, I tore up the letter and threw the scraps in the river.

'You might as well turn back now, I won't be going to the market after all.'

The ferryman cut the engine and remained motionless at the wheel, looking at me pointedly.

'What are you waiting for?' I said.

'You'll still pay me for taking you there and back?'

I nodded, sunk in thought. Slowly and deliberately, I lowered my banner with its ancient 'dream' ideogram. I almost had to laugh, in spite of everything. Then I tossed the banner into the river. It described a fluttering arc before touching down on the dark brown surface, where it drifted into an eddy and spun round a few times before being sucked into the deep.

It was a sickening letter, written in a fastidious, schoolgirl hand with a leaky ballpoint pen. It began thus: 'I cannot believe I have fallen in love at my age. But I have! I might as well tell you now that I never had those dreams about stuffed dogs I asked you to interpret. Not the first one, nor the second. I invented them from start to finish so you could demonstrate your professional competence. Do you find that endearing? Please give me a sign. If you wish to marry me, come quickly my love – Great Leap Forward Street will be ours. If you do not wish it, be so kind as to go away and never come back. Just leave me in peace, I beg you.' (The letter ran to another page devoted to news about her children and grandchildren, and yet another devoted to her parents.)

Imagine marrying a pockmarked grandmother! I would rather drown myself in the Yangtze. My God! What did I do to deserve such an honour, such love, such punishment! To crown it all, it is the first time a woman has asked me to marry her. But what a woman!

The evening after receiving the missive that put an end to his dream interpretations at the domestic workers market, Muo, the only psychoanalyst at large in China, sat in the corner of his bedroom planning a new journey. He would go to Hainan, a province declared a Special Economic Zone by the government and known locally as 'the island of desire' on account of the young girls who flocked there from the four corners of China. To achieve his goal he would travel one thousand kilometres away from the happy hometown of his parents, from Judge Di, and from the prison where Volcano of the Old Moon was being held.

He filled his pale-blue Delsey suitcase with a portable radio, a clear plastic raincoat, sunglasses (viz. a masterpiece of French optical design: a pair of thin, gold-framed lenses that could be clipped on to ordinary glasses), clothes (jumpers, shorts, several shirts), a pair of summer sandals, and flip-flops with wafer-thin soles. Then came the best part: gathering together his bedside books, his true travelling companions and trusted friends ('my spiritual nourishment: being deprived of them for more than twenty-four hours makes me ill'). Among them were a hefty hardback Larousse dictionary with gilt lettering on the cover; the two-volume *Dictionary of Psychoanalysis* in its slipcase, weighing a total of five kilos; Freud's essay on psychoanalysis in the 1928 French translation of Marie Bonaparte, revised by Freud himself and published by Gallimard; a volume in the 'Connaissance de l'inconscient' series edited by J.-B Pontalis; *Journal psychanalytique d'une petite fille*, translated by Malraux's wife (wherein Freud describes 'how the secret of sexual life emerges, indistinctly at first, then taking full possession of the juvenile soul'); Lacan's *Subversion of the Subject and the Dialectics of Desire*, which Muo held to be the best text on female orgasm; and *The Secret of the Golden Flower*, an ancient Chinese alchemical treatise that Jung studied throughout his life. As Muo wavered between *A Case of Mental Neurosis with Premature Ejaculation and Other Psychoanalytical Texts* by Andreas Embirikos, poet and father of Greek psychoanalysis, and Claude Lévi-Strauss's *Tristes tropiques*, a book slipped from the pile on to the faded carpet at his feet: Robert van Gulik's *Sexual Life in Ancient China*, which fell open at a five-hundred-year-old wood engraving by Lie-nu-chuan depicting four women in various stages of undress: two had already shed their clothing whilst a third, standing on the tip of one bound and twisted foot, was raising her leg to slip off her embroidered trousers. Muo's eye was drawn to the inclined nape of the fourth figure as she unhooked her brassiere. Taking a small card from a drawer, he jotted down the references of the illustration: upon his return from Hainan he intended to check in the library whether this was indeed the earliest depiction of a Chinese brassiere.

The act of preparing his spiritual repasts for the journey flooded Muo with a pure and innocent joy. Like a greedy child he could not resist dipping into the goodies he would have to leave behind, reading a passage or two before shutting the books again and absent-mindedly running his fingertips over the covers. Now and then he remembered having come across the same concept elsewhere and, wishing to check the source, proceeded to leaf through thousands of pages of print, as well as his exercise books. If he did not find what he was looking for, he racked his brains for any mention that might have been made of the subject by some university professor, during a lecture maybe. How to confirm this? He riffled through cardboxes filled with notes taken as a student in happier times – at university with Volcano of the Old Moon.

Sitting on his bed next to his almost full suitcase, he made a final check. The blinds were drawn, six or seven lamps were lit. He added the items remaining on his list to his suitcase: his thermos flask for his daily cup of tea, a jar of extremely hot red peppers to season cooked dishes, a jar of pickled green peppers for breakfast, some tinned foods, several packets of instant noodles, a comb with two or three teeth missing, blank exercise books for taking notes, two or three metallic ballpoints, some coloured crayons. At the back of a drawer he discovered a pencil-sharpener glowing like a gem in the dark. He tried it and, although a little rusty, it gave a satisfying crunch as the pencil-shaving curled into the air.

With his head against the wall and his eyes shut, he looked as if he were listening to music. In reality, he was having trouble breathing, and feeling stabs of pain in his stomach, possibly caused by the toxic lead in the pencil.

'I never had those dreams about stuffed dogs I asked you to interpret. Not the first one, nor the second . . .'

The words of the pockmarked policewoman came back to him without any prompting.

He got up and went into the bathroom. Without switching on the light, he stripped off his sweat-soaked clothes, leaving only his glasses. The white bathtub glinted in the half-light. The water gushed from the tap, choking and spluttering amid a cloud of steam. Muo lowered himself into it until his glasses were dislodged by the water and sank like a vessel that had sprung a leak. Again he ruminated on the humiliation he had suffered at the hands of the policewoman. He felt nauseous. Should he have guessed her ruse when she was relating her dreams? Surely not. Yet . . . she had gazed at the ground with a moony look, and her low voice had been close to a stammer. The painful truth, he told himself, was that psychoanalysis, for all its merits as the best conceptual framework for gaining insight into the human soul, was no match for a female Communist, even an uncouth, grass-roots Communist who had the gall not only to fabricate dreams, but also to turn the tables on a professional interpreter's analysis. He lay back in the tub with the water lapping his chin, cursing Mrs Thatcher and her phony limp. 'I can't let her get away with it,' he told himself, and leapt out of the bath with a great splash.

He dried himself quickly and returned to his room. Sitting

down at his desk, he took a sheet of paper, uncapped his pen and began to draft a letter.

'Dear Madam Policewoman,' he wrote in a hand that was more legible than usual, but also more guarded. 'I have the honour to declare that no one can escape the truth of psychoanalysis, not even an official representative of Law and Order. Allow me to inform you that, from the perspective of psychoanalysis, the dream you purport to have had is just as revealing as a proper dream in that it is a fabrication dictated by the subconscious. In other words, it is just as revelatory as to your fears, thwarted desires, and complexes, indeed the state of your soul: tainted, sordid, puerile . . .'

As the words poured from Muo's pen he suddenly remembered the film-dreamer, the living embodiment of all the pleasure − both physical and professional − he had experienced as a dream-interpreter. He recalled the expression on her face when she told him she had dreamt of acting the part of a girl waiting to be kissed. With wry pleasure he pictured her bare feet and the way she had rubbed the arch of her left foot up and down the mud-bespattered calf of her right leg. Ah, what a dreamer she was! A true virgin, an oriental Alice in Wonderland. How close he had come to his goal . . .

Muo did not finish his letter to Mrs Thatcher. He feared she might reply to it, causing him to get bogged down in an interminable correspondence on the significance of a fabricated dream. He tucked it away among other papers in a folder, which he packed in his suitcase.

Some days later, on a night train heading south to Hainan Island, the letter disappeared, along with the pale-blue Delsey, so ineffectually secured with a metal chain sheathed in pink plastic. It was the 6th of July.

As for what happened next, I have told you already: he crisscrossed Hainan for several weeks without success until, at the beginning of September, a chance telephone conversation with a former neighbour in Chengdu revealed to him a girl (if one can call a middle-aged female embalmer a girl) whose virginity was still intact.

II

II

Endless Night

I

The Van in the Night

A week or so after his return from Hainan, the phone rings in his parents' flat. It is past midnight.

On the other end of the line he hears the Embalmer's voice.

'He's dead. I just got back from his villa.'

'Who's dead?'

'Judge Di. It's all over. What madness!'

(At this news, all Muo feels is a prickling sensation sweeping over his body. A cold sweat breaks out in every pore of his skin. His mind races: 'Judge Di? He must have died making love, his heart must have stopped during the erotic encounter I set up for him. Will I be arrested, not as a corruptor, but as the instigator of premeditated murder? No doubt. Wait, I remember reading something about someone in a similar predicament, but where? A novel? No, a short story. But I don't recall either the title or the author. What on earth should I do now? How can I secure Volcano of the Old Moon's release from prison? I must concentrate on what the Embalmer is saying. But my brain feels all spongy. Each of her words makes my hair stand on end, but taken together they seep like an invisible liquid into the interstices of my brain until it throbs and fizzes against my cranium in a welter of conflicting emotion: relief at the cancellation of an impossible mission, and terror at the threat of imminent arrest. An inner voice sounds in my head: Go to the police and give yourself up!)

'Now listen,' the Embalmer's voice is saying at the other end of the line. 'You told me someone would come for me at the mortuary at eight p.m., but instead someone turned up at seven. Judge Di's sixth secretary, so he claimed. A nervous little man. He said we should leave at once, the judge was in a hurry. There was no time for me to change my clothes or take a shower. "Oh well," I thought, "the old judge won't be expecting a film star. The sooner we get it over with, the better for Muo." So we left right away, although I did snatch a moment to put on some of that Chanel lipstick you gave me for my birthday. We went down to the main entrance, where the judge's secretary tried calling a cab. He spent the next ten minutes shouting into his mobile, but to no avail. He was scared stiff, poor sod. He was keen to let me know he had just got back from a spell in the United States studying law. Every sentence he uttered had an English word in it – a pain, I can tell you. Just to help out I suggested, half joking, that we took one of the mortuary vans – you know, the ones that are used for transporting corpses. There happened to be one parked right by the entrance. I pointed out that it was just like the armoured police vans they use to transport prisoners to the execution ground. It was an old van with headlights like goggle eyes and a divided windscreen. The pseudo American was in a dither. He made a call to the hotel where the judge was playing mah-jong to ask permission, but was told Di had already gone home. He rang the villa but, strangely, there was no reply. It was 7.30. He took a five-yuan coin from his pocket and flipped it in the air. It bounced off the pavement and fell again. Tails, which meant we would take the van.

Looking back now it makes me laugh. Talk about omens! Just imagine: if it had been heads, or if a cab had pulled up, or if I hadn't mentioned the van at all, or if I hadn't had the key, Judge Di might still be alive. I feel responsible. And it's thanks to you that I'm in this mess.'

(The Embalmer's voice drones on and on, striving to make itself heard above the images thundering across Muo's panicky mind: a private viewing of a film, and a pair of wet trousers. The film is *Lenin in October*, screened in the Kremlin some time during the fifties. The director was sitting a few rows behind Stalin. Halfway through, he noticed the People's Little Father muttering to his neighbour. What he was actually saying was something like, 'You must send a telegram to X,' but what the director heard was, 'This film is shit.' Suddenly everything went black before his eyes. He fainted, slid off his chair and regained consciousness on the floor. When the guards escorted him from the room, they noticed that his trousers were soaked in piss. Muo thinks it strange that he should recollect this particular anecdote just now, and thanks his lucky stars that the reaction provoked in him by the death of Judge Di only resulted in an outbreak of cold sweat.)

'Once we were in the van with me behind the wheel it was my turn to be anxious. I was all tensed up thinking about what was going to happen to me at the judge's villa. You hadn't told me everything, but I'm no fool, I knew what it was all about. Muo, I want to tell you one thing . . .'

'Go ahead.'

'I hated you for it. Throughout the journey I hated you so much you have no idea. Deep down you're callous and cruel. All you care about is yourself.'

'I don't know what to plead in my defence. You may well be right.'

'You bastard! Let me continue. While I was driving, the secretary pulled himself together. He kept giving me orders, telling me which way to go, wittering on about

Judge Di. Do you know how long the judge had been playing mah-jong?'

'Before returning home to his villa, you mean?'

'Yes.'

'Twenty-four hours.'

'No. Three days and three nights. Seventy-two hours. Since Thursday evening he had been holed up in a hotel room with his cronies. The Holiday Inn – you may know it – that five-star hotel in the centre of town with fake marble columns. It's quite weird. Two twenty-storey wings, a manicured lawn and a garden with a fountain in the middle. Very clean-looking, but cold and clinical with its glass revolving doors. The secretary told me that, inside, the walls are lined with black granite, and that the lifts have doors of hammered bronze. The most remarkable experience, he said, is when you go down a corridor in search of a room. The numbers aren't marked on the doors, they're beamed from the ceiling on to the thick beige carpet at your feet. Makes you think of a crime movie. He told me he'd never seen this before, not even in the United States, and that when the hotel was inaugurated three or four years ago, Judge Di was a guest of honour. On that occasion he played mah-jong for twenty-four hours straight, without eating or drinking. He's a nutter. All he wants is the kind of arousal he felt in the old days, when he trained his gun on a condemned man. You knew what a pervert he was, and yet you threw me into his clutches.'

(Muo fumbles vainly for the switch of the bedside lamp and pulls on his trousers and jacket. He must go to the police station, or at least be ready to go. His shirt is clammy with sweat. Should he change into a clean one? He can hear something drop out of his coat pocket on to the floor, and in a flash it comes back to him: Isaac Bashevis Singer! It was Isaac Bashevis Singer who wrote that story about a man in an equally worrying predicament. Muo can recall the main drift, but not the names of the characters. The setting is a Communist country. Poland? Hungary? Whatever. A handsome young man, charming and fun-loving, an inveterate womaniser, is moved through compassion to sleep with a scrawny, fifty-five-year-old teacher who worships him. She waits for him in his house until midnight then gets out her pyjamas and slippers, takes a shower and joins him in bed. But in the middle of intercourse her body suddenly stiffens and, convulsing horribly, she dies. The seducer is left with the agonising fear of being arrested for murder. So much for the parallel. The rest of the story, Muo recalls, is devoted to the young man's efforts to get rid of the teacher's corpse in the middle of the night: after a trek through the city streets (deserted but for lurking shadows, passing patrol cars, prostitutes and roving drunks) he comes upon a frozen pond with a dog rooting around in the rubbish on the edge . . . That's exactly what I should be doing, Muo thinks, with a sharp intake of breath: getting rid of Judge Di's body. But he forces himself to concentrate on the Embalmer, whose volubility, it seems to him, must be an after-effect of holding a dead judge in her arms.)

'You know, Muo, I told you just now that I hated you from the very depths of my being and wished you dead while I was driving that van. Well, that's not strictly true. During the whole journey I kept asking myself, "Have I gone mad? Am I really to have my 'first night' at the age of forty, with a judge who's crazy about mah-jong? What kind of insane scenario have I landed myself in?" The street lamps diffused an eerie yellow light. The horns of the other cars sounded strangely distant, as in a dream – or, rather, I had the sense of re-living a drive that had occurred previously in a dream. Indeed, even now I'm not sure I'm not dreaming. A strange sort of calmness came over me, while the sixth secretary, still in excellent spirits, burbled on. He gave me a demonstration of his party trick: just by moving his mouth, lips and tongue he can imitate the sound of a mah–jong game. Apparently it has earned him the sympathy of Judge Di. And I must say he was pretty good. I could see the white mah–jong tiles, sliding apart, uniting, fighting . . . it was weird. The man actually soothed my nerves. I still felt a little tense, but it wasn't the same kind of tension as before. Like being in pain and then getting a shot of morphine. It doesn't take away the cause of the pain, but what a relief!'

(How to get rid of Judge Di's remains? A succession of film stills floods Muo's mind. First the image of a heavy body rippling the surface of a river before sinking slowly to the bottom. The rope with which it is bound becomes untied, the judge's uniform billows out. His stomach swells like a balloon, his feet give a few final twitches, before becoming rigid. One of his shoes works loose and founders in the mud, dislodging dark green aquatic plants, dead leaves, rubbish and rotting waste in a cloud of black debris. Borne along by the current, Judge Di assumes the stiff pose of a wooden doll as he floats with his long arms outstretched, heading towards the pier of a bridge. It is a concrete pier in the shape of a prow, against which the body is about to collide when, at the very last moment, it is swept into an eddy and rolls like a fallen leaf into the eye of a whirlpool. But no. A murderer like Di, with so much blood on his hands, did not deserve the kind of aquatic funeral Tibetans have practised for centuries, any more than he deserved the Yangtze River, from whose waters rise the world's most ancient prayers 'in accents intertwined two by two, waves coupled with verbs'. Who wrote that? Was it Joyce? Valéry? Had Muo got the quotation right?)

'I was driving along a road I've taken every day for over twenty years, and yet I had the sense of traversing a foreign city. We went past the open-air market, where I saw butchers cutting up carcasses, their knives flashing under the bare light–bulbs swinging overhead. I could feel a migraine coming on at the sight of them − they looked so unreal, encircled by haloes of lurid yellow. We went past the music academy. Across the grounds came the sound of a piano, no doubt a student practising in one of the grey brick buildings. 'How wonderful!' exclaimed the sixth secretary, adding that it was Beethoven's *Sonata no. 29*. For the first time I was impressed. He was eager to show off his knowledge of music, and told me about America and all his sleepless nights spent listening to the radio. He had fallen in love with jazz, and then with the piano. I told him he had good taste. He thanked me, and made a confession: he had converted to Christianity while he was over there. I was flabbergasted. In the end I actually felt sorry for him. He told me he had suffered horribly from piles while he was away, and that his condition is now incurable. They're invading his bowels. When they break there's a lot of blood-loss, like menstrual flow. Due to the unpredictability of his piles he is incapable of taking part in the mah-jong marathons held by his superiors, which often go on for days. As a result he has never penetrated the inner circles presided over by Judge Di, who picks his collaborators from among his gaming friends, and so his career is ruined.

'After the factory we turned into the road that leads to the bridge. The surface isn't as bumpy as it used to be in the days when my husband came to fetch me from work on his bike. We went past the public latrines. They aren't a shed any more, but a building with a tiled roof and white tiles on the outside. I can't tell you how I loathe that place. Nevertheless, for all its squalidness and foul smell, it is part of me, part of my life. I think of my husband, wherever he is, having assignations with boyfriends now that he is dead. At one point I asked my escort (his name was Lu): "Seeing as you're a Christian, Lu, I suppose you've studied the Bible, and all the rest?" "What do you mean, all the rest?" he asked. "Well, about paradise and such. What d'you think it's like?" "How do you mean what is it like?' he asked. "Well, would you say they have toilets in paradise? Not the grotty kind, I mean." He cut me short: "Do you really think I have time to think about stupid things like that?" He seemed annoyed, so I dropped the subject and concentrated on driving instead. When we passed the People's Park he said, "Listen here, I'm a lawyer. I don't deal in ambiguities. Pissing and shitting are what your body does. It's only your soul that goes up to heaven to join the angels. And souls don't shit or piss. So there's no need for any bogs." "Do they have them in hell then?" I asked. He said he didn't know. We both shut up after that. In the centre of Chengdu I stopped to buy something to drink. When I got back into the van, he was evidently still pondering my question. "Over in Beijing, in the Forbidden City, they don't have bogs either," he said suddenly. I was taken aback. "Oh really?" "No they don't," he said. "Have you been? If so, you wouldn't have seen any in the sections of the palace reserved for staff, nor in the inner courtyard used by the emperor, the empress and the concubines, nor in the eunuch's quarters either. No bogs anywhere, just like in heaven." "So where do they do their business?" I asked. "In a bucket?" He got angry again: "Shit! A bucket's a bucket, not a bog!"'

(Muo holds the receiver in his right hand and, with his left, feels around for the exact spot on his back the elite marksman will aim at before putting a bullet through his heart. He imagines being sentenced to death for the double crime of corrupting a judge and instigating murder. One fine morning the execution squad will take him to the wasteland at the foot of Mill Hill, a place he has seen with his own eyes, perhaps not by chance. A hole will have been dug by two low-ranking soldiers. His hands will be bound behind his back with thick ropes and he will be made to kneel with his back to the marksman, who will train the sights of his gun on the tiny square between his forefinger and thumb. Wondering whether he will wet his trousers like the Russian film director, Muo runs his fingertips over his back, pausing at the sharp, jutting triangle of his left shoulder blade, tapping his spine, exploring his frame to locate the fatal spot. Will his thorax explode the moment the bullet, popularly known as the 'killer peanut', hits him? Why peanut? Would it be the resemblance in shape? With a jolt, he remembers all the talk about 'pay-bullets' when he was a boy, about the killer bullet being invoiced to the prisoner's family. If they didn't cough up they could not recover the body of their executed loved one. If the loved one was fortunate enough to succumb at the first shot, his parents paid the price of just the one bullet, which was sixty-five fen in Chengdu, one yuan in Beijing, and one yuan twenty-five in Shanghai. Nowadays the price has gone up to at least ten or twenty yuan. 'My God,' he thinks to himself, 'my poor parents, having to go all the way across town to Mill Hill when I'm dead to settle the expense of my execution! How appalling! I can't let that happen.')

'Have you ever been to Judge Di's house? It's quite far away. Ten kilometres west of Chengdu, in the direction of Wenjiang. You follow the Yangtze until Sword Lake – you know, the artificial lake that serves as a water reservoir for the region. It's shaped like the Olympic rings. The road is quite narrow, but in excellent condition. You go up a wooded slope and come into a glitzy neighbourhood with Western-style houses (flood-lit terraces, lawns with statues, fountains, pitched roofs and rounded belfries like Russian onion domes). Pretty ugly, they are, each one kitschier than the last. Again it felt like a dream, and I wanted to turn back several times. I felt ill. The migraine was getting worse. It wasn't full-blown yet, but close enough.

'Judge Di's villa is situated halfway up the slope, behind a wall two metres high. I pulled up at the gate and the secretary got out of the van to announce our arrival on the entryphone. A spotlight flipped on, blinding me. The heavy iron door swung open.

'I didn't see the house at first. My escort told me it was a two-storey pavilion at the end of the garden. I steered the van into a dark drive that led through a thicket of bamboo. There was no lighting. Suddenly something jutted into the beam of my headlights, a strange, phantasmal creature a bit like a dragon or a tropical snake, with a ghastly flat head swaying to and fro about a metre above the ground. I thought it was opening its saw-toothed jaws, and gave a shriek of horror. My escort just laughed, telling me it was a rare chrysanthemum someone had given Judge Di. The plant is so precious that it takes four gardeners working full-time to take care of it, pruning it and watering it with a secret solution to ensure that it keeps its shape. The bloom is apparently priceless. I got out of the car to take a closer look. It was indeed a chrysanthemum, with unusually large leaves and petals curling in on themselves in a scalloped spiral. I rubbed the flower between my finger and thumb and it left a strong scent on my hand. There were more flowers of the same species in a variety of shapes – I made out one that looked like a horse.

'We turned a corner and the secretary told me we were approaching the peony garden. The van's headlights beamed over low bamboo hedges, but as it wasn't the season for peonies there was nothing much to see. I got a shock when we went past the bonsai garden, though. It gave me the creeps. You can't imagine how many there were. They reminded me of those monstrous foetuses they keep in glass jars. Some were clipped into perfectly symmetrical shapes. I can't stand that kind of thing – nature made into something unnatural. I didn't bother to stop the car this time, in fact I speeded up. But there was no end to the expanse of midgets, no escaping them: yews twisted into the shape of vases and lyres; miniature Indian fig trees with branches drooping to the ground, where they took root and sprouted more trees; elms with black boughs; I even saw a dwarf pawpaw tree fringed at the top with tiny green fruits under a tuft of leaves like an umbrella. Acacias, limes, magnolias and clove trees, all absurdly shrunken. The easiest to recognise were the cypresses, because they always keep their shape. But there were a lot of species I couldn't distinguish. Some of them had been altered beyond recognition. For instance, I took one of them to be a beech because of the grey bark, but I couldn't be sure. And so when I say I saw magnolias, jujube-trees, ilexes and green oaks, really it's just a guess.

'Well, finally the judge's villa came into view, starkly outlined against the sky. I thought we'd left the bonsais behind but there was yet another dwarf army – conifers this time – ranged in front of the house. I rolled down the window and inhaled the smell of resin and incense. Then something odd happened. A policeman in uniform stepped out in front of us, making us stop. He waved us to a parking space and ordered us to wait there. Outraged, Judge Di's secretary waved his permit under the policeman's nose. He was eventually granted permission to approach the villa on foot, unaccompanied by me.

'I was quite happy. I stayed behind in the van like someone who's arrived early for an appointment, and surveyed the house where my life would be changed and my virginity taken. The villa rising up on the far side of a lily pond was a brick building in a mixture of Western and Chinese styles, with creepers forming a little arch over one of the doors and climbing up to invade a balcony on the first floor. Through the greenery you could see large open windows lit with red drum-shaped lanterns, as if a party were underway. From time to time figures appeared at the windows, then flitted away, only to reappear elsewhere.

'The judge's secretary was a very long time coming back, so I cautiously crept out of the van. The policeman just eyed me and said nothing. I strolled around for a bit near the van. Pine-cones and broom-pods crackled under my feet. I went over to a stand of eucalyptus – I just love the fragrance, especially when combined with the almondy smell of broom.

'Looking up at the red lanterns in the windows again, I saw people hurrying from room to room. They seemed agitated. They were talking and gesticulating, but their voices were muted by the festoons of creeper. I paused to let it all sink in. There are some moments in life when you know instinctively that an impending doom has lifted. My migraine had gone. I could hear a vehicle approaching. It was an ambulance, the revolving light streaking across the tree trunks. My escort, the sixth secretary, came running. Judge Di was dead. After playing mah-jong for three days and three nights, he had insisted on playing some more when he got home. He summoned his staff and they played five matches. They were about to embark on a sixth when the judge slid from his armchair.

'Now how about that, Muo! Incredible, isn't it? Are you relieved? So am I. I'm at the mortuary. The corpse has to be embalmed by morning, before the bigwigs and the relatives arrive . . . Right, I'll wait for you here . . . Bye for now . . . Wait, bring me something to eat, will you? I'm ravenous!'

A rancid smell stings Muo's nostrils as the door of the embalming room swings open. Is it excrement? Rotting citronella? Camphor? Incense? No, it is an acrid odour that sears the nose the way hot peppers sear the palate. Whatever could it be? It is myrrh! She must have burnt some sticks of myrrh to mask the smell of formaldehyde which she knows to be nauseating and throat-constricting to the uninitiated.

'Are you all alone here?' he asks. 'Isn't there anyone else in the building? Don't you get scared?'

'Yes, I do, especially when it gets as late as this,' replies the Embalmer, without interrupting her preparations. She is wearing her work clothes and elbow-length rubber gloves.

'Excuse me. I forgot to say good evening.'

'Is it still evening?'

'Actually, daybreak is not far off.'

The room is not what Muo had imagined. It is neither stark, nor empty, nor white. Indeed, it seems less sinister than a room in a psychiatric hospital. There are five or six small lamps, all of them lit and making the shiny, chrome-plated instruments glint. There is an underwater atmosphere about the place, like the cabin of a sunken ship. This is heightened by the rush of water filling the tub gleaming in a dark corner. With a start Muo remembers a dream he once had: he was underwater, entering a submerged house. The roof was heavily encrusted with white shells, and rafts of tiny red crabs had settled on the woodwork of the door and the windows, their iridescent armour setting the dwelling alight with incandescent sparkles.

Stepping across the giant chessboard formed by the black and white floor-tiles he almost expects to hear the crunch of crabs underfoot.

'Where shall I put the food?' he asks the Embalmer. 'The shop at South Bridge was the only place still open at this hour. I brought you a peppered-ham sandwich and two tea-boiled eggs.'

'I love eggs done that way. I'm starving. Help me shell them, will you – I can't do a thing with these gloves on.'

Tea-boiled eggs have their shells cracked when cooked to allow the brown-tinged liquid to do its work. When Muo has picked the shell off, a tea-stained egg emerges with a scalloped pattern like that of a pine-cone.

'I'll take out the yolk. They say it's bad for your cholesterol,' he says.

'All right.'

She throws her head back, opening her mouth wide for Muo to drop a piece of egg into her pink jaws, where it rolls away on her tongue before reappearing as pale mush between her teeth.

'More please,' she says.

She devours the two eggs with lightning speed. In the course of this innocent indulgence Muo becomes keenly aware of the woman's eager, flicking tongue. He studies her familiar face, the curved forehead already traced with lines, the fine crows' feet, the chin betraying the beginnings of slackness.

'Come on,' she says, 'why don't you go and say goodbye to your friend Judge Di, then you can wait for me outside.'

He follows her to a semi-transparent plastic body-bag laid out on a trolley in the middle of the room. The soft glow diffused by a small lamp with a silk shade puts him in mind of an archaeological exhibit in a museum. Slowly and deliberately she begins to unzip the front of the bag. The metallic sound assaults Muo's ears. It is like nutshells being fractured in a vice. Judge Di's head comes into view, followed by his black-shirted chest.

'Damn, the zip's stuck,' says the Embalmer. 'Can you give me a hand?'

'Are you sure?'

'Sure about what? Go on, pull.'

For all the concerted and disconcerted efforts of the Embalmer and her amateur assistant, the zip refuses to budge: two of its teeth are locked in a permanent clinch. Muo can hear himself breathing. But there is also a gargling sound that he cannot place. Now and then his hand comes into contact with the judge's shirt, which is of finely woven silk and sensuous to the touch. At this close range he is able to distinguish, amid the sharp smell of myrrh, the rank odour of wine and stale tobacco typical of Parisian tramps. It occurs to him that the mah-jong addict probably hadn't washed for more than three days prior to his heart attack. Maybe a whole week.

'Wait,' says the Embalmer, 'I'll get some scissors to cut the damn thing open.'

While her back is turned Muo battles with the zip once more: he pulls the little metal clip back to the top, where the teeth mesh easily, and then down again, millimetre by millimetre. Approaching the place where it was jammed before, he gives it a tug with all his might, but once again it stops short. Suddenly he feels someone's eyes upon him. When he realises who they belong to, his chest breaks out in a cold sweat. It is Judge Di! In their grotesquely wrinkled sockets the judge's glassy eyes fix him with the dull, glazed look of someone coming back from a distant place. Terror-stricken, Muo remains poised over the judge's face, but his tormented soul seeks refuge outside his body. What vision is this? A dream? Reality? A resurrection? Can the doctor who signed the death certificate have been mistaken? Is this another Communist miracle? While these confounding questions make seismic waves in his brain, a gleam comes into the judge's eye as he catches sight of the Embalmer returning with the scissors. She freezes. The scissors slip from her fingers and bounce off the tiled floor. The judge rears up and throws his arms around her. She shrieks, but he hangs on to her shoulders to pull himself upright and then thrusts his body against her. She screams and struggles for all she is worth. He says: 'You're the Embalmer, aren't you?' She says yes, still fending him off. He smothers her with slobbery kisses. 'Don't be afraid,' he murmurs, 'every virgin goes through this to achieve true womanhood.'

The judge's words hit Muo's ears like a bombshell. He tries to separate him from the Embalmer but his arms feel like cotton wool. Then, summoning more strength than he thought he had in him, he grabs the judge by his collar so violently that he rips his shirt. 'Run for it!' he yells at the Embalmer, who flees, and the next instant a thousand stars explode before his eyes as a blow from the judge's steely elbow knocks him to the ground. Muo scrambles to his feet, but his nose is bleeding heavily and his legs give way, so he falls again. Meanwhile the judge slowly gets down from the trolley.

'Where am I?' he says, looking around in bewilderment. 'Damn! I'm in the morgue!'

Sprawled on the black and white tiles, Muo is aware of the judge making for the door and vanishing into the night. He loses track of time. Coming to his senses at last, he assesses the damage: his face is bloodied like that of the hero in a Western, and his trousers are sopping wet like the Russian director's in the Kremlin projection room.

'Not bad, Muo,' he says to himself, 'here you are, the two global superpowers united within you.'

3

The Housing Estate Called 'Light'

With his trousers and underwear soaked through, Muo has
no choice but to leave the mortuary wearing the Embalmer's
clothes, which he finds in a cupboard. The pale blue overall
is made of thick, sturdy material and is something between a
boiler suit and the robe of an ancient scholar. It is printed
back and front with the words 'Cosmos Funeral Services' (in
white), a picture of an astronaut astride a rocket (in yellow)
and the company's contact details (in red). Muo is relieved to
find that it has plenty of pockets, to which he transfers all the
paraphernalia he carries around in his trousers: cigarettes,
lighter, wallet, key-ring and his recently acquired mobile
phone, which glows and blinks in the gloom.

It is still dark. The idea of returning home is unappealing,
for he dreads rousing his parents and shocking them with his
macabre outfit. (He can already hear his mother complaining:
'Why so late? My son, when will you do us the favour of
getting married?') Instead he sets off across the slumbering
city without any particular plan. Taking the Embalmer's
route past the gate of the deserted music academy, he then

turns right and follows the long wall until he comes upon an unlit workers' housing estate with no one in sight. He would like to catch his reflection in a shop window to see what he looks like, but there are no shops in the neighbourhood. Now and then a dog crosses his path, pausing briefly to observe him and then following him along the opposite pavement. He can hear the scuttle of rats in the dustbins.

Reaching a crossroads, he is seized with doubt. Despite the warm breeze caressing his cheeks, a shiver runs down his spine. He does not know where he is. What is happening to him? He was born in this town, he grew up here. And yet he is lost. Fighting a sense of panic, he decides he might as well take a look at the changes wrought in the town by rampant capitalism. He strolls down one new street after another, all the same, all with row upon row of virtually identical concrete apartment blocks. After a quarter of an hour of indecision he decides to head north. But when he looks up to scan the sky, he can't make out where north is. To make matters worse, it has started raining. So he just carries on in the same direction as before, down a street which is lined, like all the others, with young eucalyptus trees.

'What would Volcano of the Old Moon say if I paid her a surprise visit in prison wearing this outfit?' he wonders. 'Would it make her laugh? Yes, she'd roar with laugher. She has this way of roaring with laughter that some people find alarming and others embarrassing. We'd be on either side of the glass partition, each with our telephone receivers (shit, such a poor country and such ultra-modern prisons – insane!) and this is what I'd say: "See this astronaut? My new passion." No, I'd do better than that. I'd tell her I had joined a band of professional angels, charged with escorting human beings on the last leg of their journey to paradise. To explain what embalmers do I'd say: "They are the beauticians of the dead." "Don't make me laugh," she'd reply. "You don't know a thing about beauty." I'd lean forward and she'd reach out to me on the other side of the glass and press her long, fine fingers against the little man in the spacesuit on my chest. Narrowing her eyes knowingly, she'd give me a questioning look. Then she'd dissolve in tears, having understood it all without me having to tell her a thing. She would comprehend the severity of the new setback. The finality, too. Then she'd bury her head in her arms until the screws came to take her away. They wouldn't have it easy. When she's in that position even the most die-hard warder has an impossible time. She becomes extraordinarily heavy, so that dragging her upright is a real struggle. I'd better not visit her now, and not in the next few days either. She doesn't need that. I am close to tears myself, here, in this godforsaken maze of low-rent housing.'

The first time Muo witnessed Volcano of the Old Moon in tears was when they were both studying at Sechuan university. It was bitterly cold and, exceptionally for this town in south-western China, it had snowed for several days. One afternoon towards the end of November Muo went to see Professor Li, who taught Shakespeare and considered Muo one of his star pupils. The professor's room was spacious but freezing cold, except for the adjoining study (five square metres, entirely lined with bound volumes) which was heated with a coal-burning stove, so they went in there to have an informal, friendly chat. Muo showed Li a translation he had just completed, and the professor put on his spectacles, one side of which had been replaced by a piece of string, to compare the text word for word with the original. There was a knock at the door. Professor Li stepped into the main room to answer it, and Muo glimpsed Volcano of the Old Moon as she came in. He was puzzled by her presence there, as she had never taken an interest in English, let alone in Shakespeare. She was unrecognisable, so pale and with heavily swollen eyes, she was clearly in great distress, physical or mental he could not tell. She did not speak. Indeed, she did not even respond to the professor's greeting. All she did was walk unsteadily to the table in the middle of the room, sit down on a cane chair, dissolve in tears and bury her face in her arms on the table. From his vantage point, Muo could only discern her long hair shivering between her shoulders, then tossing and rippling with each new spasm of weeping. He paced the small study, uncertain as to whether he should stay or leave. He could hear Professor Li talking in a voice suddenly bereft of the confidence and wonderful resonance that kept audiences spellbound. He was apologising for the misdeeds of his son (a student of philosophy, inordinately handsome, known as a Don Juan all over the campus, whose name often crossed the lips of female students because, it seems, he regularly visited their dreams). He dismissed his son as a rogue and a reprobate, not to be trusted, and the like. Muo approached the window and, peering at the dusty pane, discovered traces of tears on his own distraught face. The stove, which had been purring like a homely old cat all the while, had gone out. He tried re-lighting it by adding coal and blowing through the small vent but he was blinded by a gust of soot. Smoke billowed out into the other room. When the professor came to his aid, Muo left the study coughing and spluttering. The noise drew the attention of Volcano of the Old Moon, who was astounded to see him coming towards her in a cloud of smoke and streaked with soot. It was hard to say whose discomfort was the more acute: hers for being in an embarrassing situation or his for seeing her thus. Wiping his face with the back of his sleeve (which only blackened it further and made him look like a clown in a Chinese opera), Muo muttered excuses that even he could not make head nor tail of. He took a chair and made to sit down, but found himself on his knees beside her. 'Stop thinking about him,' he implored, 'forget him.' Shaking her head, she reached out to touch Muo's shoulder, no doubt to make him rise to his feet. Her despair was palpable. He wanted to tell her: 'Volcano of the Old Moon, I am short-sighted, unattractive, puny, uninteresting and poor, but I am proud and I will do anything for you, to my dying breath,' but he was struck dumb by the enormity of this statement. Lifting his face up close to her chest he could sense the anguished pounding of her heart. He managed to stammer her name as she leaned over to pull him to his feet. 'Go on, get up, or he'll see us,' she said, choking with the effort of suppressing her sobs while the tears ran down her cheeks and lips. Muo wanted to wipe them away, but his hand was all sooty. So, in a rapid movement, he kissed her on the mouth. It was not a proper kiss, their lips just met, and in that fleeting moment he could taste the salt of her bitter tears. They both drew back at once. Sitting quite still, she kept her swollen eyes fixed on him, and yet she did not see him, as well he knew. She had the dull, passive look of a patient in a hospital waiting room. In the end she drew herself up in all her grace and bade goodbye to Professor Li in the smoke-filled room.

Twenty-odd years later, trudging across town in the Embalmer's work clothes, Muo casts his mind back to that kiss – his first kiss, a kiss of love and desire, a complicated kiss flavoured with salty tears. In his mind's eye he sees Volcano of the Old Moon's black quilted jacket contrasting with the pallor of her lovely face, and he remembers her black trousers, black shoes and eye-catching snow-white rollneck sweater. That day in November has remained a milestone in his existence. He has even made a secret anniversary of it which he celebrates each year in touching solitude, appropriately attired in the same ragged blue coat and greasy cap he wore then. (At this point we may reveal the secret of our psycho-analyst friend: to put it bluntly, he is still a virgin, but not one who is eager for experience, as is clear to all whenever he is in female company.) Laden with sentiment as they are, this tattered apparel infuses him with the glow of romance as he celebrates these anniversaries of love, be it in China or in Paris.

You can hardly tell it is raining, but the drops slide down from the leaves of the trees, soaking Muo's clothes and hair. He reflects ruefully that his outfit, unlike ski clothing, does not extend to a hood. A cab draws level with him, gliding alongside the pavement in the hope of being hailed, but he prefers to ignore it, thinking he has found his bearings. Beyond a stand of spectral plane trees rising almost ethereally in the rainy mist looms an unmistakable landmark: the public toilet, the homosexuals' happy hunting ground of old, with the letters WC in neon on the roof. Upon reaching the building, Muo is moved by the curiosity of a historian to step inside. Nothing in the place seems real. Supervising the facility is a melancholy, hollow-eyed patriarch in a uniform similar to that of the mortuary, hunched like a pale ghost in the weak lamplight of his glass-fronted cubicle. 'That will be two yuan,' he announces in the tone of a museum attendant.

As he approaches the sweet factory, Muo take his mobile from his pocket and stares at it distractedly, for he cannot think whom to call. The only person in the world he feels like talking to is Volcano of the Old Moon, and she is behind bars. His thoughts shift to Michel Nivat, his French psychoanalyst who, given the time difference, should be awake at this hour. Sheltering from the rain under a tall bush with leaves as nervously aquiver as himself, he presses the digits. He hears a click, then the distant voice of his former mentor uttering a cool, tight-lipped sort of 'Oui'. As he is all too often harassed by patients suffering nervous breakdowns, Nivat has adopted the habit of answering the phone with the curtest, most neutral-sounding 'Oui' he can muster. Muo's desire to talk evaporates, and he switches off wordlessly. A few seconds later, his mobile goes off in the pocket of his overall.

'Do forgive me, Michel,' he mumbles, 'I'm so sorry to have disturbed you, but I'm up to my neck in shit.'

The voice at the other end is female, and Chinese. Muo is startled. In his muddled state he takes it to be his mother's.

'Where are you? Are you mad, Muo? Why are you talking to me in a foreign language?'

It is the Embalmer. He can't imagine why she can have slipped his mind so completely. Apologising profusely, he promises to join her at home as soon as possible.

The Embalmer. Muo is not sure quite when his upstairs neighbour acquired this nickname or who gave it to her. Everyone calls her the Embalmer nowadays, even her own parents, Mr and Mrs Liu, both professors of anatomy who have been retired for some years. They have given her their flat: two modest rooms under the eaves of a six-storey walk-up with a whitewashed exterior whose windows are protected by security grilles like cages at a zoo. Over the main entrance is a relief in white and pink stucco portraying a worker, a farmer and a soldier holding aloft a cogwheel as if it were a garland. This is the building where the 'husband' of the virgin widow jumped from the sixth floor on the night of their wedding.

After his phone conversation it occurs to Muo that he will have to have the stealth of a burglar if he wants to reach the Embalmer's flat without alerting his parents on the second floor.

As he mulls over the various scenarios open to him, he finds himself entering the vast domain of the medical university. Little India Street, planted with mighty plane trees forming a kilometre-long tunnel of greenery, cuts the grounds in two; the southern half is given over to faculty premises and the campus, the northern half to residential halls for teachers and other staff. (Chinese universities have always provided housing for their personnel, and continue to do so today. The president of such an establishment enjoys a degree of power undreamed-of by his colleagues in the West: every single decision, ranging from recruitment, salaries, promotions, reimbursement of expenses such as repairs to plumbing, electrical circuits and blocked toilets, menus and prices in the various canteens, family planning, enrolment of offspring in day-care centres and primary schools, to the allocation of flats – all depends on him. A true king. Thus, during the wave of reforms in the early nineties, the university sold its flats to the occupants, which, for the Chengdu medical faculty alone, amounted to the sale of several thousand dwellings.)

The residential halls are spread over five estates by the names of Peace, Light, Bamboo, the Garden of the West and Peach Orchard. Each of them comprises several dozen buildings five to seven storeys high, within walled precincts. It is a long way from one end of this sleeping kingdom to the other. Muo must walk down Little India Street for at least fifteen minutes before reaching Peace, after which he has the whole of Peach Orchard to cross before arriving at the estate called Light.

Despite its bright name, the estate is plunged in darkness. Muo knocks on the locked gate and shouts for the janitor, his voice echoing in the night until he is too hoarse to continue. A light flips on overhead, revealing the portal in all its solemn grandeur. Under a pitched roof of varnished tiles and cornices carved with mythological figures, the huge red double doors are overlaid with layer upon layer of brightly coloured hand-bills: opening and closing times, lists of rules and regulations, pictures of wanted criminals, announcements of residents' political meetings, the self-criticism of a thief, American film posters, slogans, appeals for AIDS donations, personal ads, public letters of denunciation dating from a different era but still perfectly legible, newspaper cuttings spanning continents and decades. The small rectangular door let into the gate opens with an ear-splitting creak to reveal the janitor, a young man Muo has not seen before, with a People's Militia coat thrown over his shoulders.

'Thank you kindly for your trouble,' Muo says, discreetly slipping the fellow a two-yuan note.

The janitor takes the money, lets him in and locks the door behind him. He raises the heavy wooden barrier and turns round to examine Muo.

'Has someone died?' he asks, staring intently at Muo's outfit with an air of suspicion.

'Yes, indeed. Liao the cripple from building 11 in the third precinct,' Muo replies, surprised at his own talent for improvisation.

Liao the cripple, the Muo family's former next-door neighbour, has been dead for ten years, but the new janitor shakes his head in sympathy and heaves a long sigh worthy of an American soap opera.

'How are you going to transport the body? Have you got a vehicle?' he calls after Muo.

'Not necessary. I have come for his soul.'

Nailed to the spot by this enigmatic reply, the janitor follows Muo with his eyes as he moves away, a ghostly silhouette in the rain. At the first precinct the silhouette walks past the entrance without glancing up at the six concrete buildings of exemplary similitude. At the second it turns left and disappears from the janitor's sight.

Muo comes upon two further entrances piercing brick walls, face to face in perfect symmetry: those of the third and fourth precincts. Both are secured by metal grilles, iron chains painted green like climbing plants, and brass padlocks dripping water. Anyone would think the buildings contained priceless treasures.

Muo ponders what he would say if he met his parents, and more particularly his mother. He knocks methodically on the left entrance. No answer. He knocks again and calls out, albeit in more subdued, disguised tones. He doesn't dare lift his eyes to the looming concrete buildings, their cloned, sombre heights vanishing into the rainy mist. Ever since he was a boy, standing by these grilles (at the time they were rusty, and closed at 8.30 rather than 11.30 p.m. as they are today) has filled him with the same dread of his mother.

The janitor who lets him in is another young man in a People's Militia overcoat, but he is shorter and thinner than the one at the main gateway. He takes the proffered two-yuan note without the least regard for either the giver or the 'Funeral Services' printed on his overall. He locks up after Muo and scurries back home to bed.

At this hour everyone is still fast asleep. The worker, the farmer and the soldier in white and pink stucco over the entrance are the only witnesses to his arrival. He slips quietly into the empty hallway, which smells of vomit as usual. Shivering with cold and wet, he cocks his ear. Not a sound.

Reassured, he starts up the stairs on tiptoe. By the second floor, however, our prodigal son is rapidly losing his confidence as well as his composure. He is no longer shivering, he is sweating. With each step the smell of home becomes stronger, an indefinable yet unmistakable smell he would recognise blindfold.

There are two flats on the second-floor landing, as in the other buildings: the one on the left belongs to the Muo family, the one on the right to the deceased cripple. Approaching on tiptoe, Muo daren't glance at either door – not that he can see anything, because he can't risk switching the light on. He advances cautiously, taking care not to make a false move, feeling around with the tip of his shoe before each step. So far so good. He knows his father's hearing is poor: ever since his eardrum was punctured he watches television with the volume turned up as high as it will go. On the other hand his mother's hearing is excellent. Since her eyesight began to fail as a result of diabetes, she can hear a cat sneeze in the building opposite, or the scuttle of cockroaches on the fridge. Holding his breath, nerves stretched to breaking point, he slopes past the flat and very nearly loses his balance. His left foot has just stepped on a plastic rubbish bag.

Rubbish spills out everywhere and a Coke can bounces off down the stairs, clattering to a halt at the bottom.

Poised motionless in the dark, Muo waits for what seems like an age for the pandemonium to cease. Once all is quiet again he is amazed and relieved to find that no one has been alerted. What a miracle! Perhaps they're accustomed to a lot of noise from marauding rats in the night. 'At home, in my building,' he once confided to his psychoanalyst, 'there are hordes of rats, and I can assure you they are the biggest in the world.'

He hurries up the next flight, and the next, quickening his pace as he reaches the top, triumphant, excited, in a state of physical lightness akin to that of a lover speeding to an assignation. He runs his fingers through his hair, pats it down as best he can, blows into his cupped hand to check his breath and polishes his spectacles.

The sixth floor comprises four two-room flats. The Embalmer's is on the right at the end of the passage. The pale light from a nearby window bathes the front door in a discreet glow, which stops Muo's hand in mid-air before he can knock. It is a strange glow, faintly yellow and with the pearly sheen of glass. He touches the door with his fingertips – it is glazed! The previous evening, when he visited the Embalmer to set up the rendezvous between her and Judge Di, this door was made of metal like all the others: reinforced, and complete with security hinges, latches, locks and spy holes.

'Has Judge Di's resurrection made me go mad?' he asks himself.

He feels around for his disposable lighter and approaches the door with its timid but effective flame. Not only is it glazed, there is also a small card pinned to the wall saying 'Mr and Mrs Wang', which is not the Embalmer's name.

His astonishment is so great that he shrinks back, descending a few treads in the dark.

'Confound it!' he thinks to himself. 'Medically speaking, I have lost my reason.'

His immediate reaction is to check the workings of his brain. The simplest, most efficient way, it seems to him, is to start with a memory test, such as coming up with words in French. It doesn't bear thinking about, not even for a second, that his knowledge of the French language, which is so difficult to learn and which has taken him so many years of hard work, could go up in smoke from one moment to the next. He prays for divine protection.

The first French word that springs to mind is '*merde*'. He recalls *Les Misérables* and recites from memory a passage where the expletive is intriguingly indicated by the initial followed by three dots, to spare the sensitivities of the French reader.

What a relief! Savouring this demonstration of his powers of recall, he thinks of another exclamation he likes very much, one which means different things in different circumstances, and which is associated in his mind with the poet and novelist Hugo. It is the word '*hélas*'. He casts his mind back to the famous exchange between Paul Valéry (his favourite French poet) and André Gide, during which the former claimed that the greatest of all French poets was Hugo, to which the latter's retort was '*hélas*'. Then there is '*l'amour*', one of those words whose resonance he finds more pleasing in French, more mellifluous than in Chinese or in English. During one of his visits to Volcano of the Old Moon, as they sat facing each other on either side of the glass partition, he told her about this personal linguistic preference, after which she repeated the word several times. As she found it difficult to pronounce the letter L, she left out the definite article and just said '*amour*', first in a whisper, then more and more loudly, until the grace and magic of the word resonated like a musical note in the visiting area teeming with prisoners and their relatives, all of whom, young and old alike, were enchanted. Such are the mesmerising, voluptuous overtones of this foreign word! It would have been taken up in chorus if the screws had not intervened.

Having verified the state of his memory, Muo conducts a fresh investigation in the hope of unravelling the mystery. Once again he holds his lighter up to the card. Not wishing to give the occupants a heart attack with his mortuary outfit, he calls the Embalmer on his mobile. She sounds panicky at the other end.

'Where are you? No! . . . Of course I know the Wangs, they teach physical culture . . . You're in front of their door? But they live in the fourth precinct, and we live in the third! Can't you even find your own building?'

Muo flies down the stairs four steps at a time, runs past the flat he had taken for that of his parents, then grins and pauses to deliver a vicious kick to the half-empty rubbish bag, making it spill the rest of the contents in the stairwell. Outside, it is still raining, and when Muo finally reaches his building he is as wet as an otter who has emerged from one hole, swum across a lake and then popped into another.

Muo can scarcely breathe. Beneath his tread the concrete stairs give way, shrinking and swelling by turns as if they were made of rubber, and he has a sense of wading through soggy marshland. It is like a dream he once had where he was crossing an expanse of marble veined with grey and black. As he walked it softened under his long strides and finally metamorphosed into a huge slice of ripe cheese.

It is the Embalmer who has put our subtle and sensitive psychoanalyst into this state, for she is at his side, holding his hand as he mounts the stairs.

When, some moments ago, he entered the building, he was unable to locate the light-switch, so there was nothing for it but to make his way upstairs like a thief in the dark. But as he neared the first floor, the light on the landing above went on. He heard the sound of flip-flops coming down the stairs, which sent a shiver of apprehension down his spine.

Holding his breath, he strained to identify their owner, fearing it was his mother. However, since leaving China he has lost the ability to distinguish, just by the sound on the stairs, what people's footwear is made of (plastic? leather? rubber?) as well as the characteristics of the wearer (man? woman? timid? violent? tender? stern?). He used to be very good at it. When someone was accepted as a Communist Party member, for instance, that person's footwear changed its tune, and for a long time afterwards seemed to sing the Chinese national anthem.

The flip-flops descending the stairs evoked a strange mix of high spirits and unconcern. The light went out again, but the darkness did not modify the rhythm of the footsteps. They reached the second floor without slowing down. Muo resumed his ascent with trepidation, the pad–pad of his shoes gradually falling in step with the crisp patter of the flip-flops until the sounds combined in a serenade of seemingly prearranged discretion.

'Is that you?' Muo heard the Embalmer ask.

'Shush,' he said. 'You'll wake my mother.'

Just ahead of him on the second-floor landing, he discerned a pale shadow coming down the stairs.

'Careful, my mother's hearing is . . .'

He did not reach the end of his sentence. The flip-flop serenade fell silent. The Embalmer clasped his hand. He could feel her sweaty palm and nervously clinging fingers, and a hard object which he realised was her wedding ring. Her face, so close to his, emanated a faintly chemical smell. He put his cheek against hers.

'What scent are you wearing?' he whispered.

'None. It must be formaldehyde.'

'No.'

'Are you sure?'

'Yes.'

'I'm glad. I loathe smelling of formaldehyde after work.'

'Can't it be iodine? Did you hurt yourself?'

'No. I put a moisturising mask on earlier. Your Judge Di gave me such a fright that I couldn't stop shaking when I got home, so I treated myself to a mask. It's quite astringent, but you have no idea how soothing it is. Look – I've stopped shaking. I've put the whole ghastly business out of my mind.'

'I almost died of fright myself.'

There followed an unsteady advance, hand in hand in the dark, groping and staggering and whispering like a pair of comedians. When they sloped past Muo's parents' flat the front door was safely shut and the lights out, but he thought he could hear his mother cough.

'How cold your hand is, you poor thing,' said the Embalmer. 'I can't get it warm.'

'I'm soaked to the skin. These overalls are too small for me. Maybe they're yours?'

'You can change at my place. I've kept my husband's clothes as mementoes. The size should be about right.'

4

Steamed Dumplings

A few minutes later, Muo's bare feet are shod in a pair of dark-blue suede slippers embroidered with three small flowers in different shades of mauve: eupatorium, sea lavender and scabious. Worn slippers, with soles that slap on the floor.

Like all Asians, the Embalmer keeps her shoes on a rack by the front door. Perching on a plastic stool in the narrow hallway, Muo has taken off his mud-spattered shoes and has lined them up alongside the pairs of trainers, espadrilles, flip-flops, and high white lace-up boots . . . They are all the same size, but quite a bit smaller than the suede slippers that belonged to the Embalmer's late husband. The slippers are too big for him: when he crosses his legs, one dangles from his big toe.

'Not bad, those slippers,' the Embalmer says to him. 'We bought them a few weeks before the wedding, in the People's Shopping Centre. Five yuan five fen, I remember clearly. Since he died I've kept them on my shoe rack. I brush them up and wear them occasionally, though they're too big.'

There are faint echoes of the mortuary in her living quarters, which are lit with five or six weak lamps disposed about the room in pale, blurry haloes, creating an atmosphere of almost subterranean confinement. She trips about with the lightness of a bird and the joy of regained youth, her face covered in the creamy mask. (Her short, pink-silk peignoir is embroidered with white birds and flowers in a golden landscape.)

'What would you like to eat? I've got some frozen dumplings in the fridge. Celery and lamb stuffing, how does that sound?'

Without waiting for a reply, she disappears into the kitchen.

'A man in the house at last,' she sighs.

The flat is pervaded by the cold melancholy of a childless spinster. It floats in the air like thin smoke, dust in a state of suspension, or burning incense. On the floor is a mat of finely woven bamboo, protected in places – next to the sofa, the television and the two leather armchairs – with different coloured bits of carpet. There is no dining table. Does she eat in the kitchen? The sofa and the armchairs still wear their protective plastic wraps from the factory. The television, enthroned on its own pedestal, has a purple velvet cover. The remote control is cased in cellophane, the telephone is draped in pale-pink towelling. A family portrait in colour, enlarged and framed, hangs on the wall. No individual photos of her or her husband, but several paper cut-outs of his silhouette. Just one picture of them together: him pedalling his bike against the wind, hunched over the handlebars, raincoat flapping, and her on the carrier, knitting a jumper that streams like a scarf behind her.

She does have one treasure in her possession: a wonderful collection of puppets. Muo is enchanted each time he peers at the small figures in their costumes of brightly coloured satin and silk: emperors in robes embroidered with dragons, empresses laden with jewels, scholars holding fans, generals bristling with sabres and lances, even beggars, all looking back at him through the dingy glass of a display case. They were a gift from her husband, who inherited the collection from one of his great-uncles. There are about twenty figures, each one more ravishing than the last. Muo could spend hours admiring them. The Embalmer's late husband installed tiny lights in the display, with individual switches secreted in the folds of velvet lining the base and sides. Muo approaches the case, sinks to his knees and opens the glass front. Entranced, he flips one switch after another, putting each puppet in the spotlight in turn. He is joined by the Embalmer, who holds a purring blow-dryer to his head. The puppets' clothing ripples in the breeze, the scholars' fans flutter, the empresses' jewels tinkle. In his rapture, Muo cannot resist reaching out to touch first the Embalmer's flip-flops and then her shapely left foot with its finely-boned, trembling instep.

The alarming sound of dumplings boiling over brings this idyllic prelude to an abrupt close. She recoils and rushes off into the kitchen. He remains on his knees, gazing as the puppets come to life in his hands. Through his steamed-up glasses Muo sees a blurred panoply of colours dancing, melting, transforming themselves into stars, flames and glow-worms twinkling in the drama of the night.

At the insistence of his hostess (a perfectionist where dumplings are concerned, she deems the taste of this delicate foodstuff ruined by over-cooking and puts a fresh supply to boil), Muo exchanges his wet uniform for dry clothes. Opening the wardrobe he is faced with a barrage of hangers. On one side the Embalmer's clothes: satin slips with scalloped hems, a fake fur coat, blouses, dresses and skirts etcetera. On the other, her husband's attire, smelling strongly of camphor: a blue Mao jacket, a slate-grey suit with matching waistcoat, a white shirt with starched collar and attached, black silk bowtie, several pairs of trousers, a worn leather jacket, belts, army caps – but nothing for the summer. The sight of these carefully hung clothes, so evocative of their dead owner's appearance, knocks Muo off course. He opens the door to another cupboard, inside which three colours prevail amongst the piles of clean, detergent-scented laundry: white, pink and blue. He catches sight of a likely garment and pulls it out. Unfolding the tracksuit, he is filled with the sense of holding a living, pulsing thing in his hands. He shuts the door and steps into the bathroom to change.

The strip light on the ceiling casts an icy pallor on the white bathtub, toilet bowl and washbasin. The washbasin has a little glass shelf bearing toothbrush, make-up bag, tubes of cream and bottles of lotion. Above it an oval mirror reflects his transformation from a man disguised as a mortician to a student of the eighties, thanks to the outfit worn by the Embalmer's late husband. (The sky-blue top, with open seams under the arms, bears the red torch and yellow insignia of the Communist Youth League. Muo remembers it as the uniform worn by the university basketball team.) He gazes in the mirror, fascinated by his new look. He recalls certain mannerisms of the clothes' former owner and imitates them by way of experiment. He is astounded by the resemblance he observes in the overall expression and the slight pout of the lips.

'The time has come to take action, Muo,' he tells himself. 'But you can't very well put an end to your protracted celibacy out of a sense of duty and gratitude, merely to honour a moral debt. No, you must leave. Even if you are missing a chance to furnish sensational proof of your virility, you must be true to your principles. You must leave. You don't owe anyone anything. Not a thing.'

He exits from the bathroom, shutting the door behind him with feigned nonchalance. The latch drops with a dull, metallic click. He listens and catches the sound of his hostess bustling about in the kitchen. If he is going to make his escape, this is undeniably the perfect moment, but he is distracted by some statement of Freud's or perhaps it was another master (his mind is so muddled that the exact or even approximate source of the quotation escapes him): 'many a murderer seeks refuge behind the mask of a war hero, just as impotence is frequently passed off as asceticism.'

'I am not impotent, thank God. Nor am I disguised as an ascetic, but as a student who likes basketball,' he chuckles, regretting that there is no one there to follow his logic. 'But can I be sure of my virility?'

He looks down at the indiscreet bulge in the dead husband's tracksuit bottoms. 'Just a minute! Think this one out. It could be a question of now or never − a prime opportunity to acquire a skill that will come in useful one day,' he muses.

But the truth is that, for all the stuffing in his head (on subjects ranging from psychoanalysis and ethics to the history of the breast or the history of sex since Antiquity), he is sorely lacking in practical experience.

Re-entering the living room, he is astonished to find that his legs are not taking him to the right and consequently in the direction of the front door, but are striding purposefully, like those of a famished husband returning from work, to the left, that is to say to the kitchen.

'Are the dumplings ready?' the surrogate husband wants to know. 'They certainly smell good.'

Standing by the cooker, the Embalmer turns to face him. Seeing her husband's clothes on someone else pierces her heart. She gives a little gasp of shock mixed with joy. She feels faint and shivery, then opens her eyes wide, taking in the tracksuit of long ago, torn and patched in places (she recognises her own hand in the mends) with its little standing collar and the V-neck above a button dangling from a thread. As Muo moves closer, the button swells until it fills her field of vision.

'I must sew it back on,' she says, touching him with one hand and stirring the dumplings with the other.

Muo lunges forward and grabs her roughly by the waist. He kisses her awkwardly but so passionately that she very nearly falls backwards against the dresser. He can feel the Embalmer's toned muscles ripple under his hands. She twists round, their tongues meet, with courteous surprise at first, and a hint of embarrassment that rapidly gives way to wild intoxication as they mingle, caress, explore, roll about like a pair of dolphins. In his innocence, Muo loses himself in the aroma of celery-flavoured dumplings, the pharmaceutical odour of his friend's facial mask, the perfume of her mouth, the hardness of her teeth (like rocks in a grotto), the murmur of the fridge, the dripping sink, the groans escaping from their throats, the steam from the saucepan rising and swathing their entwined bodies like a mosquito net of milky tulle, a floating veil, a sublime mist. Closing her eyes, the Embalmer moans voluptuously as he caresses her thighs. He is startled to see her like this, barely recognizable, absent and dreamy, her face newly radiant with a consuming lust akin to beatitude. They burn like two sticks of dry wood in a fire. They have no time to move to the bedroom. The Embalmer's hand grips the tracksuit pants and pulls them down around Muo's bony ankles. She in turn strips off her trousers and pink panties, which she sends flying with her foot. They make love on their feet, propped against the dresser whose small doors give way under this seismic onslaught, spilling fistfuls of bamboo chopsticks and plastic forks and spoons with each thrust. Then the seismic wave travels along the wall, making the wooden shelf above their heads rattle and dance, so that a bag of flour set among the pyramid of jars and pots falls on to the draining board with a dull thud. Puffs of white powder billow forth (with each rhythmic thrust), dissipating in clouds of dust mixed with bits of paper (notes? unpaid bills?), which settle on their hair, their shoulders, their faces, and even on the steaming dumplings. Some snippets stick to the Embalmer's moisturising mask. 'It's snowing!' Muo whispers but she does not respond. Again he is amazed to see her in such ecstasy. He knows that she has not heard him. At that very moment he believes he has grasped the quintessence of modern art. Here she is, the dear Embalmer, incarnating in her person all those portraits of women with both eyes on one side of the face, or heads broken up into flat rectangular planes, especially a painting by Picasso which he realises he will admire unconditionally for the rest of his life – *Woman with a Mandolin* – now that he understands the cause of the melting breast, the disjointed shoulders, the exalted frenzy. He recalls the rudimentary head, a small square filled by a huge eye emerging from a pear-shaped mandolin. Muo's first copulation, which proceeds in textbook fashion, is in danger of turning into a doctoral thesis on the work of Picasso. He dreams of becoming the great artist himself, not for his genius or celebrity, but for his penetrating, cynical, untrammelled way of seeing. Like a true hedonist, Muo casts a Picassoan eye over the dumplings dancing in the bosomy foam. On a surging tide of boiling water white horses are rearing, neighing and galloping . . . Just as the water threatens to boil over, the Embalmer seizes a spoon. Observing her hand stirring the pan and the dumplings obediently sinking to the bottom, Muo is struck by the automatism of her gesture, which proves that she is still of this world. His thoughts shift to the dead bodies that have been touched by this same hand slick with cream and sweat, this virginal, flour-dusted hand to which he has surrendered his sex. He can hear her hot, shallow breathing and her whisper of 'My man'. The effect is both numbing and seductive. He feels slightly in love with her. He wants to tell her he loves her, but the words get stuck in his throat. Then her body goes rigid and her eyes pop as she moans, 'My husband'. A complete hush descends, in which Muo hears neither the murmur of the fridge nor the water bubbling in the pan. Only that phrase resonating in the air.

He cannot decide whether the appellation vests him with the responsibility of a future head of the family, or reduces him to the status of a mere stand-in or even a victim.

She removes his spectacles, puts them down on the sink, takes his face between her hands and covers it with kisses.

'Hold me tight, my husband,' she shrieks in his ear, 'don't ever leave me.'

Without his spectacles, still thrusting, he rolls his eyes to the ceiling several times, takes a deep breath and says: 'Your husband sends you his regards.'

The Embalmer is so taken aback by this news that she looks at him blankly for a moment, then throws her head back and convulses with laughter, shaking them both. This delectable shake is Muo's undoing – it elicits a flood of sperm.

'What, already?' she exclaims. 'The dumplings aren't done yet!'

'Forgive me,' he mumbles, pulling up his pants and searching for his spectacles.

Having regained his sight, he is bowled over by the sheer incongruity of what is revealed to him. The first thing his newly initiated eyes behold is a dumpling. A dumpling with a split side struggling like a wounded butterfly, then swirling round and sinking slowly to the bottom of the pan, leaking a trail of celery and cooked meat.

He sits on the floor with his back to the door of the purring fridge. She takes a scrap of paper, bends down and wipes the rivulet of blood from the inside of her thigh. Then, with another scrap, she removes the residue of seminal fluid from Muo's skin.

'I'm no longer a virgin,' she murmurs. The tears trickle down her face, carving channels in the bluish crust of her floury moisturising mask.

'Come on,' he says, kissing her on the cheek. 'Let's eat. I'm incredibly hungry.'

'Wait, I want to have a wash first.'

The dumplings have an ashen taste, but she has prepared a deliciously spicy sauce with sweet vinegar, chopped chives, crushed garlic and several drops of sesame oil. Face to face across the low table laid with a sheet of newspaper, they munch in silence. Muo forces himself to eat all she serves him, for fear of offending her. Fortunately, she thinks of putting out a stoneware bottle of an expensive liquor called 'Phantom of Inebriation', which is famed for its potency, its exquisite aroma and its trendy container in the shape of a crumpled bag. A few gulps are sufficient to raise his spirits, thereby reducing his recent *ejaculatio praecox* to a minor blemish on his demonstration of virility. He is good-natured. All his life he has struggled to overcome his setbacks, and each time he has ended in deeper trouble. That is just the way it goes. With a Picassoan eye, he now awaits the next occasion to take up the challenge, so that he may redeem his honour and self-respect.

He knows instinctively that he has another two or three hours in which to regain his prided virility before leaving the flat and facing the world.

Eager to conserve the energy unleashed in him by the 'Phantom of Inebriation', he declines to share the water-melon she has taken from the fridge. She slices the fruit with a kitchen knife, causing the juice to run along the blade and drip on the newspaper covering the table. She spits the seeds into a porcelain bowl. With every bite she takes, the red juice spills down her chin. Muo is overcome by drowsiness. He has never had such a strong inclination to sleep, a leaden somnolence in which his mind seeks voluptuous refuge while his body feels as if it is dropping down a chute. He can barely keep his eyes open. His spectacles slide down his nose and fall on the watermelon rinds. Making a supreme effort to stay awake, he grins and puts his spectacles on again without bothering to polish them, stifles a yawn, stands up and heads for the bathroom, holding the bottle of 'Phantom of Inebriation' in his hand.

'I'm going to take a bath, then I'll be back.'

'Wait for me,' she says. 'I don't want to be left all alone.'

In the tub he dunks his head in the hot water several times to collect his thoughts. There is quite a battle ahead. He still feels languid, and notes with alarm that his member has become so small it is on the point of vanishing under a tuft of floating hair. Meanwhile the Embalmer sits on a chair with her feet on the edge of the tub painting her toenails with pearly varnish.

'I was really scared at the mortuary with your Judge Di,' she says. 'In all the years I've worked there it has never happened before – a dead man coming to life, I mean. The only time I saw anything like it was in a Hong Kong horror movie. Gruesome!'

She talks and talks like water gushing from a tap, wallowing in the blissful aftermath of love which is so conducive to confidences. She does not realise that her outpourings are concerned exclusively with her dead husband. Poor Muo doesn't come in for a mention at all. Not a word about him. He is dismayed by such a transference of identity, which he perceives as harsh punishment for his too hasty performance earlier on. 'How cruel women are! And how splendid!' the hapless stand-in thinks to himself as he lies back in the bath, immersing himself up to his ears in an effort to drown out her voice.

'Of all the embalming jobs I have done, the one I'll never forget is my husband's. In our line of work we don't normally get to treat anyone close to us, be it a member of the family, a friend, or even a neighbour. It's a golden rule. So my four colleagues were given the assignment and I stayed downstairs, waiting. They began by washing the body in preparation for massage. As he had fallen from the sixth floor, some of his veins had burst. It took a lot of concentration and careful handling to make the congealed blood fluid again. Suddenly I decided to go upstairs. I asked them to leave, to let me get on with it on my own. The hardest part was still to do: the restoration of the skull. They were glad to be spared this complicated, thankless task. I could understand why, for they knew that despite all their best efforts the result would inevitably be a disappointment to me. His head had split virtually down the middle, like a melon hacked in two. The blackened blood, the crusted brain matter and especially the cracks zigzagging over the skull made repair well nigh impossible. Like balancing on a razor's edge. At the slightest error the whole cranium would fall to pieces. No one would be able to put it together again, not even me. The worst of nightmares. I fought down my tears and barely dared to breathe at all, as I had to keep as still as possible to do the work. I selected the finest needle. The thread, imported from Japan, was the kind used by surgeons, and of such good quality that I couldn't break it with my teeth. The crack in the skull was about twenty centimetres long and at least five centimetres wide in the middle. I started sewing from the narrowest end. Meanwhile, on the ground floor, my colleagues were dancing to a tape of piano music: it was a slow, sad waltz. (You know there was a waltz craze going on at the time. A billion Chinese were dancing it. That was before the mah-jong fever.) It was the saddest tune I had ever heard, even sadder than those requiems they sing in the West on television, with flickering candles and women wearing little veils . . .'

His senses dulled by exhaustion and alcohol, Muo listens to these sad confidences made in a voice that seems to come from another world. Could this be what a ghost sounds like? He can no longer tell whether this scene is real or imaginary, whether she is talking to him in real life or in a dream.

Opening his eyes, he glimpses a little snake wriggling in the water between his thighs, and reaches out a cautious hand to grab it. It slips away. All he catches is a handful of dark hair, which strikes him as very comic. He seizes the bottle of 'Phantom of Inebriation' and pours it down his throat while his other hand resumes the game of hide-and-seek with the elusive little snake.

'The cranial sutures took ages to do. A veritable marathon. Stitch by stitch, millimetre by millimetre I sewed up his skull. The bone was hard, his hair was tangled, I had to change needles twice before reaching the end. Next I applied a coat of wax to his face. By that time the waltz had given way to a stirring tango. But still there was a hint of melancholy to the music, and even to the footfalls of my dancing colleagues. I wept. In fact I cried so much that my tears made holes in the layer of wax – supposedly weather- and climate-proof. It was awful. I had to do his face all over again. Then I put on the make-up. Some colour on his eyelids to make them look normal. I did his hair. But it all went horribly wrong. I was on the point of leaving when I was struck with the notion that I had forgotten something. I retraced my steps, and soon realised what was missing: the smile. I bent over and, with my fingertips, gently massaged the corners of his lips, but just as a faint smile appeared I heard a noise inside his skull, a loud, long-drawn-out crunching sound like that of a creaky old wooden door. It made me jump. I saw the wound opening up again, gaping and black, as the sutures snapped in succession. I took his head between my hands and screamed like a madwoman. But no one could hear me because the music had been turned up to top volume. The tango was entering its romantic phase, with soaring, dreamy chords. I had to make a tremendous effort to calm down. God knows it was difficult. Then I summoned every ounce of my courage and started again from scratch. First I had to stitch up the wound which kept refusing to close, and then there was the . . .

What's the matter, Muo? Are you crying? Wait, give me your specs. Calm down, will you . . . Tell me why you're crying. Is it because of me? Oh look at you – you've got a hard-on! Look! A hard-on in the water! Wait, what are you doing? You're mad! My clothes!' (Her entry into the bathtub is accompanied by much splashing.) 'We must be mad, the two of us. Yes, put your hands there . . . D'you like that? Go on, unhook my bra, it's all wet and sticking to my skin. Ouch! You're hurting me. You bit me! Suck me gently. I'm a she-wolf. Your she-wolf. Go on, suck some more, on the other side. That feels good. Aren't I too heavy? I'm afraid I'll crush you with my weight. I know I'm a bit hefty, but I couldn't carry out my work otherwise, could I? You need quite some muscle to lug dead bodies around. Wait, let me help, the fastening's tricky. Can you still think straight? I certainly can't . . . What on earth are we doing? . . . Keep still now. Just leave it to me. Ooh, that's nice. Mmm, really nice. My man, that's what you are. Raise yourself up a little, gently, gently. Some more, please. I'm dying of joy. Dying, dying, dying.'

The living-room window is both wide and low enough for Muo (terrestrial loser but aquatic winner) to sit on the ledge without difficulty despite his inebriation. He even has the impression he could leap through it quite easily. He leans out as far as he can, but sees only a vague glimmer down below.

Feeling giddy, he decides to straddle the window, one leg inside and the other swinging insouciantly over the mysterious void to which he feels inexplicably drawn. The rain has lifted. An invisible chaffinch twitters gaily, and a canary responds with crystalline song. In the distance the milky white beam from a television relay sweeps its horizontal cone across the night. Muo is certain that he has seen this before, without knowing where. From a hotel room? A friend's house? In a film?

Such potent stuff, this 'Phantom of Inebriation'! His throat is scorched, his chest convulsed with hiccups.

'This is it,' he thinks to himself, 'I've lost my mind.'

He regrets not having brought his exercise book. The night is almost over and he has not made any entries on this eventful day, not even a few phrases or the odd word. What a loss! He is aware that the 'Phantom of Inebriation' will blot it all out and he won't remember a thing in the morning. He clambers down from the window, steps into the husband's slippers and hunts around for a pen and something to write on. The Embalmer is still in the bathroom, humming a tune. She is washing her underwear in the basin.

He returns to the window and straddles the sill, without shedding the slippers this time. Balancing precariously, he scribbles on one of the large matchboxes he found in the kitchen:

'I am no Fan Jing. But I have truly lost my mind. In this world where success is a cardinal virtue, my insanity has nothing to do with my sexual exploits – quite the opposite.'

(Fan Jing is the name of a famous personage in *The Secret History of Chinese Men of Letters*, a withered, white-haired student who entered the annual mandarin competition year after year in vain. The day he received news of his belated success, at the age of sixty-one, he was overcome with such joy and excitation that he went out of his mind.)

Muo looks up. There is still a smell of rain in the air, but the sky has cleared, and the stars, whose names he does not know, seem close enough to reach out and touch. The white paint on the window frame is flaked, possibly gnawed by rats, as the wood is crumbling in places. He studies his face in the window pane: his hair is standing on end like a tussock of weeds. Two pinpoints of light, the concentrated reflection of lamps in the living room, dance on the lenses of his spectacles like twin fireflies. They vanish when he bows his head to re-read the note on the box of matches. His satisfaction at what he has written acts as a balm to soothe and refresh his overheated head and swelling heart. He takes a second matchbox and writes: 'S.O.S. I'm going mad. S.O.S. The revelation of my true nature is dire: every woman I want to make love to becomes the woman I love. Volcano of the Old Moon's absolute power is no more. The love of my life is in ruins. Another me resides within my body, younger and more vigorous, a type of aquatic monster, in whose existence I have just witnessed a supreme moment. Which of us is the real Muo?'

A mosquito no bigger than a gnat circles round him, buzzing like a violin, until it hits his glasses and tumbles down on to the thickly veined wrist of his left hand.

'What did you have in mind, my little friend?' he asks the mosquito.

Gently, very gently, with the fingertips of his right hand, he stretches the skin where the unfortunate insect is on the point of drawing blood. Then, abruptly, he lets go, imprison-ing the mosquito's proboscis in the closed pores. He watches the insect retract its wings and fold itself up until it has shrunk almost to the size of a pinhead, after which, with a sudden flurry of wings, it takes off like a helicopter, soars up to Muo's face, stings his nose and swoops down into the void outside.

Muo tells himself that he too should make himself scarce, just like the dapper mosquito.

His instinct and habitual cynicism tell him that the Embalmer, who is aged forty like him, is seeking not only adventure but also a new husband. Which makes sense in ordinary human terms. She wants to have a family. To be the wife of the first Chinese psychoanalyst. And what an excellent choice! Besides, she did him an enormous favour by agreeing to that rendezvous with Judge Di.

'How to get out of this predicament,' muses Muo,

shivering with cold as he sits astride the window. 'How am I to explain all this to Volcano of the Old Moon?'

He imagines strapping the matchboxes to his person and lighting them as a bomb fuse, after which he would tumble down to earth in free-fall like an aeroplane on fire, somersaulting in the void, traversing clouds and mist and trailing a ribbon of black smoke.

But through this imaginary smoke he catches sight of his other self, the aquatic monster, butting its head against a porthole, clamouring to get out.

It occurs to him to pray.

He has never done so before. How does one pray? He is in two minds whether to opt for Buddhism or Taoism. Both modes entail roughly the same manner of prayer: on the knees and with the hands joined at chest level. As for Christianity, he is not too sure. When he was a boy, religion was so strictly forbidden that his parents never took him anywhere near a temple or a church. The first time he saw anyone pray was when he was seven years old, at the height of the Cultural Revolution. One day his mother was taken away by Red Guards for interrogation. At midnight she had still not returned to the flat, which was being shared by his grandparents at the time. That night he did not sleep a wink. He got out of bed and, as he crept past the old people's bedroom, his attention was caught by a strange glimmer. Glancing inside he saw the pair of them kneeling on the bed, facing a candle (had they not dared to light a lamp?). They were praying. No one had ever explained to the boy what prayer was, but he understood instantly that that was what they were doing, although he had no notion of any faith they adhered to. Their precise gestures escape him now, but he clearly remembers the pale, vibrant glow of sacredness surrounding them like an aura, and how their lined, careworn faces beamed with passionate engagement, veneration and dignity. They looked quite beautiful.

'What can I ask the heavens to do for me?' he muses. 'Take an interest in me? Help me escape? Deliver me from this woman? Isn't it too presumptuous to expect Heaven or God to take notice of us at all? If I committed suicide right now, would God care? Would he notice the stench of my decaying corpse filling the courtyard and getting into the clothes of every resident of the building? Or would he sit back and take the credit for my deliverance from all further troubles by this total, radical act of self-destruction?

'It's probably the window that is having a strange effect on me,' his interior monologue continues. 'Is it so unusual to be tempted to jump out of a window? Or is this a window with maleficent properties? Already ten years ago it exerted a fatal attraction on the Embalmer's homosexual husband. Perhaps he didn't commit suicide at all, perhaps he just came under the spell of this window, which enticed him into the depths of some profound shame. In any case, like him I belong to that race of men (how large a fraction of humanity, five per cent, ten?) who experience this sort of stabbing sensation when looking down from an elevated platform. All my years of psychoanalysis, all that studying of Freud's books of wisdom and insight have not changed that. It is an automatic reflex, the same as a man's reaction to a woman's perfume.'

Turning these things over in his befuddled brain, Muo begins to imitate the gestures he recalls his grandfather making during that night long ago. He draws up his straddled legs and assumes a crouching position on the windowsill, like a bird on a perch. A bird with spectacles, bony talons, on the edge of a six-storey cliff. He tries to stand, only just keeping his balance, and seems on the point of taking flight when – phew! – he sinks to his knees on the window-ledge. As the rain-soaked brickwork dampens his borrowed trousers, he surveys the yawning gulf as if it were a lake into whose waters he is about to dive.

There is a buzz in his ear. An illusion? No, a mosquito. 'The little blighter's come back,' he says to himself, 'I recognise its tune.' The insect touches down on the tip of his nose, ready to plunge its sting into the flesh. Muo fends it off by tossing his head with nigh acrobatic precision, for the slightest wrong move will make him fall to the foot of the building.

A brisk wind is blowing, cold but bearable. The cloudy sky is reflected in the sombre glass. He searches for the right words with which to make a vow, reflecting ruefully that the most wonderful vow in the world would have been to keep his virginity until Volcano of the Old Moon's release from prison. But it is too late for that now. Thinking of Judge Di and the Embalmer, Muo is filled with bitterness.

He feels like a wounded, shrivelled mosquito with wings scrolled tight and legs — which are surprisingly long — crumpled up: a tiny, trembling body agonising and cowering in the hand of an unknown giant called Destiny. Abruptly, he presses the palms of his hands together before his chest and prays like his grandfather before him. But the words passing his lips are those of an old childhood ditty, which he has not sung for many years:

> *My father the canteen chef*
> *Stands accused of stealing tickets*
> *Tickets of what?*
> *Rations of rice and oil.*
> *My father kneeling on a table*
> *Bound with thick ropes,*
> *Called to account by the mob,*
> *To account! To account!*

His voice, somewhat slurred by the 'Phantom of Inebriation', is barely audible at first, no more than a murmur. But soon, gaining confidence, it resonates with joyous irony, growing louder and louder until it vies with the raucous cries of the bird answering him from its perch on the roof across the way. At the end of the first verse he hums the refrain with pouted lips in imitation of a trumpet, tickled pink to discover in his own voice the intonations of his boyhood hero and neighbour, nicknamed The Spy (the pathology professor's son, who led a gang of thieves during his re-education and who was sent to prison for twenty years for holding up a bank in the seventies). The song was much favoured by The Spy, whose cap vibrated with savage glee on top of his springy hair each time he hummed it, whistled it in the staircase or sang it at the top of his voice to attract the girls. Poor Spy! He had his own way of singing, with little flourishes.

Muo concludes the second verse with a series of tremolos and launches into the refrain, which is at once sad and merry, and which rids his mind of all the setbacks and betrayals he has suffered, as well as of Judge Di's addiction to virgins. He rocks his conscience to sleep with this thieves' chorus, until he is rudely interrupted by two strong arms grabbing him by the hips. He gives a cry of fright, while the starry sky reels, heaves, capsizes around him, and his embroidered slippers drop into the void like two heavenly bodies.

His cry reverberates among the buildings.

The two strong arms belong to the Embalmer. Seeing him balancing on the window-ledge as she came in from the bathroom, she thought he was her dead husband. She stole up to him as quietly as she could so as not to alarm him. Then she lunged forward to gather him in her arms and pull him back into the room, after which they rolled together on the floor.

She is strong. Not for nothing do her male colleagues consider her a pearl of the profession. Weeping profusely, she bundles Muo into a cupboard and fastens the metal doors with a large padlock.

'I have no intention of stitching up your skull, too,' she says in response to his kicks and desperate cries. 'It's for your own good, I promise you.'

III

Little Road

I

Don't Swallow My Tooth!

Muo gazes at the rails gleaming silkily in the sunset as they stretch away from the station of Chengdu. He is standing in the ticket office, by a window. A golden light filters through the broken, cobwebby panes. The rusty bars of the window are the colour of ancient copper, a splendid green. Thinking of the prison where Volcano of the Old Moon has now been joined by the Embalmer, he wonders whether this same light, so pure and soft, can be shining on the watchtowers (how many are there? four? one on each corner of the boundary walls?) and on the armed guards poised motionless like statues.

For the past half hour he has been queuing for a ticket, his face half hidden by a grey hood. A loud argument breaks out between two women next to him, which turns into a free-for-all spanning several generations once their relatives join the fray. There is a confusion of voices, loudspeaker announcements, the smells of human sweat, stale tobacco and instant noodles . . . The long queue shuffles forward only to come to a disheartening halt.

Outside the broken window, the world is enfolded by the night's mysterious, constricting embrace. Red and green signals flash along the track, blinking in the haze like fireflies in a fairy-tale. They remind Muo of police cars with revolving lights, which may even now be patrolling the city streets in search of a bespectacled psychoanalyst who has become the sworn enemy of Judge Di.

'Pull yourself together, Muo,' he tells himself. 'No one is going to arrest you just now. The police are too busy dining in restaurants at this hour.'

Still, the moment he spots a uniform in the doorway his legs begin to shake. The official pushes through the crowd in his direction. As he draws near the shaking in Muo's legs turns into violent twitching just below the knee. Muo heaves a sigh of relief when the man turns out to be heading to the toilets all the way at the back.

The closer he gets to the ticket window, the denser the crowd and the safer he feels in the heaving, shoving, stifling melée. Someone has lost a shoe, a woman's shoe with a hole in the sole and a broken heel. Muo's hand reaches for the chrome-plated grille over the window.

'One way to Kunming,' he shouts. 'For tonight, at nine.'

'Speak up, I can't hear you,' the employee bellows into a microphone. 'Where did you say?'

'Kunming.'

A scramble ensues, during which his hand is parted from the grille as he is shouldered out of the way. He lunges forward again, yelling the name of his destination. When it is finally his turn the sleeper tickets are sold out, so he will have to settle for a hard-seat carriage, just like the one he was in several months ago when his Delsey suitcase was stolen in the night.

A few minutes later, his head tucked into his grey hood (which, being totally unseasonal, gives him a clownish appearance), he dines incognito at a twilit fast-food restaurant, one of the innumerable booths lining the grim, colonnaded station built in the Soviet style of the fifties. A poorly lit mall has sprung up, with small eateries, souvenir stalls, left-luggage counters and news stands selling magazines with sexy film-stars on the cover, both Western and Chinese.

A fly buzzes.

No plate, no bowl, just a rectangular polystyrene box containing pieces of fried chicken, squid in red-pepper sauce and a serving of fried noodles swimming in oil, all of it cold. Cheap, too: five yuan the lot, a glass of soy milk included. Cheaper than a Métro ticket in Paris. Affordable for a man on the run. The chicken tastes of nothing at all. A disaster. He samples the fried squid, which is even worse. He chews furiously, but can't get through the hard, leathery substance. Hearing the pre-announcement crackle of the loudspeaker system, he pricks up his ears. It is a message for one Mao, a name not unlike his own. The squid meat gives up its resistance at last, whereupon he masticates it like chewing gum. Suddenly something changes in his mouth. 'What on earth?' he exclaims under his breath. He feels as if the inside of his mouth is no longer his, as if he has entered a phase that a historian or biographer would call 'post-squid'. A gap? Minutely, his tongue explores each tooth in turn: one of his incisors has gone.

The fly buzzes.

With the tip of his tongue he probes the hole, which is astonishingly wide and deep. Curiously, there is not a trace of blood.

Still with his tongue, he searches his mouth for the stray tooth. In vain. He fears he may have swallowed it by mistake, like a chicken bone or fishbone. His anxiety intensifies when even the little quantity of saliva he can muster cannot get past his gullet. Where is his tooth? Stuck in his throat? In his gut? To his relief he finds it at last, buried among the fried noodles in the polystyrene box. It is still intact, tea-coloured and almost black at the tip. It is the first time he has beheld a tooth of his own 'face to face' rather than through the intervention of a mirror. He is impressed by its ugliness and by its length, which is at least three centimetres. It has a pointed root shaped like a stiletto heel, which makes him think of the fangs of vampires in horror films. As for the other end, with which he has chewed his food for forty years, it resembles a sliver of flintstone, fissured and darkened with age.

With the caution and tenderness of an archaeologist, he wraps it in a scrap of paper napkin. He lights a cigarette, but the smoke percolating through the gaping hole does not taste the same.

Disgruntled, he leaves the fast-food counter and crosses to the far side of the square opposite the station. The girl he met a few months ago in the night train flashes across his mind. He decides to buy a bamboo mat to spread out under the hard seat later on, the way she did.

He is startled by a whiff of sickly perfume assaulting his nostrils and a female voice hissing in his ear:

'Are you looking for a hotel, boss?'

'Sorry, I am leaving in two hours' time.'

'In that case,' the heavily made-up woman persists, barring his way, 'we've got a karaoke bar, with pretty girls. Come on, boss, let yourself go a bit, life's too short.'

'No thanks. I'm nobody's boss, by the way.'

'That's the word round here for "Mister". Shall I call you something else? Something more intimate perhaps?'

'Sod off!' he barks, putting his face to hers.

The effect is instantaneous: the gaping hole in his mouth, grossly distorted in the dim lamplight, comes as such a shock that the woman flees.

The only shop that is still open does not stock bamboo mats, so he contents himself with buying one of those paper-thin plastic raincoats for cyclists, in pale pink.

The train to Kunming departs after a mere ten-minute

delay. As Muo watches the Chengdu cityscape file past the window, he tastes a moment of release. He takes out his exercise book and writes, 'When Ezra Pound was arrested, he picked up a eucalyptus seed pod as a keepsake. As for me, I will have my tooth to preserve the memory of my escape.'

The Embalmer is about to pass her first night in prison. She was arrested the morning after Judge Di's resurrection. It was a fine day. The Venetian blinds in the embalming room rustled in the air-conditioned breeze. A telephone rang. It was the mortuary director, saying in a calm voice that he needed to discuss some medical reimbursements with the Embalmer. She stripped off her gloves and, still wearing her white coat, presented herself at the director's office, whereupon she was promptly arrested by two plain-clothes policemen. She was said to be wearing handcuffs when she was bundled into one of the tribunal's black vans in front of the administration wing.

'It looked like a hearse to me,' a mortuary attendant told Muo, when he arrived at the scene in a taxi to take her out to lunch.

The two-hundred-metre walk back to the taxi had seemed without end. He felt as though he were having a heart attack. Taken with uncontrollable spasms, his calves quivered like leaves in the wind, and when he finally made it into the cab he had to press down on his muscles with both hands to keep them still.

What a quandary. Should he give himself up to the police like a repentant sinner, or should he make his getaway? After much deliberation the first option seemed the more sensible, and he decided with remarkable sang-froid to do some shopping in anticipation of serving a long sentence. In a zombie-like voice he told the cab driver to take him to The City of Books, a bookshop in the centre of town. There he purchased all seven volumes of Freud in Chinese translation (how he had changed during his sojourn in France, how unrealistic he had become: he had not even thought to find out whether books were permitted in Chinese prisons, Freud's or anyone else's). In addition he had bought a hugely expensive, two-volume psychoanalytic dictionary in French with a blue slip-case, and a book of commentaries on Zhuangzi, his favourite Chinese author. The bookseller gave the prospective prisoner two plastic bags in which to carry his spiritual provisions. Finally, in order to avoid returning home and having to say goodbye to his parents, he bought bed linen, towels, a toothbrush and a pair of heavy-duty black canvas shoes, which would serve him as work shoes. Of one thing at least he was certain, having heard it said repeatedly: prisons in China were places of work.

Another taxi dropped him off at the crossroads where the horse and mule market was held, not far from the tribunal (he thought it would be too risky to be seen to arrive in a taxi, as the demented Judge Di might consider this a provocation). He would walk the last part of the way. With each step the bags seemed to grow heavier, so that he was bent almost double. He imagined the plastic handles stretching to breaking point until a great crash made everyone turn and look as the books spilled from the bag to land on the pavement amid the dead leaves, gobs of spit and dog shit. Catching sight of the Palace of Justice on the hillside, he was seized with muscular spasms all over again, while a cramp in his calf, which would have made the steeliest character howl out loud, almost paralysed him. He halted, rested the bags on the ground, sat down on them and waited for the pain to pass, after which he set off again, limping along in a comic manner.

Forty-eight words, he had read somewhere, no more and no less, just forty-eight, were all you needed to survive incarceration anywhere in the world. How many words did he need to survive in a Chinese penitentiary? A hundred? A thousand? Whatever the case, these ten books in French and

Chinese would undoubtedly place him in the top echelon of rich and aristocratic prisoners.

'If I ever become a millionaire,' he vowed, 'I'll just buy books, books, and more books, which I'll store in different places, sorted by subject. I'll keep all the works of Chinese and Western literature in Paris, at an apartment I'll buy somewhere in the fifth arrondissement near the Jardin des Plantes, the rue Buffon for instance, or else in the heart of the Latin quarter. All my psychoanalytical volumes will go to Beijing, where I'll spend most of my time on the university campus by the side of the Nameless Lake (as that beautiful lake is known). All the other books, on subjects such as history, painting, philosophy and so on, I'll leave in a small studio-cum-office in Chengdu, near my parents.'

Suddenly remembering his current state of penury, he reflected that he had never had anything to call his own and probably never would have, not even so much as an attic room or tumbledown shed. 'Maybe these ten volumes represent my only fortune, the only riches I will ever possess,' he told himself morosely, and began to weep. He limped on with tear-stained cheeks, and would have hidden his face in his hands had they not been encumbered with heavy burdens. He tried his utmost to stem the flow of tears, without success. He sobbed so much that he attracted attention from passing cars and buses. Some people gave him worried stares. But he was worlds away.

'Unbelievable! Imagine blubbing over money!' Muo muttered under his breath. 'Here I am, about to be slung behind bars, and yet I'm so preoccupied with money that I can't help making a spectacle of myself in the street.'

In his tearful mind's eye he saw himself lolloping along, slowly, painfully, a bag hanging from each hand, like a solitary ant toiling uphill with a breadcrumb . . .

It occurred to him that, if he were filming the story of his life, this would be the crucial scene. He pictured himself entering the Palace of Justice and hearing his footsteps echo down the long hall with marble columns. At the moment the lenses of his spectacles reflected the golden sun, but soon he would be descending into the murky depths where the judges lurked in their subterranean lair. He would pass through twilight zones of deepening horror until he reached Judge Di's door. The judge, believing the plastic shopping bags to contain explosives, would scream blue murder. He would beg to be spared. But Muo (wide shot followed by pan and close up) would wearily take off his glasses, polish them on his sleeve and say quite simply: 'Go ahead, handcuff me, but release the Embalmer!' He would be like the captain of the *Titanic* who elected to go down with the ship and ordered women and children into the lifeboats first (a film can transport you anywhere, even when you're on the point of giving yourself up to the judiciary). Muo could already see himself among snoring convicts in the semi-dark of an overcrowded cell, making his first entries in his secret diary. He would write in French: 'Wherein lies the difference between western civilisation and my own? What have the people of France contributed to world history? The first thing that springs to my mind is not the French Revolution – it is the spirit of chivalry. And that is that spirit which has guided me today, for I have engaged in an act of chivalry.'

The Palace of Justice was housed in an ultramodern structure designed by an Australian architect. The dazzling glass fortress was set on a slope which, according to legend, harboured the legendary tomb of General Zhang Fei of the Three Kingdom Period. The midday sun beating down on this vast diamond set it ablaze, silvering the artificial showers sprinkling the lawn and glinting on the tower which, set against the clear blue sky, dominated the palace like a castle keep. The dazzling marble clock-face indicated three o'clock. (It cannot be denied the architect had a sense of humour: everyone in the town associated the clock tower with an old

Chinese saying said to have been uttered by the powerful king of the underworld – 'When it's time, it's time.')

One, two, three . . . With bowed head, Muo huffed and puffed as he counted the steps to the entrance of the glass fortress. Several soldiers, some of them armed, stood watching his laborious ascent in silence. The plastic bags strained under the weight of the books. Halfway up the steps he paused to muster his forces. He looked up at the soldiers, their dark silhouettes standing out against the glass façade. One of them, who was unarmed, descended a few steps, put his hands on his hips and shouted in the manner of an authoritarian overseer, 'Tired already?'

'Done in.'

'Come on, keep it up.'

The soldier stood with arms folded, following Muo's slow progress with an air of amusement.

'What are you humping around in those plastic bags?'

'Books,' replied Muo, relieved to hear his voice sounding calm and neutral. 'I've come to see Judge Di. I take it you know him.'

'Bad luck. He's just left.'

'I'll wait in his office,' said Muo, adding solemnly, 'I have an appointment.'

He had another dozen steps to climb, when his glasses slid down his nose. In a reflex, he let go of his bags to catch them – which he succeeded miraculously in doing – whereupon Freud's great works tumbled out of one plastic bag and the Zhuangi commentaries out of the other. With his heart in his mouth Muo watched them, or rather heard them, spill down the steps, first in close formation, then fanning out in all directions.

The soldiers roared with laughter, jiggling and shaking like puppets. One of them cocked his rifle, aimed at a book and pretended to pull the trigger. He simulated the jolt that firing the gun would cause to his jaw, trained his sights on another book, mimicked the sound of a shot and affected triumph at hitting the mark.

The Gillette shaving foam, the anti-dandruff shampoo and the toothbrush that Muo had purchased earlier tumbled down in the wake of the books, the shaving foam making a particularly spectacular descent as it clanged and clattered down the steps. Muo retrieved his scattered possessions, then wearily recommenced his ascent clutching the toiletries for his future prison life. As he did so he noticed a tall, gaunt figure with a bulging leather briefcase under his arm, bending double to inspect one of the fallen books. He was aged about fifty, with a small, pointed head and a long neck. He resembled a stork.

'Are you familiar with these books?' asked the Stork.

Muo gave a nod of assent.

'In point of fact, my boy, I want a straight answer. Just say yes or no,' he said in a somewhat hoarse, reedy voice. 'I shall repeat my question.'

'Yes, I am familiar with them,' said Muo.

'Don't reply until I have repeated my question. Now, are you familiar with these books?'

'Yes I am.'

'Do they belong to you?'

'Yes.'

'Follow me. I have forgotten my reading glasses in my office, and I need them to check some details.' The Stork took out an identification card with his picture on the front. 'I am Judge Huan, President of the Commission for the Prevention of Clandestine Publications. Freud's books are strictly forbidden.'

'But I just bought them in a bookshop.'

'Precisely. In point of fact, I need to establish by whom and under which false licence number they have been published.'

Unlike his colleague Judge Di, who preferred an underground office, the Stork had opted for a perch on the fifth and top floor of the glass fortress.

In the lift going up, a misunderstanding arose. At Muo's mention of Judge Di, the Stork assumed that he was an acquaintance of the judge, possibly his advisor in matters of psychology. Wishing to make up for his authoritarian behaviour earlier on, he adopted a friendly tone and became quite talkative, complaining of the lack of staff in his department and of having to work so hard in monkish solitude, often late into the night. The usual small talk. It was a somewhat wearisome conversation because he was unable to utter more than three sentences without saying 'in point of fact' (a phrase frequently employed by the General Secretary of the Party, also Head of State, in his televised interviews). He spoke of his modest origins as a Communist school teacher and his good fortune at having been singled out by the Party in the late nineties to pursue a career in the judiciary. He had resigned himself to being at a disadvantage vis à vis certain colleagues, who were drawn from the ranks of the Army.

'In point of fact,' he confided in a fawning voice edged with bitterness, 'the omnipotent Judge Di, with whom you have your appointment, frequently makes me very uneasy.'

The entrance to his department, which bore the name of the commission, was secured with three locks: one on the sturdy, shiny protective grille and two others at different levels on the double doors with glass panels. The Stork took out a bunch of keys which jangled in the silence, then deactivated the alarm system by pressing the numbered buttons on a panel set in the wall. The click of the locks being turned, the squeak of the grille, the swish of the glazed double doors gave way to the hum of an air conditioner. But the ventilation did nothing to dispel the powerful odour stinging Muo's nostrils as he stood in the doorway – an odour of self-righteousness, morality, power, secret lives, incarcerated bodies and exquisitely desiccated corpses.

Entering the offices of the Commission for the Prevention of Clandestine Publications, Muo found himself in a vast room that was for the most part shrouded in darkness due to the blinds lowered over the windows. After a moment or two it dawned on him that he was surrounded by forbidden books (some worth a fortune) jumbled together on shelves that stretched floor to ceiling. A smell of mildewed paper wafted about the room. In the middle of the ceiling was a small opening – a traditional feature of Chinese architecture – through which a cone-shaped beam of greyish light was projected on to the middle of the floor, leaving the walls in shadow. Muo felt as though he had stumbled upon a long-abandoned library. The cheap plywood shelving sagged under the weight of books, with the bottom shelves so weighed down by the mass of tomes that they dipped down to the dusty rug.

Arriving in the centre of the space, where the light was strongest, Muo took advantage of the Stork's momentary inattention to put down his bags and reach for the nearest book. It was a copy of the memoirs of Mao's personal physician with a black-and-white photograph on the cover showing the author in shorts, smiling ecstatically, beside Mao in a floppy shirt and wide trousers, screwing up his eyes against the glare of the sun. Furtively, Muo opened the book and happened on a page devoted to a sexual disease that, although not affecting Mao personally, he had passed on to all his sexual partners. The physician had advised him (with the same ecstatic smile?) to bathe his member regularly, to which the President of the People's Republic had replied that he preferred immersing it in the sexual organs of a woman. Muo shut the book and replaced it on the shelf. He walked on, passing shelves crammed with political books. There were many reports and analyses of the events of 1989 in Tiananmen Square, but also documents pertaining to power struggles in the bosom of the Party, the suspicious death of

Lin Biao, the true personality of Zhou Enlai, the famines during the sixties, the massacres of intellectuals, the re-education camps, cases of revolutionary cannibalism . . . Muo, whose head was reeling, lost himself in this archive of blood-curdling cruelty and connivance, before finding himself afloat in a sea of erotic novels, licentious writings by libertine monks, the works of de Sade, old sexual manuals clandestinely reprinted, albums of pornographic wood engravings from the Ming dynasty, various editions of the Chinese Kamasutra, and several dozen versions of *Jing Ping Mei* (the novel that had so inspired Muo when he read it in France that he almost devoted a psychoanalytic dissertation to it – although the idea had never developed beyond occasional jottings in exercise books). There were even two stacks filled with antique volumes of handmade paper sewn with thread. Muo inquired what kind of subjects they dealt with and why they had been banned.

'They are esoteric Taoist studies in ejaculation,' replied the Stork.

'Do you mean masturbation?'

'No, ejaculation, or rather non-ejaculation. For centuries they studied ways of making human sperm circulate in the body during sexual congress, with a view to drawing the fluid to the brain so that it could be transformed into some supernatural energy.'

Muo almost took out his exercise book to note down the titles of the ancient volumes. 'A pity I can't have them with me in prison,' he mused. 'I'd be able to write tome after tome of commentaries.'

They passed into a second room, smaller than the first, but in the same state of semi-darkness. There were no shelves or books, just a mass of film storage cans, hundreds and thousands of them stacked in piles like a mountain of sad corpses. Some of the towers had toppled and film had spilled from the cans, coiling out like snakes, blossoming into enormous knots. It was calcinated in places, or furred with greenish mould.

The Stork, president and sole employee of this commission, held office in the third room. Having put on his reading glasses, he pored over Muo's copies of Freud, craning his neck to examine each volume and noting down the doubtful references in a large ledger bound in fake black leather. Meanwhile Muo discovered documents that were even more bone-chilling than those of the two preceding rooms. There were letters of denunciation everywhere. 'My private collection,' the Stork declared proudly.

The letters that he had dealt with were labelled, classified and locked away like museum exhibits in seven glass-fronted cabinets of richly carved ebony. Each cabinet had its own speciality. The first contained denunciations of fathers by sons and vice versa, the second of husbands and wives, the third of neighbours, the fourth of colleagues at work, while the fifth and sixth were reserved for anonymous denunciations. Within each cabinet the letters were ranged according to subject in coloured folders, creating a vivid rainbow effect. Red was for political subjects, yellow for money matters, blue for extramarital fornication, violet for homosexuality, indigo for sexual abuse, orange for illicit gambling, green for thievery and housebreaking.

The seventh cabinet contained the letters of self-denunciation. Seeing the key in the lock, Muo ventured to ask permission to open it. The majority of the letters dated from the Cultural Revolution and were long, some running to over a hundred pages and resembling those relentlessly confessional novels in which the author reveals the darkest recesses of his being, complete with lascivious fantasies, hidden desires, secret ambitions.

Stacked in the corner were cardboard boxes with red labels containing all the unread letters. The Stork was clearly appeasing a private passion.

'Perhaps,' said Muo, 'I might add a letter to your collection.'

'Whom do you wish to denounce?'

'Judge Di.'

The Stork could not help laughing out loud. Turning back to his work, he said, 'In point of fact, I know why Judge Di told you to come here with those books of Freud's.'

'Tell me.'

'He is hunting a criminal, some sort of psychoanalyst who organises assassinations in local mortuaries. He probably thought Freud could give him some clues.'

Once again, a searing pain shot through Muo from his calves to his ankles and up again towards his kidneys.

'Do you think Judge Di will have the psychoanalyst shot?'

'In point of fact, he will undoubtedly pass a life sentence.'

'Would you mind telling me where the toilets are?' Muo asked, forcing himself to remain calm.

'At the end of the corridor, on the left.'

Upon leaving the department of the Commission for the Prevention of Clandestine Publications he headed straight for the stairs for fear of crossing Judge Di in the lift. Despite his limping gait, he flew down the steps four at a time. He was on the run. 'I bet the judge has alerted the airport,' he thought to himself. 'I'd best take a train.'

Ignoring his aching limbs, he sketched an escape route in his mind: by train from Chengdu to Kunming, and by bus from Kunming to the Sino-Burmese border, where he would have to find a smuggler to lead him into Burma on foot. Then Rangoon–Paris by plane.

From the shadows a locomotive looms larger and larger with a deafening roar and fills the entire window before disappearing. Next a succession of gigantic, teetering freight cars cast their shadows on the glass. The last carriage is filled with armed guards crowding round a single green lampshade, whose feeble glow rapidly dissolves in the darkness.

The dark reflection of an old man appears in the window, blurry and vague at first, then coming into focus as the train enters a tunnel. Clearly mirrored in the glass is a dental topography: the tip of a tongue runs the length of dingy teeth in an upper jaw, then probes a black hole in the middle. The gap, which looks enormous, grossly distorts the man's countenance.

'It is my own reflection,' Muo ascertains with narcissistic fascination, tears welling up in his eyes. 'A foretaste of what will become of me, twenty years hence – Grandpa Muo, or else Convict Muo slaving down a mine. But for now, all is well. To be on the run is to be alive.'

Suddenly, in the glass, he catches sight of a girlish figure pausing in front of his compartment on her way down the corridor. He has a feeling he has seen this girl, who can't be more than eighteen, somewhere before, and she too seems to recognise him. He whips off his glasses, shrinks back into his hood, lowers his head and feigns the deepest of slumbers. Not daring to move a muscle, he remains thus until the train rumbles out of the tunnel, by which time she has vanished. He can breathe freely again and indulge in the luxury of eavesdropping on the animated chatter of the couple next to him.

The topic of his neighbours' conversation is the ethnic minority known as the Lolo (or Yi, in Mandarin) who inhabit the mountainous region that is filing past the window. Muo knows little about these folk other than that the men wear voluminous cloaks, a sort of outer garment made of canvas, which they are seldom seen without and which they use to wrap themselves in at night. The true home of a Lolo, he has heard it said, is his cloak. Another passenger, a workman familiar with this stretch of the railway, recounts the adventure that befell him a month earlier. It happened in broad daylight, between the stations of Emei and Ebin. With a detached, impersonal smile, he describes how the carriage he was in was looted – 'common currency' in these parts. It was attacked by a gang of about fifteen knife-wielding Lolo in black cloaks. Three of the bandits blocked the door at one end, two or three others posted themselves at the other, while the rest raided the car. There was no shouting. All the passengers kept quite still, even the children. The Lolo split up into two parties to work their way down the carriage from opposite ends like ticket inspectors. With a knife to their throats, the passengers had no choice but to turn their pockets inside out and meekly surrender their handbags, briefcases, peasant hods and suitcases for the steely-fingered Lolo to dig into. They took pleasure in flicking their fingers against people's heads, spectacles, chests and private parts, which was very painful. Suitcases that were too large or too stuffed for their taste were tipped out on to the floor. Their booty was all the more considerable given that bank cheques are not used in the countryside and everyone travels with cash, which can range from housekeeping money to the savings of a lifetime. The whole operation had taken no more than ten minutes. When the Lolo were done they simply jumped off the train, easy as pie. They didn't even wait for it to reduce speed going up an incline, no, they didn't care, they leaped to the ground while it was going at full speed. It had been mad, quite mad.

'I've had more than enough of being chased by the law,' thinks Muo. 'Being taken for a ride by the Lolo, that would really take the biscuit.'

Fear creeps into his heart. He fears for the dollars hidden in a secret pocket of his underpants. The lush, slumbering landscape sliding past the window, which filled him with nostalgia a moment ago, suddenly appears hostile. He has the impression of travelling in a foreign country: lofty mountain ranges, mountain peaks, mountains as far as the eye can see, all of them akin, in his mind, to the dark cloaks of the Lolo. The passing forests, marshes and gorges teem with phantom shadows casting looks filled with racial hatred, that most implacable of passions. Even the few lights twinkling feebly in a hamlet clinging to the mountainside or in the depths of a distant valley seem resentful.

If only the train would speed up, if only he were out of here.

The conversation beside him becomes more heated. He rises from his hard seat and moves to the smokers' corner.

His cigarettes taste decidedly different since his tooth fell out. The first inhalation has an unpleasant aftertaste, and there is a general absence of aroma and subtlety. Instead of sliding in between his teeth and caressing his tongue and palate, the smoke is funnelled in through the central gap and passes directly to the back of his throat. His mouth has been reduced to a conduit, a vent, a chimney flue.

The smokers' corner is at the very end of the carriage and sheltered from inquisitive looks. He takes out his tooth from its paper napkin. With much fumbling he pushes it into place, pressing the root upwards into his gums. By a miracle it stays put, wedged between the teeth on either side. The hole has gone.

He rediscovers the taste of Marlboro, which he savours with little puffs as if it were some delicacy. At his side, the door of the toilet swings in the draught (a sleepy occupant has forgotten to shut it), letting out whiffs of fetid air. But nothing can spoil his enjoyment now. As the train enters yet another tunnel the power fails and the carriage is plunged into total obscurity. The glowing tip of his cigarette in the pitch darkness reminds him of his first smoke a lifetime ago, when he was a boy. Thirteen he was – no, fourteen. The name of the brand was Jin Sha Jiang (River of Golden Sands, thirty fen a packet). The opening lines of a naïve and clumsy little poem he had composed at the time resonate in his head. It was in praise of that first cigarette, and he had given it the title 'Little Four Eyes'.

Ah, my first kiss
On the fine sensual thigh
Of a River of Golden Sands
Glowing in a February night

He rejoices in the vibrating echo of the train in the tunnel, exults in his restored tooth, relishes his boyhood reminiscences, and before he knows it the light has come on again. Suddenly he hears a female voice behind him.

'Hello Mr Muo!'

Silence. Muo is transfixed with fear. Everything seems to freeze: the air, the train, his body, his brain. 'That's it, a female police officer,' he mutters under his breath, feeling faint.

The voice repeats its greeting, accompanied by a mysterious clicking sound. What can it be? A bunch of keys? Ah, handcuffs more like. 'I'm finished,' he tells himself. Putting his hands in the air, he swings round in theatrical slow motion, expecting a Chinese Jodie Foster to hold a gun to his temple, in a Sechuan version of *The Silence of the Lambs*.

'Take me to . . .'

He is about to say 'Judge Di' but stops mid-sentence. He can't believe his eyes: it is the girl he saw reflected in the window earlier on.

There she stands, gaping at him. Her mouth seems larger than life, indeed everything about her seems larger than life: the denim jacket, the red polka-dot trousers, the bright yellow backpack, and even the Heineken six-pack under her arm. The cans vibrate to the rhythm of the train, which explains the mysterious clicking sound earlier.

'Don't you remember me, Mr Muo?' she says. 'You interpreted a dream for me at the domestic workers market.'

'My name is not Muo,' he responds gruffly. 'You are mistaken.'

No sooner has he spoken than he ducks away, quickly stubbing out his cigarette in an ashtray affixed to the side of the carriage. Lacking the courage to look her in the eye, he turns on his heel and walks away. On no account must he be seen to act furtively, so he does his utmost to retain a gentlemanly demeanour. His consternation is so great, however, that he takes the wrong direction and steps into the toilet by mistake. He slams the door behind him. 'I'm going nuts,' he rages, grabbing hold of the washbasin as he doubles up, sick to the stomach. 'I must be stark raving mad. Of course it's her. How could I not have recognised the country girl who dreamt of being in a movie? Damn and blast! How dare she disturb my meditation, that most sacred, most noble of activities!'

In the course of his vituperation something falls out of his mouth into the washbasin. It takes him several seconds to realise that it is his tooth. Fortunately the washbasin has been blocked since goodness knows when, and his tooth has rolled to the bottom of a blackish pool with white foam floating on top. After much patient underwater groping he succeeds in locating it with his fingertips. He cleans it and dries it several times over, but the penetrating smell of drains, trains and latrines will not go away.

Suddenly there is a ruckus in the corridor. Putting his ear against the door he can hear ticket inspectors shouting and the film-dreamer responding in a thin, tearful voice. She is travelling without a ticket. They fulminate against her as if she were a thief caught red-handed. She has no defence. She has no money, she stammers. In all the eighteen years of her existence this is the very first time she has done this. She swears she will never do it again. They say they'll take the pack of Heineken as security. She pleads with them, explaining that it's a birthday present for her father and that it

192

represents two months' earnings as a domestic worker. But the inspectors are adamant. They can't wait to get their hands on the beer. One of them tries to wrest the pack from her. She resists, in her desperation letting out a terrible, piercing cry like a wild beast in agony. (For a long time afterwards, whenever he thinks of her, Muo hears this feral cry ringing in his ears.)

He opens the door and steps out into the corridor, wishing to intervene in her favour but unsure how to go about it. She turns to him beseechingly.

'Mr Muo, please, please explain to them what happened just now when I was fiddling about with my ticket. You are the only person who saw it being snatched away by a gust of wind when I put it on the ledge by the window.'

Muo confirms her words at once, takes out three ten-yuan notes from his pocket and gives the three ticket inspectors one each.

'For you, my friends,' he says. 'Ten yuan each and we won't mention it further.'

The voices of the train passengers seem to come from far away, as far away as the boat in which Conrad's Marlow navigates the heart of darkness in search of Kurtz. Muffled, somnolent voices. Men sifting the endless repertoire of anecdote. Swags of talk floating amid bursts of laughter, coughs, a spectacular sneeze, then dying away in a low sigh or a yawn. Hard to tell who speaks and who listens.

Crouching under the wooden banquette, his ears pressed against the floor of the carriage, Muo listens to the wheels. When the train heads up a long mountain slope he can hear them skating on the rails, now with the dull rumble of thunder, then with ear-splitting screeches, transforming his secret sleeping-berth into a bird's nest in the eye of a storm.

He can almost see the sparks flying. But once the train rolls down hill, devouring the night, the wheels produce a more muted sound, a smoothness of cadence that is barely perceptible. The echo returned by the mountains is distant, ethereal, like the sound in a conch shell held to the ear: the murmur of a calm tide lapping a shore of polished shingle, blue-grey in the morning light. Best of all is when the train pulls into a station. You can hear a long sigh passing through the wheels, one after the other, like someone breathing in their sleep – some living creature in the undercarriage, you would think, so near that you can almost feel its tepid breath.

Snatches of the insomniacs' conversation reach Muo's ears. According to one of them, whose low voice evokes the storytellers of old, each mountain range and each mountainous district breeds its own folk, just as each ocean breeds its own sailors. The Lolo in this region all have a talent for jumping on trains. It is a natural talent, an inborn aptitude which, in some, approaches genius when they perform their death-defying, acrobatic leaps to get on and off trains hurtling at top speed. By this talent, the Lolo distinguish themselves from other folk. They are at their most spectacular when they assault a goods train, for not only do those carriages lack proper doors and foot-plates, they are also secured with iron bars and padlocks. A party of Lolo will be strolling nonchalantly along the track looking very much at ease, though maybe a little weary or tipsy. A train goes past. One of them breaks into a run. After a few paces he takes a flying leap, describing an arc perfectly calculated for him to grab hold of one of the iron bars and cling to the side of the carriage, with his large black cloak slapping in the wind. He takes a hammer from his pocket, smashes the padlock, lifts the iron bars, gives the heavy sliding door a push and slips inside. A second or two later he reappears with a television set. He takes another leap, in free-fall this time, or rather in lyrical suspension, with his cloak floating in the air and his loot in his arms. Like a ski jumper, he lands without losing his balance and hands the television to his cronies, who have come running. They tie it on to his back with ropes, and off they all go. Sometimes there are guards who go after them taking pot shots, but when a Lolo takes to his heels on the mountain, even with a television on his back, he is unassailable. Bullets go haywire or arrive too late, missing the moving targets which have the magical elusiveness of birds.

'Are you there, Mr Muo?'

It is too dark to see anything. His mind is quite blank for a moment, then he identifies the voice: it belongs to the girl who spoke to him earlier, the film-dreamer from the domestic workers market. His drowsiness is instantaneously and totally dispelled. Mindful of the disaster that happened the last time he rode a similar night train, he decides to keep silent. A fugitive he may be, but a virtuous one. An ascetic.

The girl repeats Muo's name two or three more times, in a low voice, for fear of rousing the other passengers. But the softness of her tone does nothing to conceal her good humour and affectionate nature. Muo, the ascetic fugitive, tries his best to snore convincingly, but the rhythm of his breathing is too erratic. For all that he cannot see her, he knows that she is even now insinuating herself into his secret sleeping-berth.

'Not bad, this little cubby-hole,' she says, crawling towards him.

She knocks into him in the dark. Both of them cry out.

'Not so loud,' he says.

'It's all right, everyone's asleep.'

'What is it you want?'

His voice is as cold as ice.

'D'you like jujubes? I've brought you some.'

'Not so loud,' he repeats, girding himself to keep his ascetic vow. He doesn't want to smile, even if she can't see him.

'Keep them for your father,' he adds.

'Don't worry, I've got some more. Go on, have one. They're clean. I washed them.'

'Well, just one then.'

But in the gloom she misses his outstretched palm.

'Where's your hand?'

After a fair amount of fumbling, one jujube changes owner. Muo puts it into his mouth with caution, so as not to dislodge the loose tooth.

'D'you want another?'

'Wait.'

A midnight feast. He chews the fleshy fruit-gum carefully.

'I want to show you a book I bought,' she says. 'You can tell me what it's worth. Got a light?'

He strikes a match and the girl appears in the light of the flame, very close to him, her back hunched, her elbows propped on the floor. 'How pretty she is,' he reflects.

Another match is needed to light up the book: a slender volume, shiny with wear, and, on the cover, six Chinese characters: *Elementary Grammar of the French Language*. Some pages have folded-down corners and comments written in the margin.

Muo remains silent and keeps very still, scandalised by his physical reaction: his penis is erect. It is the first time this has happened since he lost his virginity. He can't tell whether it was triggered by the taste of the jujube or by the sight of the book.

As the match burns down, a long, soft ember drops on the cover of the book, bounces up and falls again on the plastic raincoat he is using for a mat. Deftly she extinguishes the spark.

'It must be worth five yuan, don't you think?' she asks, engulfed in darkness once more. 'I bought it second-hand. To impress my father. He paid for my brother to go to secondary school, not me.'

'How are you going to impress him, not knowing any French?'

'I will tell him what you explained to us at the domestic workers market: that French is a language of words whose sole purpose is to please women. How did you put it? To woo them. I don't give a toss about not knowing the language. All I want is to get my father's goat. He has a husband in mind for me, the village headman's son, someone I don't fancy at all.'

'Maybe he is in love with you.'

'I don't want him loving me.'

She paused. Although Muo cannot see her, he can feel her eyes on him.

'Muo, why are you hiding?'

'What?'

How cunning she is! Taken by surprise, he is so busy thinking up explanations that the anxiety gets the upper hand and his erection subsides.

'You keep hiding,' she says, 'because you're scared of the police.'

'Do you want to know the truth? Will you swear never to tell a soul? I am leaving the country. And as I loathe farewells, I have decided to give the land of China a final hug from the floor of a night train. I am a patriot.'

'Never!'

'You know Burma? Well, that is where I want to go. A wonderful country where people spend their time chewing betel nuts and spitting out jets of blood-red juice. There are temples everywhere. I shall enter a temple. Become a monk. Buddhist monks are allowed to eat meat over there. I am very partial to meat.'

'Don't make me laugh. No temple will accept an interpreter of dreams like you. You're running away. It's obvious. You even told me your name wasn't Muo.'

She changes the subject.

'May I lie down beside you? I'm knackered.'

'Be my guest, you can share my raincoat. The floor is dirty.'

After that he holds his tongue. He listens to jujubes being chewed in the dark. She chews like a peasant, making such loud smacking noises that Muo is convinced they can be heard at the other end of the carriage. Little by little, the sound of chewing dwindles away until it is replaced by the regular breathing of sleep. The noise of the train hurtling down the track blends with the burble of passengers and muffled snores. Suddenly he wakes her.

'I don't even know your name.'

'Everyone calls me Little Sister Wang. Why d'you ask? Are you getting off at the next stop?'

'No. I want to ask you something, but if you prefer not to answer, I will understand.'

'Go on, ask.'

'Are you a virgin?'

'What?'

'A virgin. Someone who has never made love to a man.'

'Yes, I'm a virgin.'

In the dark he can hear her spluttering with laughter.

'Honestly?' he asks.

'Of course.'

'If you save us, my friends and me, I'll take you to France.'

'What d'you want me to do?'

'A magistrate in Chengdu by the name of Judge Di has sent two of my friends to prison. Now he's after me. He has been offered money. He declined. He's got plenty as it is. All he wants is to meet a virgin girl.'

Having made his statement, he awaits her outraged reaction, imagining the ear-splitting, almost feral scream she unleashed on the ticket inspectors. But nothing happens. She doesn't make a sound, he can't even hear her breathe. An unspeakable despondency hangs in the air, to the point where he loses all hope and finds himself wondering, with a lopsided smile, why she hasn't made off. All of a sudden, she asks him haltingly, 'Will you really take me to France afterwards?'

'Yes.'

'All right then, I accept . . .'

In the gloom, he thinks he is going to faint. Forgetting the ascetic fugitive, he takes her in his arms before she reaches the end of her sentence.

'Thank you,' he mumbles in a fatherly tone. 'Thanks a million. I'll teach you French.'

This puts him in mind of long-forgotten poems by Hugo, Verlaine and Baudelaire, which he cannot hold back now. He lets them pass his lips as he covers the girl's hair, her eyes, her nose with kisses. She keeps her head down, in the dark. But she does not push him away. Abruptly he kisses her hard on the mouth. A wild jujube all swollen with sap!

'What's this?' she murmurs. 'There's something in my mouth. It's come from you.'

'My tooth!' he exclaims, so forcefully that he sprays saliva through the ruins of his teeth. 'Don't swallow it!'

2

The Head of the Dragon

Chengdu, 5 October

My dearest Old Moon, my splendid Volcano,

Have you kept your taste for enigmas? Or has it been spoilt
by your lengthy imprisonment? My dear little champion, the
cleverest of all the female students, riddle-solving rival of
Oedipus who won the end-of-year puzzle prize: a juicy red
watermelon weighing five kilos, which was shared among
the eight occupants of your ten-square-metre dormitory.
There was no knife. Everyone rounded on the poor fruit,
jostling and laughing, battering it with spoons. The following
year you won a book, which you gave to me: a dictionary
of the slang used in novels of the Ming dynasty, a rare
book which I love leafing through and have read and re-read
so many times I could write a novel in the Ming style
myself.

Here is an enigma for you to ponder: my motive for
writing a letter of as yet undetermined length in a foreign

language, i.e. French, of which the esteemed recipient understands not a word.

My surprise at finding that my hand – still swollen, but we will come to that – had begun writing this letter in French soon passed into excitement at the ingeniousness of this spontaneous gesture. I was quite enchanted. Really impressed, not to say filled with self-admiration. I am sorry I didn't think of it before. It's such a pleasure to envisage the reaction of the screws charged with censoring your mail. I can already see their long faces when confronted with letters written in French by a tireless correspondent, a passionate and mysterious lover. Given their strict budget and the rising number of prisoners, I am sure they will not bother to have this cabalistic missive translated. (At Chengdu, the only three or four people who understand the language of Voltaire and Hugo are professors at the university of Sechuan. 'Tell me, professor, how much would it cost to translate one page?' 'About a hundred and twenty yuan.' 'No!' 'That's the going rate.')

From now on, my dear Old Moon, my splendid Volcano, we can look to a foreign language to unite us, reunite us, tie us together in a magical knot that blossoms into the wings of an exotic butterfly. An alphabetic language from the other side of the world. Its spelling, complete with apostrophes and diacritic signs, gives it an esoteric touch. Your fellow prisoners, I imagine, will be jealous of you for passing the time with my love letters, extracting meaning from them. Do you remember those wonderful times we had when we were students, sitting together listening to recordings of our favourite poets: Eliot, Frost, Pound, Borges . . . Their voices, each with its own personality and sonorous beauty, enveloped us, uplifted us, made us dream, even though neither of us understood English or Spanish. Those accents, those incomprehensible phrases remain with me, even today, the loveliest music in the world. Music filled with the spirit of romance and melancholy. Our music.

Do you know what blows my mind as I write these words? That I did not learn other, less widely spoken languages. Vietnamese, for instance. I have a smattering of that six-tone language with its complicated, subtle grammar. Just think if I wrote you in Vietnamese . . . Even if Judge Di were prepared to pay for an expensive translation, he would never find anyone to do it, not even at the university of Sechuan. Or another language, even more cabalistic, such as Catalan. Could anyone capable of translating a letter in Catalan be found in this province of one hundred and fifty million inhabitants? You know what I would like to do? Study languages reputed for their esoteric dimension, such as Tibetan, Mongolian, Latin, Greek, Hebrew, Sanskrit, the Egyptian hieroglyphs. I would like to penetrate those inner sanctums, kneel down with three sticks of burning incense and pray for us in the languages of the holy of holies.

We made off together: Little Sister Wang with her six-pack under her arm, and I, Muo of the blissful smile and ruined teeth, fugitive from justice, who had abandoned his escape to Burma after several hours on a train, a Muo who had emerged from his rock-hard hiding place accompanied by his new recruit, his potential saviour, his true and oh-so-precious virgin.

It was three o'clock in the morning when we got off the train at the station of Meigou. The platform of beaten earth was full of puddles from a recent downpour. A dismal place wedged between two high mountains. When the Chengdu–Kunming train, my train, pulled out of the station and disappeared into the night, the echo of the stationmaster's whistle lingered in the air, reverberating among the rocks until it blended into the wind, the rustle of leaves, the lapping waters of an invisible river.

The most urgent business at hand was to contact the son-in-law of the mayor of Chengdu – you remember, the bloke I told you about many times, the one who started this whole virgin nightmare. He was our only means of contacting Judge Di, but we had to wait until morning to telephone, because, despite being a restaurateur during the day, he spends his nights in a prison cell like you, with his mobile switched off.

Meigou is the name of the river that flows past the small town of the same name, not far from the station. The long thick trunks of trees felled in the mountain forests floated downstream, heaving and colliding to a strange, phantasmal rhythm. As we walked along the riverbank, our footsteps sounded alien. Our breathing, and even our speech, took on a different rhythm. We felt apprehensive, as if we were entering a foreign land peopled by shadows and hostile sounds, where we ourselves were ghostly intruders. On the bridge at the entrance to the town there was an ancient stela, with still legible inscriptions in Chinese and in the language of the Lolo, stating that the river's source was at the summit of the Meigou Mountain, a deep spring of divinely limpid waters. In times of drought, it was enough to throw something dirty into it for the rain to come down in torrents all over the region.

We were in luck. A karaoke bar in the high street was still open. It was hard to believe that such a backwater would boast a bar called Shanghai Blues that stayed open past 3 a.m. Extraordinary. I wish you could have seen the little film-dreamer sing. Her pretty face beamed with a triple glow: youth, coquetry, and love of music. It was hot and dark inside, too dark to see the other punters. She took her jacket off and moved close to the screen, like a star on a film set. For a country girl she is not shy. Her slight frame in her floppy T-shirt, her flat chest, her graceful arms, her whole skinny body has an adolescent charm that even my myopic eyes can appreciate. The more I looked at her, the more she reminded me of you. I am not saying she looks like you, but there is an echo of you in her profile, notably in the curve of the skull, the high forehead, the elongated eyes, and in the way of pausing now and then to scratch the roots of her hair, which is cropped along the ears, like yours. In her voice, too, there is an echo of yours: low, a little husky. Her imitation of black blues singers is beyond compare. She knows a fair number of popular songs, which she must have learnt when she was working as a maid for some people who ran a karaoke studio. Some of the songs she chose were terrible, but others were great, such as 'I Take This Road But Once In A Thousand Years'. The melody, the lyrics, her voice, they killed me. You know I always sing out of tune, but I actually went so far as to take the microphone myself and sing along with her, ruining the song. I congratulated her. She was radiant. She knows she has a nice voice and that she sings well. In my elation I told her that, as far as artist's names go, 'Little Road' sounded better, smarter, than 'Little Sister'. She repeated the name 'Little Road' several times after me.

'All right,' she said, earnestly. 'From now on, you can call me "Little Road".'

Superstitious as I am, each time I think back to what happened the next day, I wonder if the song was a premonition. It was indeed the rarest of roads, a road one never travels more than once in a lifetime.

The proprietor of the karaoke bar, an amiable thirty-year-old, seemed quite taken with Little Road. When all the other customers had gone home he asked her if she liked dancing. She said she knew hip-hop, she had learnt it when she was employed in a house with a balcony overlooking the quadrangle of a technical college. She had watched the students hip-hopping during break-time every day, and in the end she could do it herself. The owner of the bar offered to take the role of DJ while she danced. He played a track called 'I Have Nothing In The Whole World' by Cui Jian, the rock star of the eighties. The hoarse, despairing cries of Cui Jian were magically modernised by the deft manipulations of the stand-in DJ. He played those switches like a drummer in a jazz band, letting Cui Jian work himself up to a pitch of agony before he attacked. Carried away by the music, Little Road smiled as she pranced and twirled across the dance floor. Soon her limbs were jerking spasmodically in a trance-like manner. Next record. This time it was a Chinese rap artist. I'm sure you know the famous poem in the novel *The Dream in the Red Pavilion*, which opens with the line 'Everyone loves money'. Sung by a rapper, it's fabulous. Little Road made a backward flip, and as she jumped her T-shirt rode up, baring part of her abdomen, which was so flat you could see her rib-cage. It was the cue for a change of dance steps and rhythm. Putting her hands flat on the floor and holding her head down, she spun round on her arms. Round and round she turned, bending and stretching her legs in the air, faster and faster until wham! her head replaced her arms as the pivot and her body – what a body, lithe and vigorous! – rose straight up with her feet in the air. I applauded. Before she got too carried away, I thought I'd chip in myself. 'Let grandpa here show you a revolutionary dance,' I said. And I danced an old-time jig for them, you know, that silly, old-fashioned dance we learnt at school about the valet of the evil landowner who goes round collecting the rent from starving peasants. (It was because of my ugly looks, I have no doubt, that this ungrateful role was forced on me throughout my teenage years. It became my trademark, my emblem, and plunged me into such loneliness that I nearly became homosexual.) I gave them the full works: side-stepping like a crab, pirouetting, cavorting, cracking the whip (I used my belt), but in the end I lost my footing in the middle of a jump and fell flat on my face. You know what the DJ played for me next? The music of that revolutionary ballet, *The Girl with the White Hair*. Honestly. The Shanghai Blues at Meigou stocked records of every description: from the Beatles to U2, Michael Jackson, Madonna, and even Red Sun of our Heart, Red Orient, and speeches by Chairman Mao sung by Hong Kong techno stars.

By sheer luck I got through to the mayor's son-in-law at the first try, right after breakfast. The condemned man was busy serving his accursed sentence in a taxi. I had the impression that he was surprised to hear my voice, although he did not show it. He listened patiently to all I had to say. In conclusion I asked him whether he thought an encounter between Judge Di and a second virgin might alter the situation, or at least help bring about the Embalmer's release.

There was a moment's pause. I thought he was pondering my question. Suddenly he burst out, 'How are you doing, sexually speaking?'

I was taken aback.

'I'm doing all right,' I said modestly. 'I have even made some progress in that field.'

He laughed. It was not Homeric laughter, but I heard him none the less.

'Bravo! Listen to this: according to old Sun, the shrewdest convict I have ever known, life boils down to three things: eating, shitting, fucking. If you're doing all three, everything's fine.'

'An amusing definition.'

'Come here as soon as possible, with the girl. What is she called? Little Road? Nice name. Give me a ring as soon as you arrive. In the meantime I'll set things up with the judge.'

Then, switching from our dialect to Mandarin, he added an afterthought. I had a feeling he was imitating one of his fellow detainees:

'Muo,' he said, 'this is a veritable bombshell.' And with that, he hung up.

My heart pounded with joy. I wanted to shout at the top of my voice, it was insane. I knew my parents would already have gone to work at the hospital for the morning rounds of injections, but as I had no one else to call, I dialled their number anyway. Of course there was no reply, but it calmed me down. I decided to concentrate on getting back to Chengdu. It was then that we stumbled on the Blue Arrow.

The Blue Arrow was the name of the Chinese pickup truck that was parked at the entrance to the town. Splattered with mud and with the paintwork all chipped and flaking, it was actually more like a yellow arrow – that's how unrecognisable it was. The back of the truck lacked a tarpaulin and was so battered that the tail board was tied up with a piece of string. Little Road and I ran into the driver in a greasy spoon where we had breakfast. It was impossible to tell his age – anything between thirty and fifty. He was bearded, or rather unshaven, stooped, sallow-faced, and racked with fits of coughing. Once the fit had passed he cleared his throat and spat out great gobs of phlegm, which he ground with the sole of his shoe while he went on talking. He was a caricature trucker, and acted the part to the hilt.

As there would not be a train to Chengdu for another five or six hours – and any delay might seriously compromise the plans of the mayor's son-in-law – I decided to make the journey in the Blue Arrow. After some negotiation and a twenty-yuan note, the trucker agreed to take us on board.

I will remember to the end of my days this drive through the Mountains of the Great Cold. The clapped-out vehicle set off along the most potholed road in the world, jolting and bouncing all the way. The seat next to the driver had been gutted and repaired in places with sticky tape. I might as well have been sitting directly on the springs, which creaked like those of an old mattress and catapulted me to the ceiling of the cabin with each pothole. Worse than a boat tossing on the waves in mid-ocean. Funniest of all was the radio, on which all the knobs were missing, and which reacted badly to the bumps. At one point the sound went off altogether, during which time we forgot all about it until it suddenly blared again at top volume. As it happened, the song was 'Let Us Crush Our American Enemies,' which, as I'm sure you remember, tells of a badly wounded soldier, gun in hand, making straight for the American front while the bullets whistle past his ears and an inferno of shells explode at his feet. Now and then, when the music fell silent, it sounded as if he must have been hit, for all you could hear was a sinister crackling noise which might well symbolise his death throes. But the next pothole set it all off again. The soldier was resuscitated and carried on singing while the machine gun continued firing blanks. Stunning! I did not light a cigarette, for fear that the smoke and ash would fly into Little Road's face beside me: the window on the driver's side did not close fully and there was a five-centimetre gap at the top through which the wind rushed in. Little did I know how grave the consequences of this innocuous-looking gap would be. Life is certainly full of pitfalls.

The trucker asked me to tell him some dirty jokes, for he had not slept the previous night and with all this bumping around on a 'shit road' he was in danger of falling asleep at the wheel.

'You know, stuff that'll give me a hard-on,' he said.

I replied coolly that my profession gave me access to people's dreams, and that although they often had a strong sexual component, they were never laughing matters.

If you had only seen his face! But I resigned myself and racked my brains to remember the kind of smutty stories you hear in changing rooms and communal showers. Try as I might, though, I could not think of anything.

'Telling such jokes,' I said, 'is a bit like undergoing psychoanalysis.'

'Meaning what exactly?' he asked suspiciously.

'I mean that one is required to descend into the sub-conscious to locate them.'

We were driving through a pine forest recently devastated by fire, when suddenly flowering azaleas and rhododendrons came into view, splashing the mountainside with colour.

'Shall I have a go?' Little Road suggested.

'A kid like you, what would you know?' said the king of the road with a lecherous grin.

Little Road asked if I had any cigarettes left. She fancied a smoke, she said, to refresh her memory.

You should have seen how she smoked that cigarette. Unlike me, she did not fill her lungs with smoke, she just inhaled a small amount, which she savoured quietly before letting it out gently through her nostrils. Her delicate fingers with unvarnished nails elegantly held the cigarette to what may best be described as her 'budding lips'. To be honest, she did not seem in the least countrified. You'd never have thought she came from a poor family.

This is the story she told:

Once upon a time, very long ago, a solitary monk lived on a remote mountain with an orphan, entrusted to his care since the age of three. Time passed. The child grew up without any contact with the outside world. When he was sixteen, his master took him to see what the outside world looked like. They went down the mountain and, after walking for three days, reached a plain. As the young man knew nothing, when they came across a horse the monk told him, 'Now that is what you call a horse.' In the same way he pointed out a mule, a buffalo, and a dog . . . Then a woman appeared, heading in their direction. The youth asked his master what this creature was called.

'Lower your eyes,' the old monk said. 'Don't look. It's a tigress, the most dangerous beast in the world. Don't go near, or you'll be devoured.'

That night, when they returned to their mountain refuge, the old monk noticed that the novice was wide awake, tossing and turning in his bed as if he were lying on hot embers. It was the first time the old man had seen him in such a state. He asked what the matter was. The novice responded: 'Master, I can't stop thinking about that man-eating tigress.'

I laughed. The girl could not be denied a sense of humour.

But there was no reaction from the king of the road. I tried to prolong my laughter in the hope of it being infectious, but he maintained his impassive reserve. In the end, he pronounced the following verdict:

'It's funny, but too vegetarian to my taste. I prefer something meatier.'

I looked outside. The unpredictable car radio resumed its transmission of the music programme. We were high up on the mountain. The Meigou River, which we had been following for some time, was now to be seen in the depths of a ravine, a thin ribbon of sparkling yellow. The driver announced that he was going to tell us a joke.

'I bet you can't wait to hear one of mine,' he said.

That was when the trouble started.

Peering through my glasses, I spotted a heap of large, black stones obstructing the mountain pass ahead. The dark mound stood out grimly against the blue sky and the yellow earth of the road.

'Shit,' cried the driver. 'The Lolo! Shut your window, quick.'

While Little Road followed his instruction, he tried winding up his own window, but the five-centimetre gap remained.

As we neared the pass, the black stones loomed ever larger, becoming increasingly imposing, superb, majestic even, until we could make out their cloaks fluttering in the wind like the banners carried into battle by warriors of old.

'Are they bandits?' Little Road asked.

'They are true-blue Lolo,' I said.

'True blue?' scoffed the driver. 'We'll see which is truer and bluer – these savages or my Blue Arrow.'

And this is what the champion of modern technology proceeded to do: he stepped on the accelerator and honked furiously in the hope of scattering the Lolo. But the road was too steep for the rickety old vehicle to gain speed, and even the blasts from the horn, reverberating through the Mountains of the Great Cold, made little more impression than the drawn-out, plaintive wailing of an exhausted camel in the Takla-Makan desert, the endless desert of death.

The shadowy figures stood stock-still, sinister silhouettes against the yellow earth. As the truck lurched forward, a strange optical effect occurred: the shadows lay down under the wheels. Little Road and I yelled at the driver to brake. But he seemed not to hear. The Lolo remained motionless. A huddle of black rocks. The moment of truth had arrived. The Blue Arrow charged, jolting violently over the bumpy road. In a final spurt, it lunged at the Lolo like a tiger, sending us flying to the ceiling of the cabin.

I shut my eyes. The driver slammed on the brakes. Thank goodness. Disaster had been avoided by a hair's breadth.

There were about thirty Lolo between the ages of eighteen and thirty, long-boned and muscular to a man, undoubtedly past masters at train-jumping. They crowded round the truck shaking their fists and cursing the driver in a stream of incomprehensible invective peppered with the odd phrase in Chinese (not Mandarin but Sechuanese): 'You bastard', 'Just you wait', 'We'll get you', and so on. The windows of the truck were filled with swarthy, glowering faces, so coarsely featured that they seemed hacked out of wood. Their earrings glittered. After a time they drew back and regrouped around a young man swigging beer, who seemed to be their leader. He held the bottle out to the others, after which it circulated. A low rumble of voices was all we could hear.

Discreetly, the driver took out his wallet and tucked it under his rump, in amongst the springs and shreds of padding of his ragged seat. I wondered if I should do something about the dollars stashed in my underpants. But it was too late.

The leader of the gang stepped forward. His angular face was disfigured by a long scar. A mean fellow, you could tell.

He hammered on the windscreen with his beer bottle, spilling white froth down the glass.

'There's a tired horse for you!' he roared in Sechuanese, baring his blackened molars and the back of his throat in an explosion of triumphant laughter.

Then the others raised a chorus of imprecations against the Blue Arrow.

'Who do you think you are, you bastard? Thought you'd run us over, did you? If your truck had so much as touched a hair on our heads I'd have smashed your face!'

The humiliated driver said nothing, but a tremor passed through the seat as he tensed his muscles to rev the engine.

'Do you know where you are?' Scarface went on. 'This is Dragon Head Mountain. Open your eyes and look. This is the place where we Lolo slaughtered thousands of soldiers during the Qin dynasty.'

On the accelerator, the driver's foot began to jerk about, as though resisting the message coming from the brain.

'We're going back to our village,' Scarface said. 'Will you take us there?'

'All right then, get in the back,' the driver said, still not daring to look the Lolo in the eye.

The truck started up again.

Scarface had told us that the mountain was called Dragon Head, and the farther we travelled the more we saw how apt the name was: beyond the fateful pass, the mountain rose up in the shape of a strange prehistoric beast, a gigantic crouching body stretching from east to west which, in the light mist, seemed to be lying in ambush. Suddenly the predator reared its head – or was it a trick of the light? It was a proud head, splendid, menacing, with a rocky skull and scaly forehead. His chin bristled with foliage sprouting from the clefts in the rock, clinging to the cliffs, swaying in the wind. From a distance, it resembled the bearded dragon in the cartoons of my boyhood, or the dragon pasted on my parents' door.

'Do you know the expression "to drop a bombshell"?'

The driver eyed me as if I were mad.

'Turn the car round as soon as you can,' I said, 'then head back to Meigou. The Lolo can't stop us going back where we came from.'

'Coward!'

The master of the old jalopy rejected my sensible idea. What I dislike about men is that, as soon as they get behind the wheel, they tend to be arrogant, irritable and violent – as if it's not just a steering wheel they're holding in their hands, but power and regal authority. Even Little Road was worried. You could tell: she kept clapping her hand to her mouth. I should have offered the driver something extra to persuade him to change his itinerary. Each time I think back on this journey I bitterly regret not having done so. It was not out of miserliness I swear, but out of forethought. I might still have had to escape to Burma, it was impossible to say. And all things considered, I didn't have much money anyway.

The Blue Arrow toiled up Dragon Head Mountain, stopping several times to muster its resources before arriving at the summit. We were in for a shock: beyond the crest there were two more dragon heads awaiting us with the same implacable scorn. Ah, the Lolo! I can't help being fascinated by them. To think they spend their entire lives in these mountains. Not my cup of tea at all. Just looking at them gave me vertigo.

'Hey, you two,' said the king of the road, 'shall I tell you what I was thinking about just now, when we were set upon by those savages?'

Neither of us responded. He persisted:

'If you were in my shoes, what would you have thought?'

Our silence did nothing to discourage him.

'Well, I'm going to tell you. I was thinking of a really meaty joke.'

He gave me a look as if he had just beaten me six-nil on

213

the football pitch. I wanted desperately to snore, or to screw up my eyes, anything to stop him launching into one of his dirty stories.

'The Lolo are shouting in the back,' Little Road observed. 'They'll be wanting to get off when we reach the summit.'

At this moment one of the Lolo in the back banged on the roof of the cabin. But the driver took no notice, so engrossed was he in the telling of his tale. It was an autobiographical joke:

Two years ago, he was working as a driver for the army (he had joined up for eight years) at the headquarters of an infantry regiment. One day he chauffeured a Communist commander on an inspection tour. The trip was to last four days. On the second evening they checked into a shabby hotel in a small town. The commander, a temperamental man aged about fifty, spent the night with a fat, ugly whore, the only one the hotel had to offer. He must have been in dire need to go with the likes of her. The driver said he himself had passed the night in 'vegetarian' mode.

Our driver's voice, interspersed with fits of coughing, was accompanied by thumps on the roof of the cabin. When we reached the top of the second dragon head I told him to stop the truck so that the Lolo could get off. He turned his head and threw me an authoritarian look.

'What are you playing at? Running scared are we? This is the place they have chosen to attack us, to strip us of everything but our underwear. They take me for an idiot.'

He pressed the accelerator. Once over the top, the Blue Arrow plunged down the steep gradient, while the driver continued his story.

'The next day, as we were driving along, the commander told me that the whore had cost him two hundred and fifty yuan, and that some way had to be found of squaring the army accounts. I couldn't think of anything, but he was quite calm. He said he had an idea: I was to file a report saying that, in the course of the inspection tour, our vehicle had come into collision with an old sow, and that her owner had claimed two hundred and fifty yuan compensation.'

With that he burst out laughing.

'You have a sense of humour, don't you, chief?' I ventured. 'But listen! There's someone stomping around over our heads. I can hear him.'

'Oh I'm suffocating! This is too much,' he spluttered, between guffaws.

Leaning back in his seat, he held his side with one hand and the steering wheel with the other.

'He couldn't have put it in a better way – an old sow indeed! I'm sure that's exactly what he was thinking the night before, when he was having it off with the whore: an old sow!'

At that moment the interior of the cabin darkened, as though a solar eclipse had caused a sudden, maleficent darkness to descend. In fact it was the black cloak of a Lolo, held by an invisible hand, trying to cover the windscreen. This mobile black screen put an end to the driver's laughter.

'I told you one of them was up there.'

'Do stop the truck,' begged Little Road, clapping her hand to her mouth.

But the driver had no intention of admitting defeat. Swearing under his breath, he pressed on, bobbing his head this way and that to peer through the almost entirely obstructed windscreen. He was a madman – a madman who had spent eight years in the army, undergoing guerrilla training in clapped-out vehicles on bumpy roads.

During one of the countless jolts the car radio, which had been silent for a while, suddenly came on again with Ravel's *Bolero*. Unfortunately for the former army chauffeur and for us as well, by this time we were no longer careering downhill but zigzagging up the third dragon head. The Blue Arrow spluttered and slowed, providing the Lolo with an ideal opportunity to renew their assault. A face appeared at the top of the windscreen. Although upside down, it was instantly recognisable as Scarface. His cronies in the back of the truck had to be holding him by his feet.

Scarface kept shifting his cloak to obstruct as much of the trucker's view as possible. Primordial hatred, racial contempt and a marked taste for violence and blood – all those traits were written on his steely features. In a way he scared me more than Judge Di. Ravel blared the accompaniment. What music! It could have been the trumpets of Jericho.

'Don't do anything stupid now!' my voice quavered.

'I'll get you, you filthy Lolo!' the driver shouted through the glass.

He was like a boxer dodging punches, leaning this way and that to catch a glimpse of the road ahead. Now and then we were in complete darkness, at which times he just drove on by instinct. In moments of visibility he steered the Blue Arrow perilously close to the edge, exploiting the least hump in his path, the least boss of earth or rock, in an attempt to jolt his adversary off the truck.

From time to time I looked sideways at Little Road. Both of us being excluded from the combat, we wore the same numbed look of fear and helplessness. The *Bolero* provided a rhythmical accompaniment to Scarface's exertions, turning them into carefully devised choreography, a dance of the black cloak, while the two combatants exchanged mutually unintelligible curses and dark threats.

Taking advantage of the strong headwind which flattened the cloak against the glass, Scarface managed to cover the entire windscreen. You would have thought a curtain had fallen. A black curtain edged with sunlight. Nevertheless, the crazy driver resisted: hanging on to the wheel with both hands, he leaned over almost horizontally, resting his head on my knees and peering out at the road through the luminous but extremely narrow slit beneath the black curtain. Finally the wind dropped. The cloak started flapping again, and the driver sat up.

'I'll get you, you scarface shit,' he hissed through clenched teeth.

In a reflex, he cleared his throat and aimed a gob of phlegm out of the five-centimetre gap in his window with virtuoso precision. This was a gesture too far. A fatal gesture. I caught a flash of rage in Scarface's eyes.

At one stage the sides of the road rose to several dozen metres in height. Suddenly, Scarface's cloak was gone. Inside the vehicle our spirits rose. Now and then the cliffs gave way to fields of yellow earth planted with maize or spindly wheat or to slopes miraculously dotted with paddy fields. In the end we approached the peak of the third dragon head. Once again a precipice, a drop of several hundred metres this time, stubbed with bushes and rocky outcrops – and below, the Meigou River, like a yellow shoelace.

We zigzagged down the other side of the summit. Suddenly ten fingers, gnarled like eagle's claws, appeared in the gap at the top of the driver's window. The window shook, seemed about to break under the pressure. Then, out of nowhere, Scarface appeared on the other side of the glass.

It all happened with such breathtaking speed and such heart-stopping violence that I cannot now recall whether there was any exchange of words between driver and assailant. The driver's first reaction was to try to unclench the eagle's claw but, finding himself unable to prise them loose, he hammered them with his fist so hard that the blows resounded in the cabin. Scarface held on. He wanted to get his whole hand inside to reach for the door handle, but the gap was too narrow and his fingers got stuck. The driver let go of the wheel and tried again to dislodge the intruder's fingers. In the course of this duel the Blue Arrow began to rock and skid out of control. Once the driver had managed to steady the vehicle his eyes lit on a bend in the road with a rocky promontory alongside. He stepped on the accelerator and headed straight for the towering rock. He thought to swerve away at the last fraction of a second, thereby crushing his assailant to death against the rock. I told you he was crazy! A few metres short of the promontory, Scarface let go of the window, took a flying leap and landed safe and sound on a neighbouring outcrop, while the Blue Arrow collided with the rock face. The windscreen shattered with a deafening noise. I barely had time to take Little Road in my arms and push her head down to protect her from the impact. I myself was hurt on the side of my head, my chest and my knees, but I did not lose consciousness. A hail of shattered glass submerged us as the truck bounced off the rock, glanced off a tree on the other side of the road and collided once more with the rock face, after which we skidded towards the edge of the road where the ground fell away. Thank goodness the truck did not overturn. It came to a standstill, smoking, on the brink of a precipice.

My body was paralysed and there was an excruciating pain in my skull. Had I suffered a head injury? Would I be mentally handicapped for life? Road accidents can turn people into brainless zombies. The worst possible scenario. Do a test. Right away. A memory test, for instance. Ask yourself a question, such as 'When was Freud born?' The question alarmed me. I didn't know the answer. I had almost lost hope when four digits appeared in my mind's eye: 1856.

I went on quizzing myself in the severe tones of a teacher. 'When did Freud die?' The answer came: '1939'.

My improvised self-test was interrupted by the sound of moaning coming from close by. It was Little Road, the sacrificial virgin. She mumbled something, but I could not make out what it was.

'Do you remember your date of birth?'

'My left leg is broken.'

Worse was to come. The Lolo attacked the door on the

driver's side, but the handle had snapped off and the lock was jammed, so they couldn't get it open. As for the driver, he was leaning forward with his head in his arms over the steering wheel, as if he had metamorphosed into someone else.

He was not wounded, apparently, but said not a word and did not react when they belaboured him with their fists. He just gripped the wheel with all his might. Outside, gathered on the top of the promontory, were Scarface and his cronies with a collection of hefty stones which they held up in the air and shook menacingly. In the barely recognisable, clipped accent of regional Sechuan, they issued the death sentence: 'These stones will smash your skull, your brains will splatter on the ground, your vile corpse will be left for the vultures, dogs and worms.'

I brushed the broken glass aside and clambered out through the windscreen on to the bonnet. Before jumping to the ground, I raised my arms and shouted, 'Help! My daughter has broken her leg!'

Although baseless, my claim to paternity brought tears to my eyes. No one took any notice. There were trickles of blood in the back of the truck – two or three Lolo were badly hurt. One of them, bleeding profusely from the head, was helped down by his comrades. A horde of Lolo peasants materialised out of the blue, their cloaks flapping as they charged down the slope, screaming and brandishing picks and other farm implements as though attacking an imaginary foe. Within a moment or two the Blue Arrow was surrounded by swarthy, angry faces.

I stepped up to Scarface, who was conferring with his mates, and grovelled before him like a beggar, pleading that the important thing was not to punish the driver but to help the wounded – 'those on your side as well as my daughter'.

An enraged old Lolo pushed through the crowd towards me. He was at least sixty and wore the 'Lolo horn', the turban-like headdress fashioned with black ribbon. Despite my protestations that the accident in which his son had been injured was not my fault, he clenched his fists and made ready to let fly. Fortunately, he was so slow in gathering his strength that I had time to take off my glasses before receiving a violent blow to my right ear. His bony fist was so hard that my head reeled and buzzed and I almost lost my balance. I showered him with abuse, calling him an old cretin or something of that ilk. His response was a sharp kick in the belly. I had not been expecting a blow below the belt from an old-timer wearing the traditional headdress. It literally took my breath away: I doubled up, completely winded.

The shame of it! Hot tears of boyish cowardice sprang from my eyes and trickled down my cheeks. I drew myself up and heard myself sob and cry, 'Why did you hit me? Why attack a Frenchman?'

Not a very impressive performance, and I knew it. I was filled with self-loathing. But I would have said anything to save my skin. Having embarked on this lie, I could not stop.

'I am not an overseas Chinese, but a Frenchman come to fetch his adopted daughter. You have attacked a French citizen. Do you realise where that will get you? In jail! I warn you: you will be dealt with by Judge Di. You know who Judge Di is, don't you? The King of Hell!'

The word 'French' was picked up by the Lolo, who raised a chorus of mutterings. Some of them were familiar with the word, others not.

'Can you prove it?' Scarface asked, defiantly.

'I don't believe you,' growled the old man in the headdress.

There was a pause.

'Go on then,' he said, 'say something in French.'

I did as I was told. I could have insulted him in that language, but I chose not to. What I said was – and my memory is vivid – 'France is situated in Western Europe.

The earliest inhabitants were the Gauls. Their name lives on in a popular brand of cigarettes: Gauloise. The greatest contribution of France to global civilisation is the spirit of chivalry . . .'

That was the spiel I gave them, like a professor in a lecture hall. I did not look at them while I spoke. I was quite calm; I narrowed my eyes and focused on the three peaks, the three sombre, savage dragon heads. The Lolo listened attentively. They put down their stones and sat on them, the better to immerse themselves in the intonations of my French discourse. I took my wallet from my pocket, pulled out my French residence permit and presented it to Scarface. Needless to say, I was not going to tell the truth.

'Here is my French identity card,' I said.

He got up from his stone to inspect it and compared the face on the card with mine, like a customs official. Then he passed it on to his cronies. While it was going from one dark, callused, mud-encrusted hand to the next, I showed Scarface the rest of my cards: credit card, student card, library card, and so on. His attention was caught by something tucked into a corner of my wallet.

'What's that?'

'It's called a "Carte Orange" – it entitles you to take the Métro in Paris.'

I handed it to him. A gleam came into the eyes of the king of train-jumping.

'The Métro is an underground train. It rides in tunnels.'

'Only in tunnels?'

'Only in tunnels.'

He stared at me as if I were from outer space.

'Never in the open air?'

'The whole network consists of tunnels. Endless underground tunnels.'

'Not a country for the likes of us then,' he concluded.

He could not be denied a sense of humour.

The others, no doubt virtuoso train-jumpers to a man, roared with approving laughter.

'That much is certain, it's not a country for the Lolo.'

Are they really the savage bandits people think they are? I am not so sure. The Lolo possess certain virtues. They are known for not attacking Westerners, even pretend-Westerners who have neither blue eyes, fair hair nor big noses. They are chivalrous in their own way, and outgoing – but also sensible. They would not wish to run unnecessary risks, in the knowledge that the Chinese police take the safety of tourists seriously and that the slightest misdeed can carry the death sentence.

After handing over two-hundred-yuan compensation for their wounded (which came from my pocket, not the driver's), the Frenchman, his adopted daughter and their mad driver were permitted to go, leaving behind the remains of the Blue Arrow for the driver to collect later. Better still, Scarface and his cronies pelted the first vehicle to pass by with stones to make it stop – it was a minibus belonging to a hydraulic power company.

'Take them to hospital double quick – the girl has a broken leg!' The command echoed through the mountains.

During the ride Little Road lay on the back seat while I knelt by her side to steady her broken leg with my hands, for the least bump in the road made her howl with pain. Little by little the world settled back into normality. The hurricane of threats, shouts and tears made way for the sunny calm of a purring engine, the rush of air conditioning, and a chauffeur clearing his throat. ('I nearly messed my trousers, I was that scared!' he confided in me.) The minibus flew down the yellow track like a silvery bird darting among black rocks, dark trees, green grasses, and azaleas in flower. A bird in free flight, as light as a sunbeam.

The deposed king of the road told the chauffeur his joke about the sow. When I looked out of the rear window I noticed that, seen from the vantage of the minibus, Dragon Head Mountain had ceased to be the monstrous beast of legend sprawling from west to east. The three crests that rose up above the green swathes of forest looked very different: the one in the middle was cone-shaped, while the other two resembled the splendid dark-veiled breasts of a twilight goddess. A poem, whose author and title escape me, came back to me. We used to read it together, you and I:

> *And the sun high on the horizon*
> *Hiding in a bank of cloud*
> *Lines the clouds with saffron.*
> *Dove sta la memoria.*

3

The Flying Sock

In the days and nights following the Dragon Head episode, Little Road is visited by nightmarish visions: of a giant cobra lying coiled on the ground and suddenly rearing its head by half a metre, opening its serrated jaws to bite her leg; or of a quivering arrow cleaving the air on its way to pierce her with its poisoned point. In her dreams she hears the vibration of the invisible bow, thrumming like a dying note of a cello. The arrow pierces her leg. Always the left leg. Sometimes, the images of the serpent and the arrow conflate with that of a human bone, fleshless and phosphorescent – her fractured tibia, exactly as it looks in the X-ray photographs.

The X-rays are taken in the finest medical establishment of Sechuan: the Hospital of Western China, renowned for its department of osteopathic surgery. It occupies a ten-storey building with thousands of beds and several operating theatres fitted out with American, German and Japanese equipment.

Five hundred metres to the north stands the Palace of Justice. From the window of her ward, Little Road can see the glass palace, often wreathed in mist, especially in the mornings. Judge Di is not there. According to the mayor's son-in-law, the leading magistrates of the country are all in Beijing to attend a fortnight of conferences.

'When I return,' Di had told the mayor's son-in-law on the phone, 'I will be glad to receive the gift from your psychoanalyst friend.'

('Judge Di was so excited,' the mayor's son-in-law reported to Muo, 'that even at the other end of the line I could sense his marksman's fingers burning with desire to check the girl's virginity.')

With his silvery hair, impeccably starched white collar and wire-framed spectacles hanging from a little chain round his neck, Doctor Xiu, Head of the Department of Osteopathic Surgery, is the living embodiment of authority. His success with the first finger re-attachment in the late sixties brought him nation-wide fame. Rumour has it that even today, at sixty years of age, he still hones his grafting skills at home (in the kitchen?) by re-attaching the limbs of dismembered rabbits.

Trailing a bevy of doctors and nurses, he makes his morning rounds through the dozen wards on the eighth floor, including that of Little Road, who was admitted to hospital yesterday. He gives a barely perceptible nod when introduced to Muo, the patient's adoptive French father. After studying the X-rays he delivers a swift and unequivocal diagnosis: a fracture of the tibia, necessitating an operation in the coming days to insert stabilising metal pins. Then a splint for two months, followed by another surgical intervention to remove the pins. Potential loss of limb length, possibility of some degree of permanent lameness in the patient.

Little Road frowns, turns pale, then blushes. She asks Doctor Xiu if he means that she will be a cripple for life. He does not give her a straight answer, nor does he meet her gaze as he hands her the X-rays. 'Take a look for yourself, my dear. It's not good news.'

Muo has the impression the world has come to a standstill. No sooner have Doctor Xiu and his retinue departed than the air is filled with the condescending, pessimistic comments from the other patients and their visiting relatives, as well as from the nurse taking the orders for lunch. The full import of the doctor's words begins to dawn on Muo.

He dashes into the corridor to catch up with Doctor Xiu.

'Oh Doctor, you must help me, I beg you. I have already bought plane tickets for my daughter and myself. We have to be in Paris in two weeks' time. It's extremely urgent.'

'Just a moment, sir. You who have come from France are no doubt far more knowledgeable than I regarding Flaubert's novel *Madame Bovary*, in which her husband is considered an excellent osteopath for having set his prospective father-in-law's broken leg to rights within forty days. Considerable progress has been made in our field since then. However, the elderly Frenchman's fracture was simple, no complicating factors whatsoever. Your daughter's case is far more serious. The bone is broken in two. All I can do is give you my assurance that I will carry out the intervention personally and will do my utmost to restrict the visible consequences.'

Every night the mayor's son-in-law heads to the Provincial Penitentiary No. 2 to sleep in a private room.

The prison is a brick building in the shape of the Chinese character meaning 'sun' or 'day'. The south wing – representing one of two horizontal calligraphic strokes – is entirely taken up by a printing plant operated by prisoners, the north – the second horizontal stroke – by a cannery manned by those awaiting trial. These are joined by two vertical strokes at the east and west containing the dormitories of the three thousand inmates. Each side is five storeys high. The empty spaces between the factories and the dormitories are the exercise yards. Through the middle runs a building that consists of a ground floor only, and is given over to the cells of privileged prisoners who, unlike the others, have neither shaven heads nor a number. (Normally, as soon as you enter into prison, you are given a number – 28,543 say – which is your sole identity until the end of your term. A guard entering your cell will not call out your name, but rather, '28,543, time for mess!' or '28,543, interrogation call!')

Come ten o'clock this October evening, convict number 28,543, nicknamed 'the Kalmuk', is sitting on his pallet in cell 518 on the top floor of the east wing, absorbed in the fabrication of a flying sock, the secret of which is known to all prisoners.

The Kalmuk enjoys the privilege of working outside the prison two days a week, in one of the restaurants managed by the mayor's son-in-law.

Using a ballpoint pen he notes down the message that his boss and friend has instructed him to transmit: 'The mayor's son-in-law is looking for a doctor who can fix a broken leg in ten days.'

He stuffs the scrap of paper down to the toe of the sock and adds a half-empty tube of toothpaste for ballast. Then he ties up the top with string. Finally he attaches another piece of string, longer and thicker this time, after checking its strength with his teeth.

When he sings a line from a revolutionary opera at the top of his voice – 'My husband's low wages have no effect on my ideology' – all the prisoners know it is the secret code announcing the launch of a flying sock.

The prisoner on the look-out by the door signals that it is all clear in the corridor. Holding the sock, the Kalmuk clambers on to the shoulders of another cellmate, the sturdiest of the lot, who hoists him up to the small window. The bars are too close together to allow more than a hand to poke out. Nevertheless, after much deft twisting and turning, the

Kalmuk succeeds in getting his whole hand out and then, centimetre by centimetre, the rest of his forearm, allowing him to dangle the sock over the void.

With the skill of a puppeteer he manipulates the string to make the weight swing slowly from side to side in front of the barred windows of the fourth-floor cells. Another hand comes out to seize it in mid-swing. The Kalmuk waits. Keeping his fingers quite still, he sings another revolutionary song:

> *The Communist lover is truly amazing.*
> *Like a Thermos flask,*
> *Cold on the outside,*
> *But scalding inside.*

Like an angler sensing a catch, he feels his flying sock twitch at the end of the string, in token that the message has been received. He hauls the sock back in, but when he looks inside it all he finds is his own note plus the tube of toothpaste. He ties the sock up and casts it back into the void, making it swing with the precision of a metronome in front of the windows of the third floor. Then he lowers it further to the next level, past one window after another in the hope of it being seized again. Now and then the wind plays up, sending the sock on a wild journey like a darting sparrow who ends up flying into a plate-glass window. At times too, the sock (which is nylon) snags on some protrusion in the bars or brickwork and resists all efforts to tug it free.

An hour elapses. When the Kalmuk finally pulls in his sock he discovers a note inside, which reads: 'No. 96,137, cell 251, knows someone. 100 yuan for the info.'

4

The Old Observer

The X-ray photograph crackles in the hand of a man known as the Old Observer as he holds it up to the light. It is a coarse hand – dark-skinned and gnarled, with crooked bony fingers resembling the twisted roots of a tree, and sharp, thick fingernails (cut with a sickle?) encrusted with mud (or excrement?).

At the sight of Little Road's shin-bone shimmering on the negative, the Old Observer's clouded expression lifts. Muo's gaze is riveted on the old man's ravaged, furrowed face, his wispy white moustache, thin lips and flattened nose. He registers the faintest twitching of facial muscles, the least hint of an expression or gleam in the eyes. The pair of them are seated on a tree trunk in the muddy forecourt of the old man's abode, which is perched on a forested mountain two thousand metres high, away from the main footpath, in a clearing fringed with giant bamboo. Over the double doors is a white-painted signboard bearing the words: 'Observation Post of Panda Droppings – Bamboo Forest'.

The old herbalist continues his scrutiny of the X-ray which

shows, if her adoptive father is to be believed, the leg of the young aspiring ballerina who is to take part in the national ballet championship in ten days' time. The air is filled with the rustle of bamboo.

Muo's face darkens when he realises that the old man is holding the X-ray upside down. A cruel, revealing insight. He snatches the photographs, puts it the right way up, and points his finger at the top end of the tibia.

The old man resumes his examination with the same blank expression as before, seemingly unaware of any change.

'What do you call the big bone that is broken in two?' Muo asks, bolstering his courage.

'I don't know.'

'Do me a favour, stop playing around. It was a fifteen-hour bus journey to get here. Don't you know what a tibia is?'

'No.'

'An old mate of yours from prison, no. 96,137, claims that you once used a poultice to mend someone's broken shin-bone after an accident in the printing workshop. That was ten years ago.'

'I don't remember.'

'96,137 – doesn't that number ring a bell? Serving a life sentence, he was, and in return for fixing his leg you demanded that his family pay the school fees of your daughter, who was living with her mother in your home province.'

'I don't remember anything like that.'

The rain is coming down in sheets as Muo, having left the Observation Post of Panda Droppings, makes his way down the mountain to the trunk road where the bus passes only once or twice daily. He takes shelter under a jutting rock. Then, as it is getting late and he is soaked to the skin, he decides to seek refuge in the dormitory used by the bachelor workforce at a bamboo furniture factory nearby.

The medieval-style factory is not far from the Observation Post, and all the workers are acquainted with their solitary neighbour, the taciturn old man bowed by past hardships, who served five years in prison for attempting to cross the border illegally. It seems he was trying to get to Hong Kong after the 1989 handover. (He spent all night swimming across the sea. He could already make out the lights of Hong Kong. But he failed.)

According to the workers, his job is to patrol the forest, which is inhabited by the last panda bear in the region, one of the mere thousand surviving panda in the world. The panda, being even more solitary in its habits than the Old Observer, is rarely if ever sighted. The old man is charged with collecting the droppings and sending them on to the regional centre for analysis to gauge the creature's need for alimentary or medical assistance.

The rain stops, but the drops sliding off the trees keep pattering on the corrugated iron roof. A mountain stream gurgles behind the dormitory. Inside, the workers play cards by the flickering light of spirit lamps. The air is thick with smoke. Muo fills a dented copper kettle with water, which he puts to boil over the crackling fire in the hearth hollowed out of the earthen floor. Huddled on a wooden bench beside the singing kettle, he dozes off. He has a dream in which he hears the name of Bei Le – a very ancient name with two sonorous syllables – being intoned in a palatial environment (the Forbidden City? the glass Palace of Justice in Chengdu?), while the enthroned Emperor, robed in yellow, grants his morning audience to his ministers, generals and courtiers, among whom is Bei Le, the country's leading expert on horses. Bei Le has reached retirement age and wishes to recommend one Mr Ma to the Emperor as his replacement at court.

'He is a genius, your imperial majesty,' Bei Le says. 'He knows more about horses than I do. No man is better suited to take over from me.'

His curiosity thus aroused, the Emperor sends Mr Ma to the imperial stables in order to pick out the best mount from among thousands of horses. The Emperor is a tyrant: unpredictable and given to violence. For Mr Ma (whose traits, posture and habits strongly resemble those of the Old Observer of Panda Droppings), the slightest error will be fatal. He heads to the stables, inspects the horses and unwaveringly makes his selection. When he displays the steed of his choice to the Emperor and his courtiers they all burst out laughing: not only does the horse lack the famous white forelock, classical sign of purity and nobility of race, but it is also an unprepossessing mare: scrawny and dun-coloured. The Emperor summons old Bei Le.

'How dare you play games with me, the supreme sovereign of the land? Your crime deserves the death penalty: the man you recommended cannot even tell the difference between a stallion and a mare.'

Before being executed, old Bei Le asks to see the mount selected by Mr Ma. Setting eyes on the mare, he heaves a long sigh.

'Mr Ma is truly a genius. I do not even reach his ankle in stature,' he tells the Emperor.

Sure enough, two years later, when the tyrant has been killed in a popular uprising, the mare is adopted by his successor and turns out to be the swiftest mount in the land, capable of covering a thousand *li* daily, like the winged horse of legend.

Muo awakes with a jolt to the realisation that the old Emperor is none other than Judge Di, that Bei Le is the mayor's son-in-law, and that Ma, the all-time equestrian expert, stands for the Old Observer of Panda Droppings. Then the new Emperor, surrounded by guards in full armour, casts off his disguise and his false beard, thereby revealing himself to be none other than Muo himself, while the winged horse in the guise of a scrawny mare fuses with the X-ray of the broken shin-bone.

'Mr Ma is obviously not taken in by appearances,' Muo reflects, 'so what can the Old Observer have been looking for in the upside-down X-ray?'

At daybreak he climbs up to the Observation Post once more. He finds the old man with a hod on his back, on the point of setting out on a tour of inspection.

'May I accompany you?' Muo asks. 'It would give me an opportunity to see a panda in the wild rather than in a zoo.'

'And take idiotic photos, I suppose?'

'No, I don't have a camera with me.'

'I warn you that you'll be wasting your time.'

Muo cannot remember where he read that men of action are always taciturn. In that respect, at any rate, the Old Observer of Panda Droppings is a great man of action. When he talks to him, Muo has the impression the old man wants to put his fingers in his ears. At first he takes this to be a mark of contempt. But the deeper they penetrate the Bamboo Forest, which is so dense that the old man has to slash a path through the sun-obscuring undergrowth, the more he realises that keeping quiet is part of the job description. The old man can hear everything he cannot see. His big, hairy ears are in excellent working order. Suddenly he stops, listens, and says he can hear the panda in a pine wood nearby. They head off in the direction the sound came from, and after twenty minutes' brisk walk arrive at the pine trees, where, among spills of russet pine needles and pine-cones smelling of damp and decay, they find fresh paw-prints on the soggy ground. Prints as large as the palm of a hand, with the opposable thumb pointing away from the fingers. On some of them, more distinct than the others, it is possible to distinguish the shape of the heel-pad and the claws.

'Could you really hear it from the other side of the mountain, more than a kilometre away?' Muo asks admiringly.

As the old man fails to respond, Muo continues, 'I'm nearly blind as it is, but thanks to you I have now discovered that I'm deaf as well.'

Wordlessly, the Old Observer stoops to draw a measuring tape from his hod, squats down on the ground and, in the manner of a tailor taking fabric measurements, proceeds to ascertain the length and breadth of a pawprint.

Muo breaks the silence. 'Perhaps you do not wish to prescribe treatments because you lack medical qualifications and because you think you'll pay dearly for the slightest error. But I assure you, I swear to you, and I can give it to you in writing, that if you do not succeed in mending the leg of this ballet star-to-be I will not hold it against you.'

Pretending not to hear, the Old Observer extends the tape measure to note the precise distance between two pawprints. The distance is short: presumably the panda was running. Then he draws himself upright and goes after the other marks on the muddy ground.

Muo follows at his heels. But the old man quickens his pace, as though trying to shake him off. He crosses streams and takes flying leaps from one rock to another with an agility that reminds Muo of the Lolo. He can barely keep up. When he loses sight of the old man he is forced to scan the ground himself for panda tracks to show him the way. Here and there they become dense and confused, suggesting an animal trampling the ground in hunger and distress, or a deliberate game of hide and seek. Perhaps the solitary panda was leading the Old Observer a merry dance by leaving traces that suddenly change direction, go back on themselves and run out on the bank of a stream.

Muo eventually comes upon the old man under a tree, apparently inspecting the trunk. It is a common birch tree.

Around it the lianas have been disturbed, leaves have been crushed, and at the base of the trunk the smooth silvery bark has been shredded and flaked off in places. A smell of aniseed fills the air.

'Shaking me off isn't as easy as you think,' Muo says, quite out of breath. 'But don't worry. I have just one more thing to say to you, then I won't bother you any more.'

Without deigning to look at him, the Old Observer puts his nose close to the scratchmarks, sniffing the pungent aroma of the sap with flared nostrils.

'I have a confession to make,' Muo says, then pauses as he reconsiders revealing the truth. He holds his tongue, convinced that the word 'judge' would, to this former convict, spell torture and despair.

Instead he says, 'For the past ten years I have been studying psychoanalysis in France. This is the deal: if you can put the girl's leg to rights in ten days, I will teach you this new revolutionary science from A to Z.'

For the first time the old man turns his head and throws him a quick glance of appraisal.

'It is a science invented by Freud, which lays bare the secret of the world.'

'Which secret is that?'

'Sex.'

'Say that again.'

'SEX.'

The old man bursts out laughing. He is so convulsed he nearly collapses at the foot of the birch tree.

'We should get Mr Freud to come here,' he gasps, pointing to the scuffed bark. 'Then he could tell us why the panda rubs against this tree.'

'Maybe it's hungry. Freud would say it's suffering from material frustration.'

'Not at all, young man. All the panda wanted was to scrape off his balls.'

Stunned by this news, Muo stands gaping at this evidence of auto-castration, a practice he has come across in books. The sun's rays project leopard spots on the enchanted tree trunk. He is disappointed to note that, as usual, the interpretation he came up with was mistaken. He is filled with self-reproach. The Old Observer simply presses on along the footpath.

A good hour later, another surprise awaits him. Since morning they have seen masses of butterflies of different species, each one more beautiful than the last. These have not awakened the slightest interest in the Old Observer, but now he stops in his tracks, motioning Muo to be silent: his attention is riveted on a tiny, innocent-looking butterfly flitting down the muddy, bamboo-lined path among the tufts of black centaurea and yellow tansy, plants that are known for thriving in wet surroundings. With the satisfied grin of an entomologist finally discovering the species he is looking for, the old man declares:

'We can go home early today.'

Wary of what the old man might have up his sleeve, Muo makes sure his concentration is worthy of a brilliant disciple of Freud. Wordlessly, they follow the butterfly as it zigzags among the shrubs, toadstools and grasses lining the dappled path, on which the mud is ankle-deep in places. Muo stares so intently at the butterfly that his vision blurs, causing the white and grey markings on its wings to blend into the ferns nestled amid the pale, gnarled roots of bamboo.

Suddenly the butterfly quickens, whirling and gliding in febrile flight while its beauty grows increasingly resplendent. It seems blissfully intoxicated. By an exquisite fragrance? The scent of a female? Muo is about to offer a Freudian comment on this phenomenon, but to his intense disappointment the insect swoops down into a ditch, where it settles on a heap of dung, wings palpitating with excitement.

'What good luck!' the old man exclaims. He jumps into

the ditch, peers at the fragile creature, and murmurs, 'Enjoy your meal, little one. Still got a weakness for panda droppings, eh?'

This confrontation shakes Muo to the core of his being. Animal droppings, a butterfly, an old convict – there is, in this timeless trinity, a touch of the sublime, of eternity. Suddenly his life, his books, his dictionaries, his notebooks, his emotions, his worries all strike him as futile and superficial. The same goes for his sexual betrayal, his deceit in the mountains of the Lolo, and above all his idea of returning to China with a mission of salvation.

The dampness drifting in the forest coats the dung with what looks like brown varnish. Once the butterfly has gone, the Old Observer takes out his utensils, gathers up the droppings and puts them in a plastic bag. Muo watches him stash everything in his hod.

Together they make they way back to the observation post, where the old man lays a bamboo mat on the ground in front of his house. He spreads the panda droppings on the mat for them to dry in the sun, goes inside and returns with more dung-filled plastic bags, each tagged with a date.

'My house is too damp, so I have to keep bringing them out here to dry,' he explains. 'The centre only sends someone round to fetch them once a fortnight.'

The old man spreads out his entire collection of droppings on the mat, neatly arranging them in chronological order. Although they have not yet lost their colour, the damp has made them spongy, and the remains of half-digested bamboo leaves are visible. Suddenly the old man bursts out:

'Would you be prepared to spend your life with a peasant woman?'

'What do you mean? I have no idea what you're getting at.'

'If I manage to set the dancing girl's broken leg to rights within ten days, will you marry my daughter?'

5

Sea Cucumber

Since Judge Di's arrival in Beijing for the conference of
Chinese jurists and magistrates at a four-star hotel called The
New Capital, his habits have been abstemious, not to say
ascetic. He is following a strict diet based on sea cucumbers,
prescribed by a sexologist in anticipation of the carnal delights
shortly to be supplied by the psychoanalyst Muo. However,
to this boorish glutton, being deprived of the daily pleasures
afforded by the unlimited consumption of food represents an
unbearably cruel torment, which undermines both his
physical and mental well-being. Already in childhood Di had
a reputation as a greedy-guts. Before each meal his mother
was obliged to put aside an egg, a piece of meat or a chicken
leg, so that she could feed it afterwards to the smallest of his
sisters, whose stunted growth was aggravated by her inability
to stand up to her fiendish brother during the distribution of
food. In those days the future judge's greatest talent was
concentrated in his right hand, notably in the index and
middle fingers with which he deftly manipulated his chopsticks (the same steely index finger that would, in later years,

pull the trigger of his sure-fire gun). Plunging his chopsticks into a pot, he was capable of seizing a pound of noodles in one go, leaving nothing for the others. In one go, never two. Pure genius. As his family were of modest stock, they did not go in for refinements such as serving dishes: the mother placed the cooking pots directly on the table for everyone to dip their chopsticks into. As soon as the prospective judge moved his chopsticks towards the spicy vapours rising from the grease-ridden pots and pans, his siblings would pummel him mercilessly, but they were always defeated. Once a grown man and elite member of the execution squad, Di retained this supremacy in the barracks mess, where the soldiers squatted round a single iron pot to consume their coarse victuals.

In those days he would often take solitary walks in town, making a stop at The Donkey Pot. He would go straight to the kitchen, where a side of donkey was invariably stewing in a gigantic pan. The cook knew what was expected of him: without a word he would take a prong and plunge it into the pan to extract a chunk of steaming meat. Using a huge carving knife he would slice it into a bowl filled with stock, to which he added finely chopped chives, pepper and salt. Finally he would pose the ritual question, a sort of code between them.

'Do I add some donkey's blood today?'

If Judge Di nodded his head in assent, it meant that he had shot at least one condemned prisoner that day, in which case the cook would take the bowl through to the restaurant area, where he would seat himself on a low stool to slice the congealed blood into squares of red jelly which would then bob on the surface of the stock. The judge adored – and indeed still adores – the taste of these soft, bloody lumps melting in the mouth. He would devour the meat, swallowing the gristle whole like a man starving, or crack a rib with his teeth to suck out the marrow, before noisily slurping the soup. Some years later, when his life was all sunshine (not thanks to the light cast by Chairman Mao, despite the song sung by billions of Chinese for half a century – 'The sky reddens in the East. The sun rises. It is he, Mao, our president' – but thanks to the sun of the West, that of Capitalism in the Communist mode), he donned the garments of magistracy. Since that time, being wreathed in the auras of power, money and the indiscreet charm of the bourgeoisie, he has been initiated into Western gastronomy. With a white napkin tied round his neck, amid the clatter of forks, knives, spoons and the strictly regulated changing of plates with each course, he dines on *lapin chasseur, chou frisé à la duchesse*, kidneys in Madeira sauce, salmon *à la crème* . . . To him, this exotic cuisine is a pageant worthy of the cinema, a 'good show' (he has a smattering of English and loves the word 'show', which he pronounces as 'sow' with a strong regional drawl). He has discovered that the cuisine of the West revolves around the notion of 'sow', as does their civilisation, in which even going to war means putting on a 'sow'. This is contrary to his spirit. He is a man of the nitty-gritty, not of 'sow', since he is in the business of passing sentence. Back in his villa of an evening, the satisfaction at having destroyed yet more lives, and with that entire families, makes him feel young again. His step grows more assured. He makes such a racket as he stamps up the stairs you would think an army were invading the residence. At the sound of his approach, his wife emerges from her quarters and throws herself at his feet, crying out in the long-drawn-out tones of a Chinese opera, 'You have returned, your honour?'

(Author's note to female Chinese readers preparing for marriage: this instance of a wife addressing her husband by his official title strikes me as uncalled for and untypical, especially in the intimacy of the home. The phrasing of the question, however, is ingenious. Here we have the key to the art of matrimony that has provided such a solid basis for our families over thousands of years: never ask a question that might embarrass. Never ask a man where he has been or what he has been up to. Never. It is sufficient to establish the fact of his return in the interrogative form, thereby attesting not only to your solicitude regarding his welfare, but also to the miraculous good fortune that has brought him back to you. So moved are you by this miracle that you cannot utter more than a few syllables. The same principle applies to social intercourse. When you address someone over breakfast, you do not ask what they are having, which might be embarrassing if the dish they have ordered is cheap, you merely say, 'Are you eating?' That is very subtle, and quite perfect.)

One type of Western food to which Judge Di is especially partial is charcuterie. Sometimes he has breakfast at the Holiday Inn, which is the best hotel in town. The buffet is set up in a rectangular garden. There he gorges himself on sausage (his favourite), along with dressed ham, breaded chops, smoked chicken breast, salami and black pudding. To him, these are tasty appetisers, not filling enough for a proper meal, especially when it is a question of satisfying the acute hunger, both physical and moral, aroused in him by condemning people to death. The moment of condemnation is even more intense and thrilling than the actual execution, which is merely the carrying out of an order. Putting a man to death is a unique and very masculine sensation, but in the courtroom the manly thrill of wielding power over life and death is enhanced by the pleasure of playing cat-and-mouse, which is a more feminine game, full of innocent candour and childish cruelty. He is the cat toying with a mouse: he lets it go, just a little, just enough for it to catch a glimmer of hope. The mouse can't believe its luck, it trembles and cowers. The cat remains obligingly aloof. The mouse makes a run for the skirting-board. The cat waits and watches and, just as the mouse thinks it is free at last, he lashes out with his merciless claws and *wham*, the game is over. After such strong stimulation, every organ, every muscle in his body aches to be recharged, in the same way that some men, after having sex, dive into the refrigerator with bulimic ardour.

That is how Judge Di became a devotee of pork offal. He likes to conclude a session at the tribunal or at the mah-jong table by feasting on offal: hearts, lungs, stomachs, kidneys, livers, entrails, tongues, tails, ears, trotters and brains. He even employs a live-in cook from Shanghai at the tribunal's expense, who is on call twenty-four hours a day to prepare a Shanghai delicacy known as 'tripe with spirit', which requires stewing on a low flame in a sauce of chopped ginger, osmund flowers, star anise, cinnamon, grilled tofu, yellow wine and a handful of the glutinous rice that is normally used as a fermenting agent. Now, in his Beijing hotel room, the repast comes back to him in his dreams. His mouth waters at the thought of the earthenware cooking pot sweating droplets of glistening grease, and especially of what it contains: entrails in every shape and form, red, viscous, fatty, spongy, steeped in alcohol and flavoured with herbs and fiery spices, both salty and sweet, each morsel akin to a sliver of honeycomb complete with grubs working up the gravy.

The sea cucumber recommended to him by the Beijing sexologist is everything his favourite dish is not. An invertebrate mollusc related to the sea urchin and star-fish, the sea cucumber inhabits coral reefs. It is hard to come by, expensive, and exotic, for it is to be found mainly in the Indian Ocean and the Western Pacific, where coral divers descend to the sea bed to search the reef by touch in the hope of encountering the spines of this marine creature erroneously named after a vegetable. The diver returns to the surface with his catch, which he lays out on the shore to dry in the sun. Once out of water, the sea cucumber, which is fronded with quivering feet much like a centipede, shrivels into a viscid jelly. It has to be salted forthwith to preserve its shape and skin-colour, after which it looks like a human penis ten to fifteen centimetres long, veined, ridged, and knobby. When cast into boiling water to cook, it inflates to reveal a glans at the tip.

The phallic appearance of the sea cucumber earned it a position of splendid isolation at the pinnacle of ancient Chinese pharmacopoeia. It was used at the imperial court to restore the energies expended by successive emperors on their thousands of concubines. Known as 'marine manhood' during the Tang dynasty, it was later given the official name it bears today: 'ginseng of the sea'. The democratic dissemination of this seafood was very long in coming. During the dynastic period, the Emperor would offer small portions of the delicacy to ministers or generals to assure himself of their loyalty at times of political crisis or military conflict. In the early years of the twentieth century, after the collapse of the last dynasty, one He Gonggong, a eunuch-cum-cook (slandered by some as a eunuch-cum-hairdresser) opened a restaurant named Happy Virtue by the north gate of the Forbidden City and, for the first time in the history of Chinese aphrodisiacs, the aroma of sea cucumber rose up over the palace wall and wafted across Beijing. But it took another hundred years and the advent of Chinese-style capitalism for its democratisation to reach today's levels. Now medium-quality 'ginseng of the sea' is considered quite normal fare at the banquets of the new rich.

The only problem with this rare commodity, this fabulous remedy, is that it has no taste whatsoever. Generations of imperial chefs have made strenuous efforts with all manner of spices to do something about this, but without success. The sea cucumber tastes bland – disgustingly, nauseatingly so. No wonder Judge Di does not suffer his diet gladly. Each morning, the restaurant across the road sends a waiter to his room bearing a chrome-plated receptacle with a tightly sealed lid. It contains a bowl of rice-stock made with 'ginseng of the sea'. The stock, which is regularly topped up with water, is left to simmer and reduce for hours until it is impossible to distinguish a single grain of rice. But notwithstanding this recipe from one of Hong Kong's finest restaurants, the sea cucumber remains bland. Come midday, the same waiter brings the same receptacle, this time with a serving of 'ginseng of the sea prepared with red oil', or 'sliced ginseng of the sea with carrot gravy', one of the traditional imperial dishes that were on the menu at He Gonggong's Happy Virtue Restaurant. But the taste is no different. In the evening, the same receptacle is brought to him again, this time with ginseng-of-the-sea soup made with savoury mushrooms and bamboo shoots. Bland enough to make you weep.

At last, on the fourth day of his diet, Judge Di begins to feel some effect. He becomes aware of a faint stirring in his member, which has been stone cold since the incident at the morgue.

'I think I'll bring forward the date of my return to Chengdu,' he tells himself with glee.

6

The Oriole

For all that the ointments concocted by the Old Observer-cum-herbalist are contained in a tin can, a jam jar and a flask (vessels as innocuous-looking as cruets of salt, pepper and chilli powder), their appearance on Little Road's bedside table enrages the doctors and nurses of the Chengdu Hospital osteopathy department. These believers in the primacy of the lancet to the exclusion of all else inform the young patient and her French mentor, orally and in writing, that they risk a heavy fine and expulsion from the hospital if they do not get rid of these suspect, nay scandalous items at once.

Persuaded by this ban on herbal medicine and the fact that time is running out, the couple move into The Cosmopolitan, a modest hotel in the southern suburbs of Chengdu. A quiet place, with hardly any other guests, run by a peasant couple who struck it rich growing hothouse blooms and who converted their old farmhouse into an eight-room hotel, with a hallway containing a shrine to the god of riches and a multitude of clocks indicating the time in New York, Beijing, Tokyo, London, Paris, Sydney and Berlin. The hotel courtyard boasts a large cage – not one of those wicker affairs that hang on a nail in the wall, nor a bamboo one suspended from the branch of a tree, but a metal cage in the shape of a pagoda, no less than two metres high and painted dark green – with a bird roosting on the perch. An oriole. It wakes up to sing a few notes of greeting to the two new arrivals. The girl is hopping on one leg with the aid of crutches. When her bespectacled companion, weighed down with luggage, makes to assist her, she haughtily declines his offer and quickens her pace with the air of a distraught young lady of noble birth with a short-sighted, clumsy old retainer at her heels.

Muo thinks she has changed over the past few days. She has grown unpredictable, irritable and generally ill-tempered. Her mood swings are a bane to him. When he inquires what she would like for lunch she says she couldn't care less and goes off in a sulk. She chews her lips, twists a lock of hair around her finger and glares at him like a spoilt child. He puts up with this change of temperament in the knowledge that disability always makes people irritable. Pain affects the mind. How can she be expected to keep her spirits up and go on being the vivacious, feisty little film-dreamer when her leg is broken and she is racked with pain at the slightest movement?

Little Road's room is on the first floor, and is so dingy that the bare light-bulb hanging from the ceiling has to be kept on all day. The walls are running with condensation.

She is lying in bed with her left leg on top of the covers when Muo enters the room with a basin of hot water. Squatting down, he delicately rolls the girl's trouser leg up to her knee. The limb is badly swollen and the skin has a morbid sheen, slightly phosphorescent, with dark blotches.

'The bruising is worse than it was yesterday,' she observes. 'I can't stand it. My leg looks like a patchwork of countries in an atlas.'

Muo smiles. She is right: the blue, black and violet stains do indeed bear some resemblance to a map of the world.

'I shall start with Darkest Africa,' he says.

He smiles again, glad to have come up with a pleasantry to hide his dismay at the sight of this accusing, battered limb. He slips some cloths under the leg, soaks a compress in the basin of hot water and dabs at the blotch in the centre of the map, a horrible expanse of black veined with purple, blue and red, which resembles a sacrificial tortoise held aloft by its hind legs so that its triangular head dangles in the sea.

At the very heart of this dark continent there is a visible dent with two sharp ridges. 'That is where the tibia is broken in two,' Muo tells himself. Being possessed of a good bedside manner, he resorts to prevarication.

'They say that the Old Observer's most spectacular achievement was with a disfigured hunter, whose left cheekbone has been smashed in such a way that there was a deep hollow where the bump used to be. Not only did the old man repair the breakage, he also succeeded in remodelling the area into a jutting cheekbone.'

'How did he manage that if he didn't operate?'

'By applying the same poultices he gave me for your leg, that's all. They're made with magnetic herbs which pull the bone shards together.'

When he has finished cleaning the affected leg, Muo takes a bunch of keys from his pocket. Selecting the pen-knife attached to the key-ring he prises the lid off the tin can, releasing a fusty smell of damp and moss, mud and bog, which rapidly pervades the air.

'What a stink,' says Little Road. 'Reminds me of the smelly old well in my village.'

The recycled can, whose original contents cannot be known since it lost its label long ago, is filled with a black, blubbery substance.

'This is the first stage, according to the old man.'

Using his pen-knife Muo scoops the ointment from the can and spreads it on the pad he has prepared by folding a piece of white cloth several times. Then, with a delicate gesture, he applies the compress to Little Road's leg and secures it with gauze bandages.

That night, he is woken by the young girl knocking on the partition between their rooms.

'Does it hurt?' he asks in the dark, putting his mouth so close to the wall that his lips brush the paintwork.

'Yes it does, but not too much. Could you give that poor bird something to eat? It's hungry.'

'Which bird, my lame princess?'

'The oriole in the cage.'

He pricks up his ears. The scuttle of a rat along the rafters. A moth bumping against the window pane. The croak of a frog. The honk of a car in the distance. And down in the yard the cry of the oriole: metallic, shrill, agitated, slicing the air like a scythe in the night.

'You can tell it's a domestic oriole,' Little Road says from the other side of the partition. 'Wild orioles don't sound like that.'

'How do they sound?'

The imitation she gives is more like the high-pitched squawking of fledgling sparrows, which Muo finds amusing. Wide awake now, he gets out of bed, takes some biscuits from his bag and goes down to the courtyard. She was right, the oriole is famished. It swoops down from its perch like a shot, a golden arrow flashing in the dark, splashing Muo with water from the drinking-trough. Holding on to the bars with its claws and folding its wings, which are more splendidly feathered than the body, the oriole quivers with excitement as it pecks the crumbled biscuit from Muo's extended hand. It devours the offering down to the last crumb without the least token of gratitude, then regains its perch, visibly fortified. After that it pays no further attention to its benefactor and sets to work preening its feathers with a show of intense pride. Muo is disappointed, and turns to leave.

Suddenly he hears a sound like a parody of a human voice rising from the cage. He wheels round to face the self-obsessed bird, which, for the next second or two, utters various combinations of distinct syllables, unintelligible but sharp and bright as diamonds.

In the morning Muo asks the proprietors of the hotel about the oriole. The woman explains that the bird's parents were orioles of a noble species which were kept by a Christian pastor. Fellow oriole-keepers flocked to his home with their own birds, bearing gifts of money and goods in the hope of being permitted to place their cage next to his, so that their bird might listen to the pair in his possession and learn to sing like them. But the pastor always refused. After he died, the oriole's parents did not survive for long. The orphaned chick, however, grew up happily and, from time to time, utters a phrase remembered from its parents. A phrase in Latin, apparently. Something the pastor said at the close of each service. Some say they are the last words spoken by Jesus Christ.

Like his fellow psychoanalysts in the West, Muo studied the Bible, but he can't think what this last phrase uttered by Christ can be. He goes to the trouble of making a note in a new exercise book, and promises himself to check the holy book for the answer to the enigma. Then it slips his mind.

Despite the thick padding, the smell of mud persists in the lame princess's room for three days. Each time she wants to take a shower, her loyal, short-sighted attendant kneels humbly by her bed to wrap her leg in a sheet of clear plastic, which he secures with big pink elastic bands. The smell of the poultice makes his head spin.

On the fourth day, when he removes the soiled bandages and washes the leg in readiness for the next poultice, he notes that the bruising has faded somewhat. Darkest Africa has become slate-grey, and its size, like that of the other continents, has shrunk considerably. The inverted tortoise has lost its long neck, leaving the triangular head as a small island in the ocean.

A wave of joy and excitement sweeps over the patient as Muo unscrews the lid of the jam jar containing the second remedy. The jar is old, the glass scratched and dull. The contents, dark brown this time, give off a strange smell, remarkable for the diversity of components. It is a chaotic assortment of grease, opium, bee's wax, incense, tree bark, roots, herbs, poisonous mushrooms, ink, ether, resin and a hint of the dung-heap. Spreading the paste on the fresh compress, Muo can make out fragments of leaves and mushroom.

'Is it true that your old shit-collector succeeded in fixing a broken cheekbone which had left a dent in the person's face?'

'Yes. And you know what the key to his success was? The X-ray, he told me. He could tell there was still an invisible filament linking the extremities of the broken bone. His ointment succeeded in getting the bone to fuse by means of suction. That's the word he used: suction.'

'Is it the same with my shin-bone?'

'I think so, yes.'

'Where did he learn all that stuff? Did he tell you?'

'When he was a boy he was apprenticed to a herbalist, who brought him into contact with a practitioner of traditional medicine in the same town. This traditional doctor was unsurpassed when it came to curing cataracts with an acupuncture needle positioned in a particular spot in the gums. He proposed sharing his secret with the young apprentice on condition that he marry his daughter. The apprentice assented, thereby gaining possession of the secret cure. Years later, during the Cultural Revolution, he fled to the Emei mountains, where he fell into a ditch when he was out collecting herbs, and broke a leg. A Buddhist monk put his leg to rights in ten days. They became friends, and the herbalist exchanged his acupuncture secret for the monk's bone-setting recipe.'

It is two days later. The mayor's son-in-law has sounded the alarm: Judge Di wishes to bring forward his return to Chengdu. A catastrophe. Thank goodness for some reason he changes his mind and the alarm is cancelled a few hours later. Everything settles down again.

The state of Little Road's leg is improving by the hour.

'There's a sort of draught coming from my shin-bone, I can feel it in every pore,' she says. 'Just now I thought I felt a worm under the bandages, wriggling up from my ankle to my knee. And now it's going all the way down again.'

The third and final poultice is applied on the sixth day, in keeping with the Old Observer's instructions. Time to clean off the residue of the previous ointment (Muo the male nurse now knows this leg like the back of his hand), to slip towels under the damaged limb, and to open the flask (she wants to pull out the stopper with her teeth, but he won't hear of it: 'The old man told me it contains powdered peacock gall, which is essential but also toxic, not to say lethal. In the olden days it was used by Mongolian and Manchurian nobles to commit suicide.')

Once the stopper has been carefully removed with the aid of the pen-knife, the flask exudes an acrid, savage smell with a hint of gunpowder. The ointment is a dingy green colour, thicker and more viscous than the previous ones, and consequently harder to spread on the compress.

'What is the poison called?'

'Biliary vesicle of peacock.'

'What a beautiful name. Everything about peacocks is beautiful, not that I know what a biliary vesicle is.'

'It's a small, black bladder-like sac in the liver. If you've dressed a chicken, you will have come across it.'

'I love peacocks. They're like kings . . .'

'They say that death by peacock gall is gentle, sweet and painless. Which reminds me of an ancient poem: "Death in the shimmering fan of a giant peacock's tail".'

A man's face appears to Muo: long, angular, glowering like a gun.

Is it Judge Di? The courtyard light has been switched off. Hard to tell. Maybe he needs new glasses. Maybe his eyesight has worsened again. If this goes on he'll be blind by the time this is all over.

The crunch of leather soles on the gravel. Brand-new Italian shoes bought in Beijing? Or a gift from one of his victims?

The shoes stamp up the stairs like a triumphant army. This is not a swift ascent, there is a deliberate pause between each thundering step. Footfalls resonate on the landing and stop at Little Road's room. The sound of knocking. The door opens with a long-drawn-out, high-pitched squeak, accompanied by the voice of Judge Di speaking of himself in the third person.

'Judge Di to see you, my dear.'

'Please come in. Have a seat, your honour.'

'No hidden mikes or cameras?'

(Footsteps going round the perimeter of the room, then approaching the bed. He is probably kneeling down to look underneath.)

'Do you know where Judge Di has just been? In Beijing. He wanted to return earlier, but was unable to.' (The scrape of a chair as he takes a seat.) 'The organisers of the conference prevailed upon him to address the assembly. All the jurists and magistrates of China were eager to hear about how he had solved a criminal case by posing as a corpse in the Chengdu morgue. A thrilling story, which is apparently to be adapted for television.'

'Will you be playing yourself in it, sir?'

'Why not? If it's realism they're after . . . But what's this? You look a bit under the weather, my dear.'

'Yes, that's right. I'm not in the best of health. I have just had an operation.'

'Just goes to show that Judge Di has a discerning eye. Nothing escapes him. What is your name?'

'Little Road.'

'Not an attractive name. Today our fatherland is rich and prosperous, we don't have little roads any more. People advance proudly on the great and sunny road of socialism. You must change your name. Judge Di will call you Great Road.'

(Silence. She's quite right not to answer. Where is she now? Sitting on the bed? Standing against the wall? The tyrant rises to his feet.)

'Come on, Great Road. Here, my jacket. Put it on a hanger in the wardrobe.'

'There isn't a wardrobe here. I'll hang it on the door knob.'

(For the first time, Little Road moves away from the partition, heading slowly towards the door.)

'What are you playing at? Tottering around like a little old woman with bound feet. Come here, so that we . . .'

(The judge is interrupted by a long groan from the girl.)

'Aha! So you like Judge Di, do you? Makes you swoon, does he?'

'Forgive me, it's not my fault . . . The Lolo . . .'

'Incredible! A Lolo maiden! Great Road of the Lolo – that'll be your name in full. I love seeing Lolo girls dance. They're so spirited, so full of rhythm and joy. Go on, dance for me!'

'I can't.'

'Don't be shy! Every Lolo girl can do it, just hold out your

253

arms. Come on now, we'll dance together, like sweethearts at the torch festival in your home province. What's this smell? You smell of gunpowder. Come on, let's dance the *Golden Mountains of Peking*.'

(Hardly has he launched into the first bar of this revolutionary song when she is betrayed by her convalescent leg and collapses on the floor.)

'What's going on? Do you realise what you're doing? You're passing up the opportunity to dance with Judge Di. His patience is running out. Go and take a shower. Afterwards, you can join him in bed.'

(She scrambles to her feet, letting out little moans. Her footsteps recede. The bed creaks under the weight of Judge Di. Then a crash is followed by the cries of the girl, who has fallen again.)

'Stop playing games. Judge Di is not amused.'

'I'm not playing games. I broke my left leg in an accident.'

'Well I'll be damned! That bastard psychoanalyst has set me up with a cripple! How humiliating. Judge Di never sleeps with cripples!'

(He jumps up from the bed, uttering a stream of curses and abuse. Then the door slams so violently that the walls shake. Finally he stomps away down the stairs and Muo awakes from his dream.)

For a moment, in the haze of semi-sleep, he wonders whether it was indeed a dream. He is reassured by the shrill cries of the oriole in its pagoda cage. He puts his ear to the partition and hears Little Road breathing regularly on the other side.

'What a wonderful sight!' Muo reflects, studying the X-ray upon which the segments of tibia have finally fused to form a single long and luminous shape. The image calls to mind a pirate's flag, brazen signal of rebellion both savage and mythical.

It was early in the afternoon when he arrived with Little Road at the hospital for her X-ray appointment. As the results would not be ready for three hours, he offered to wait and gave her two hundred yuan to go shopping: 'Buy yourself a present. My treat.'

When he finally leaves the hospital bearing the X-ray, his mind is full of questions: 'Where is she now? Is she still shopping? Has she bought anything? Lipstick? Earrings? Clothes? A pair of shoes?'

For a while he walks in the street without being conscious of his feet touching the ground. He is floating, skimming over the surface. He goes down People's Road, the city's main traffic artery, then turns left to walk beside Brocade River as far as the old South Bridge. He smiles at everyone he sees — men, women, children, old people, and even the dreaded policemen. He wishes he could make them all stop and look at the X-ray which proves the Old Observer's great achievement, this miracle that he has wrought.

'If I ever get married . . . (But to whom? Volcano of the Old Moon? The Embalmer? Little Road? At this euphoric moment in time I am in love with all three, indeed all four if you count the daughter of the Old Observer whose acquaintance I have yet to make. If they so wished I would marry them all, despite my physical inadequacies.) But let me stick to the subject: should I ever get married, I will put this X-ray up on the wall of my house. I will have it mounted and framed and I will light it with a soft, diffuse glow so that it may be admired by all as a great work of art.'

It is late afternoon. The sun is veiled. A warm fug rises from the polluted waters of the murky river. How it has dwindled, the silky Brocade River of his boyhood, which used to be so limpid, such a wide expanse of shimmering water. It was too wide to swim all the way across, but what good times they used to have, he and his friends, lounging about on the half-submerged island in mid-stream. He is a different Muo today from the short-sighted, awkward adolescent forever engaged in imaginary conquests. As a boy, his conquests were merely fictitious. In his recurrent, naively erotic dreams, he saw himself falling in love with one girl after another: a cousin, his teacher, the maid's daughter, a school-mate . . . the list went on. Fate has decreed that Judge Di should be the one to help Muo realise his ideals, spurring him on in his quest, driving him to combine – he hopes – revolutionary romance with proletarian realism. What a great leap forward! Great leaps are nothing new in the Communist world, but this one is truly forward. If Judge Di had not been looking for a virgin, Muo would probably have remained a virgin himself and would have spent the rest of his days in intellectual masturbation over his psychoanalytic text books. As it is, he is in love with four admirable, real-life women. Scanning the faces of the men crossing his path on foot or on bicycles, he wonders whether any of them has been as lucky as he. Judging by their expressions, he thinks it unlikely. For a normal person, being in love with two people at the same time is stressful enough. There can hardly be anyone capable of loving four in perfect synchrony. Walking along, he ponders this thought, which has never occurred to him in this form before.

'What a pity Volcano of the Old Moon is not in the same penitentiary as the mayor's son-in-law. (The Embalmer is no longer there either, but she vanishes from my mind from time to time, which is something Volcano of the Old Moon never does.) Nevertheless, perhaps he knows someone in the women's prison who could launch a flying sock on my behalf? Some little cotton sock – preferably blue, but another colour will do just as well – still warm from the anonymous owner's foot, threadbare at the heel and toe, in which I could put a note saying, "Message for 1,479,437, cell 5,005. Judge Di returns tomorrow. You leave the day after." Or, on the safe side, I could dispense with words and draw a picture instead. A drawing of a girl, my Volcano of the Old Moon, pole vaulting over a barbed-wire fence. Underneath I would write "J-2", nothing else. In the days when we were students she was a member of the athletics team and won three bronze medals at the inter-university games. I remember her training courses, the cloud of dust at her heels as she ran, her sleek jumpsuit emphasising the curve of her hips and thighs, the long pole planted in the track and bending into an arc, the nervous tension, the kinetic energy stiffening her body and sending her flying. Each time, I expected her to stay up in the air, evaporating into a puff of smoke or turning into a swallow.'

Muo has been visited by a terrible nightmare of late. It recurs every two or three days, and always begins the same: pitch darkness, a smell of stagnant water, and a voice groaning, 'However constipated I may be, I'll never succeed in shitting in a collective soil bucket.' Then a stool drops into the utensil with a clattering sound that fills the dark space. There are three of them in the cell: the prison director, the prison doctor and Muo. The voice belongs to the prison director. The reason for their incarceration is the pregnancy of convict no. 1,479,437 of cell 5,005 (also known as Volcano of the Old Moon), who has been behind bars for the past two years. As they are the only three men to have had any contact with her in the past months, one of them must be the perpetrator of the crime, unprecedented in the history of the Chinese prison service. The director, who is inclined to wax confidential during his interminable defecations, has confessed that he almost fell in love with her because of her physical resemblance to Madam Tian, the great dancer of revolutionary ballet whom he idolised as a boy. He summoned the prisoner to his office and made her dress up as the heroine of *The Girl with the White Hair*, complete with the white horsehair wig symbolising the effects of spending twenty years on a mountain hiding from a landowner seeking to take her virginity. He put on a record of the ballet music, but Volcano of the Old Moon was incapable of dancing. 'I possess neither the willpower nor the strength of toe to dance on points like Madam Tian.' The tale of the prison doctor, who spent most of the time crying in a corner, was simply another version of the eternal quest for virginity. He had noticed no. 1,479,437 during a gynaecological examination. At thirty-six years of age she was still a virgin, a condition increasingly rare in present-day China and unique among the prison population. At first, she was no more than a curiosity to him. But then, reading a new edition of an ancient book, he came across the secret recipe for the 'red pill' developed by alchemists of the Ming Dynasty to prolong the life of the Emperor. The main ingredient was the menstrual blood of virgins. A retrial after eight centuries might be interesting, he thought. So he summoned the prisoner and, claiming to have encountered something untoward during his previous examinations, instructed her to supply him with a sample of her menstrual blood for additional tests. The sample never arrived on his desk, however, as the prisoner had suffered from amenorrhoea since the beginning of her sentence. Although he had done nothing wrong, the prison doctor was arrested one morning – to paraphrase the opening sentence of Kafka's *Trial*. But, despite their perversity, neither he nor the prison director could have made her pregnant, for the simple reason that they had both responded to a government appeal twenty years earlier and, being dutiful supporters of the one-child policy, had presented themselves at the hospital for permanent male contraception, that is, to have a vasectomy. As for Muo, he has never seen his girlfriend anywhere but in the visiting area, under the strict surveillance of female wardens and in the presence of other prisoners and their families. The nightmare always ends with the jangle of keys, the squeaking of hinges and the cell being invaded by members of the firing squad with the red star of China on their caps and eyes glinting as coldly as their guns.

The first time he had the nightmare, Muo awoke to feel the blood rushing to his cheeks. He got out of bed and went over to the window. He was at The Cosmopolitan. The pagoda-shaped cage stood in the courtyard below. A car rumbled in the distance. A street lamp cast a pool of yellow light on the ground. The realisation hit him that his subconscious had just manifested itself in the form of a dream, and that it contained an indictment of Volcano of the Old Moon. In Freudian terms this was a sign of 'the beginning of the end of love'. Why now? What could have brought it on? The presence of the sleeping girl with the bandaged leg on the other side of the partition, whom he watched over day and night? An icy chill – no, a presentiment, a premonitory shiver – ran down his spine.

No one can truly comprehend a dream.

Not even Freud.

Intermittencies of the heart. Who talked about that? Proust, probably: *In Search of Lost Time* (the French equivalent of the Chinese novel *The Dream of the Red Pavilion*). But not even artists, who are a separate race of mankind, understand the meaning of dreams. They merely create them, live them, and end up as the dreams of others.

Arriving at the South Bridge, Muo the agnostic, would-be polygamist and polyglot, decides to buy a gift for Little Road at the open-air market. Vendors shout bargain offers under the darkening sky, hungry chickens flap their wings in their cages, fish wriggle free from their bed of ice and fall to the ground, open-mouthed. Cinnamon. Star-anise. Absinth. Vermouth. Peppers. Exotic fruits. Genetically manipulated fruit from America. Vegetables from local farms. What could he surprise Little Road with to win her heart?

It could have been taken for a blob of black oil-paint in water, or a tadpole. It is the biliary vesicle of a white-spotted snake, which the salesman has put in a clear plastic bag filled with Chinese spirits. The vesicle has sunk to the bottom, where it curls and undulates in the alcohol.

Muo has opted for this organ not as a substitute for the peacock vesicle, which is incomparably more precious and toxic, but on account of the specific merits of the snake vesicle, which is commonly known in China as a highly efficacious fortifier of fractured bones. But his choice is also influenced by the legendary properties of this organ with regard to blowing up a person's courage to kamikaze proportions. On both counts – bone-fortifier and courage-booster – the vesicle of the white-spotted snake is reputed to be superior to that of the peacock.

But it will never be ingested by Little Road, for whom it is intended: within an hour of its purchase, a blind beggar shambling along the side of the road catches a whiff of alcohol. He sweeps the point of his cane from side to side over the pavement until it hits an obstruction: an abandoned plastic bag. He bends down, picks it up and sniffs. The fluid has been spilt, but there is still something left in the bag. Holding the bag in his hand he steps into a nearby grocery shop, whose manageress has installed domestic and international telephone lines for her customers in the hope of making some extra money.

'That must belong to the man with the spectacles,' she says, identifying the bag with a quick glance. 'He came to make a phone-call here. The battery of his mobile was flat and he wanted to phone a hotel in the suburbs. I told him that the suburbs was the same rate as the provinces: long-distance. He paid up. From what I gathered he got some bad news, because he turned quite pale, and kept saying, "But that's impossible . . . Tell me it's a joke!" But it wasn't a joke, because he slammed down the phone and dashed out into the street to hail a passing taxi. He was very nearly run over. When he discovered the taxi was occupied, he stopped someone riding a bicycle, took out some money and bought the bicycle there and then. I don't know how much he paid for it, but it must have been plenty, because the cyclist, clutching all those bank-notes, was beside himself with glee. The little man wearing spectacles jumped on the bike and sped away. He left an envelope with an X-ray in it by the phone. When I saw him he was carrying a plastic bag in his hand. He must have dropped it by mistake.'

'What's in the bag? It's ages since I was able to see.'

'Let me have a look. What on earth can that little black thing be? Wait, let me get my reading glasses. My eyesight isn't very good . . .'

'You're too modest. I can tell that you have an extraordinary personality.'

'It looks to me like the biliary vesicle of a snake.'

'What luck!'

The blind man takes the plastic bag, holds it to his lips and proceeds to funnel the vesicle into his mouth. He rolls it around his tongue, savouring the taste.

'The real thing, nice and bitter.'

The vesicle bursts between his yellow teeth, filling his mouth with dark juice.

It starts to rain.

The rain trickles down Muo's glasses as he pedals, almost blinding him. He can barely see the front wheel as he charges ahead, plunging into puddles, splashing pedestrians, over-taking one ghostly cyclist after another in the downpour. He is racing to the station to catch Little Road who, so the proprietor of The Cosmopolitan told him, left the hotel earlier that afternoon, limping slightly.

'She was wearing a newly bought pair of dark glasses and had a six-pack of beer under her arm. She said she wanted to go home to her parents. Before she left she offered us forty yuan for the oriole. She opened the cage, reached inside with her hand and set the bird free. She watched it fly away until it was out of sight.'

Muo has no time to search his memory for signs of her planning a getaway. There is no time to lose, not even a second. The train to her home province, the same one he met her on a fortnight ago, leaves at 9 p.m.

But the nearer he draws to the station the more he is filled with admiration for Little Road's strength of character. Making a choice like that, which will affect the rest of her life, demands respect.

'If I were in her shoes,' he reflects, 'I'd make off too, I'd refuse to have my virginity taken by Judge Di.'

His legs slow down. The rain lifts a little. His glasses are no longer steamed up. Then suddenly, as if to prove to himself that he has not gone completely to the bad, he turns full circle and heads back to the hotel.

He sleeps little that night. 'What a relief,' he thinks as he twists and turns in bed. 'Perhaps the heavens have intervened to save me from my polygamous leanings. The morality of pure, monogamous love has prevailed.'

At that moment he fancies he can hear the familiar cry of the oriole. Distinct syllables, bright as diamonds.

'What a bird! Can it be telling me that its generous, liberating benefactress has returned?'

The oriole and its puzzling utterances renew Muo's enthusiasm for his plan to win over Judge Di – his virgin-strategy. 'I'll call my strategy Helia,' he thinks to himself, 'after the Greek goddess of virginity.' The meeting with Judge Di is due to take place in less than twenty-four hours.

He runs down the stairs. The pagoda-shaped cage looms large and solitary. It is empty – just as it was when he went to bed. After a moment of spine-chilling calm, Muo throws a terrible tantrum, shaking the cage with all his might, punching it with his fists, banging his head against the bars, vainly trying to lift it up and push it over on its side. He takes a flying Kung-fu-film leap and kicks it.

His cathartic fit of rage is cut short by the near dislocation of his right foot, whereupon he gives up. Instead, wreathed in a beatific smile of childhood regained, he opens the door of the cage and crawls inside.

'I'm a bird,' he crows, convulsing with laughter.

His head knocks against the perch, his spectacles slide off his nose and he curls up on the floor of the cage like a captive pheasant destined for the pot.

He breathes in another world: cold metal bars, flaking paint, droppings, straw, dead leaves, grains of maize . . .

'This is my night of preparation. A practice run for my future in a prison cell. I feel sick. Why not take my life tonight? If I had jumped out of the Embalmer's window, like her husband, I would have saved myself so much humiliation. If Little Road came back and found me in this cage, would she set me free? Where is she, anyway, the little minx? On the train? Did she buy a ticket this time? Probably not. Fare dodging is the sport of the poor. Perhaps she didn't leave after all. Perhaps she's gallivanting around town with some local boy, or she's found herself a job as a waitress or cleaner. She'll be back. I have the feeling she's in love with me. Perhaps she fled because she loves me too much. Please come back, Little Road . . . What's this? Something has landed on the bars of the cage? A grasshopper?'

Suddenly the phrase that has been eluding him for days

comes flooding back. The last words spoken by Christ on the cross, which the bird has been parroting: 'Father, into thy hands I commend my spirit.'

How he regrets not being able to say them in Latin, like the bird. Muo, you must learn Latin. Indeed I shall – later, in my prison cell. I will even be able to write poetry – and my last will and testament.

The next day he goes to his parents' flat to spend his last hours of freedom with them. At four in the afternoon they leave him to go out shopping. Alone in the flat, he hears a knock on the door. He is doubtful at first, he could be hallucinating. But the knocking continues. Opening the door, he finds a girl on the doorstep. No doubt some peasant come in response to his mother's advertisement for a domestic worker.

'It's too late,' he says.

She blushes and shyly hangs her head, rubbing the arch of her right foot up and down her left calf.

'My father asked me to tell you . . .'

'Who is your father?'

'The Old Observer.'

Muo staggers back. It is as if a bombshell has exploded. All his life he will remember this moment. Covered with embarrassment, he wants to ask her to come in, to take tea with him, but his tongue betrays him and he hears himself ask, 'Are you a virgin?'